Kerstin Trimble

TRANSGRESSION

oder

Der Mann an Ludwigs Stelle

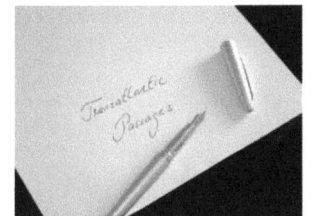

Transatlantic Passages 2015

© 2015 Kerstin Trimble

Transatlantic Passages

www.transatlantic-passages.com

Herstellung und Verlag: BoD – Books on Demand, Norderstedt.

Cover art: Noah Leo and Emily Witczak

ISBN: 9783734793561

Für meine Großmütter

Thank you, Samuel Harris

"Thank you, Samuel Harris. Samuel Harris."

The older one tapped his forehead with his index finger, as if to say: *Won't ever forget that name.* Bud was shifting around, getting nervous, inching backwards to signal his urgent desire to get this over with and the hell out of here. The Brits were looking at them in a funny way, but did not comment on the curious presence of two black American soldiers, with two Kraut in tow, yet without a superior officer, a warrant or a transfer order. Their British captain gave a simple nod to two of his soldiers, who then tapped the Germans on the shoulders and escorted them to the old factory building where new prisoners were being registered and processed. On their way into the factory hall, the older one of the Krauts turned around once more. Sam could see the expression in his intelligent, short-sighted eyes behind dirty, black-rimmed glasses: He understood very well what had just happened. He bid his American captors farewell with another tap on his forehead. *Samuel Harris*, his lips mouthed soundlessly. Sam stood and watched them go, hands in his pockets. He felt the little piece of paper the German had slipped to Sam as he was ushering him out of the Jeep. He had not looked at it yet.

When their Jeep returned to the country bakery that served as their makeshift quarters, Sergeant Rhees came lumbering out of the front door, his face speckled with officious anger:

"There you are. What the hell is going on? I was about ready to report you as deserted!"

"No, sir, we're right here," said Sam in a casualness that was meant to take the wind out of Rhees' sails, but had the opposite effect.

"Fuck it, Harris. Where are the fucking prisoners?"

"Gone, as ya tole us, sir."

Rhees stared past Sam's eyes straight into his mind and knew that Sam had not gotten rid of the prisoners in the fashion that Rhees had suggested.

"You set them loose, didn't you."

"Why would I wanna do that, sir?"

"You set the *fucking enemy* loose."

"No, sir."

"How are they 'gone', then?"

Sam made no reply.

"You stay right here 'till I have time to deal with your shit," Rhees ordered, confining them to the same flour-dusty backroom that had contained the two German prisoners just a couple of hours ago.

"Thanks. Thanks a million," gnarled Bud between his teeth. He was sitting on the flour chest, avoiding eye contact with the man who dragged him into this mess.

"Ya saw the pictures of those women. They need their men to cum home."

"My woman needs me to cum home, too. Five minutes later and Rhees woulda reported us as fuckin deserters."

A pause.

"Damn. At least gimme a cigarette."

"Ain got none left."

"You had half a pack this afternoon."

"Ain got none left now."

Bud finally raised his eyes at him, in slow realization: "Ya gave'm to them Krauts! To them bloody Krauts! Ya insane. Ya headed to the nuthouse. That is, if ya doan get yaself killed before that."

They sat in silence, and the cigarettes that would have occupied their idle hands and wordless mouths were sorely missing. Bud picked up a piece of straw from the floor and started chewing it, hard, as if it required concentration.

"Ya know, we coulda just not *seen* them Krauts in the first place."

Yes, Sam *had* actually considered this for a moment, yesterday, as they were being slow-cooked in their sweltering, reeking armored truck in the mid-day heat. When Sam squinted towards the horizon and instantly wished he hadn't seen ... what he had just seen. Yes, he *had* wondered if he could just ignore them. But Bud had been squinting at them, too:

"Was that a person?"

"Hm. Two o'em."

"Dadgummit."

"What we spose to do?"

"Ya reckon it's Krauts?"

"They was runnin, so I guess so."

"They still behind that bush?"

"Where else would they be?"

The meadow was wide and plain, therefore, the frantic figures who had just scurried behind a bush had to still be there. When they reached the bush, Sam stopped the truck, ever so slowly.

"Ya goin out?" asked Bud.

"What the fuck else is there to do? Ya got ma back?"

"Sure."

Sam pushed his glasses back up the sweaty bridge of his nose, opened the door, and emerged very slowly, gunpoint first.

The men were not trying very hard to hide. Neither of them had a shirt on, and as far as Sam could see, they were unarmed. One was soaking wet. Sam relaxed somewhat. There was nothing menacing about these two half-clad men squatting under snowhite elder blossoms.

One of them had to be around forty, with silver-rimmed glasses that suggested scholarship, unlike Sam's horn-rimmed glasses, which merely suggested he had bad eyesight. His look was melancholic, with little fear in it, considering the fact that an American halftrack had just pulled up right next to him. The most intriguing thing about him was the way he was looking at Sam. He was looking at him – well, *casually*. Most Germans met Sam with almost childlike bewilderment. The younger man right here being a case in point: Crouching slightly behind his older companion, he was in a state of wide-eyed astonishment. It was the mesmerized look of a Nazi-bred youngster who had never been face-to-face with a black man before, much less expected to ever be vanquished or captured by one. Sam had grown used to this look, and therefore found it quite intriguing that the older German exhibited no visible reaction to the fact *who* was capturing him.

"Are ya guys alone?" Sam asked, while trying think of German words that would convey the same point. „Mehr Soldat hier?"

"No. Just me and my friend here."

"Cum on out. Hands on ya head."

They emerged from the bush. The younger, dripping wet one had problems with his balance. He was wearing nothing but his drawers. The other one was shirtless, but at least he had his pants on.

We're taking prisoners, Sam realized gravely.

"Can we…? Our clothes?" asked the older one, with a gesture towards the elder bush.

Sam nodded awkwardly. As the man scrambled back under the dense branches, Sam realized, in a fit of panic, that he might have just allowed the enemy to whip a hidden gun out of the bush. He hastily raised his weapon. Yet the German merely retrieved his companion's pants and their tunics. Sam exhaled slowly.

"Bud. Cum on out and check that bush while I watch them."

Bud clumsily tried to emerge from the truck while simultaneously keeping his weapon pointed at the prisoners.

"Bud."

"Hm?"

"I got them. Lower ya gun and look in that bush."

Bud hopped down and started poking around the elder.

"Check their clothes, too."

Bud found a nice watch in one of the pockets, and put it on his own wrist with a grin. He also took a pocket watch from one of the jackets.

"What ya doin there, Bud?"

"That's what ya spose to do."

Disarm them, not steal their valuables, thought Sam, but in light of the fact that one of the Krauts understood English, he preferred not to have a discussion in front of him. The older man now helped the younger one into his pants with much circumstance. The younger one's foot was bleeding profusely. As he was trying to maneuver it into the pant leg, his face twisted in obvious pain. Sam climbed back into the driver's cabin and found their first-aid kit. He gave it to the older prisoner, who immediately used it with obvious skill. He nimbly dressed his comrade's wound and returned the kit with a nod of thanks.

"Where's all ya stuff? Ya gotta have some stuff."

"Yes, we have a car. Over there."

"There?"

"Yes, in the woods. It's camouflaged."

"Sit on the hood."

They drove the short distance to the place the German soldier had indicated, both prisoners perched on the large hood of their vehicle. They found the German *Kübelwagen* with the Krauts' equipment and belongings. Sam piled it all up in two separate heaps; one with the prisoners' military gear, one with their personal effects. He slid a side-glance at Bud, who was inspecting the items with the eyes of a scavenger. Sam began to slide important-looking objects into his own pockets before

Bud could get them, a fine tobacco tin, a silver cigarette case. Next, he found their wallets. One contained the picture of a middle-aged woman, dirty-blonde, serene, confident. The photograph was in the same immaculate condition as the woman in it. The older German kept it carefully tucked in a perfectly-sized pocket in his wallet. Out of the younger man's wallet tumbled a tattered, dog-eared, love-worn photograph. It showed a rustic young woman with blonde, firmly braided hair, in a plain dress and blouse that had been pressed with great care. She had the somewhat apprehensive, flustered expression of someone who hardly ever gets her photograph taken. Her mouth was sweet and soft like a child's. The deplorable condition of the photograph was clearly the result of countless caresses and kisses.

Sam's mind was flooded by the horrid insight that those two prisoners were actual *people*. That somewhere in Germany, the radiant middle-aged woman and the sweet fawn of a girl were sitting at kitchen tables across from empty chairs where these two men belonged.

Ever since he had waded from the landing craft into a blur of carnage, there had been only shadows on the other side of this war, dim outlines that had to be gunned down before they could gun you down.

Sam was not supposed to look into a wallet and discover a human being.

When he glanced back up at those men, Sam felt a little woozy. He smiled at them. Then he carefully reassembled their wallets.

He and Bud gathered the two piles in two bundles and loaded them onto the truck. Their prisoners climbed back onto the hood.

"Let's go."

♦

"What the *fuck*, Harris, is that?"

Lieutenant Rhees' pale face was speckled with red splotches, as always when he was either angry, in combat, or drunk.

"They were right in front of us, sir, we couldn…"

"What part of 'no prisoners' do you not understand?"

"They were right in front of us."

"You've had Krauts right in front of you before, Harris, and you knew what to do *then*."

"Yes, but these two were all by themselves and unarmed."

"And what do we do now? How many men are we, Harris?"

"Twelve, sir."

"A-huh. How many men can we afford to spare to

guard, and feed, and take care of them?"

"We can spare no one, sir."

"And yet, there you are, riding around, picking up Krauts. *Injured* Krauts, on top of that."

"Only one ofem's injured, sir."

"Shut the fuck up!"

The scarlet spots on Rhees' otherwise pasty face were dancing, and despite his discomfiture, Sam found this phenomenon mildly fascinating. He was wondering how exactly it worked, what strange condition made Rhees' blood hop rather than flow through his veins.

"Get rid of them."

Rhees started to walk away.

"How, sir?"

Rhees stopped and turned, disdain in his look.

"What kind of a stupid question is that?"

"But sir…"

"Did *I* pick up those fuckers or did *you*? You get rid of them the way y'all should have gotten rid of them when you first saw them, and I wanna hear no more about it. Tomorrow at noon we move on, *without* any fucking additional baggage."

He retired to his makeshift commander's office in what used to be the baker's living room. The other soldiers who happened to be in the parlor with Sam and Bud were staring at them, their expressions ranging from malicious glee to uneasy sympathy.

"What ya gonna do, Sam?" Bud asked.

"What ya aksin *me* for?" Sam snapped back. He left the parlor and wandered down the deserted village street, kicking dust, chewing on an unlit cigarette.

Rhees wanted him to kill those Germans.

Was there anyone he could appeal to? Their company commander, maybe? Nonsense. He didn't even know where Major Miles even was. Not to mention the fact that Normandy was a burning hell. This was not a good moment to inquire about the lawfulness of shooting two Germans whom he had picked up in their underwear. Bud wouldn't be of any help. Nor anyone else. Loneliness was clawing at Sam's chest. He had been ordered to kill two men. So what? How many Krauts had already sunk to the ground in the crosshairs of his gun sight? The problem was – he had looked into their wallets.

Sam returned to the bakery and entered the room that used to be the baker's office, and which now served as their clinic because there was slightly less flour dust in the air than anywhere else in the building. Ray, the medic, was taking care of the younger Kraut. Sam grunted. Ray probably did not know that he was wasting his time. He was extracting a pretty large, sharp object from the German soldier's foot. The prisoner clenched his teeth with a sharp inhale, in boyish stoicism. Man, how old was that kid? His girl in the photograph was almost a child, too.

"How did that happen?" Sam asked him. The prisoner scowled at him in dark rancor. He wouldn't answer even if he knew enough English to do so.

"Where's the other one?"

"Storage room," said Ray.

Sam left the clinic, went to the cook and obtained his ration for the night. Those who were on good terms with the field cook, like himself, did not have to wait for the official meal times. Then Sam made for the storage room where they had taken the older German. Bud was guarding him. Their assignment to eliminate the German prisoners was written all over his miserable face.

"Really?" he asked when Sam made a move to enter, blocking his way.

"Jus wanna talk to him."

"I doan think that's a good idea."

Sam didn't budge. Neither did Bud.

"Doan talk to that Kraut any mo'e. Ya makin it harder."

"What am I makin harder?"

Bud glowered. "What we gotta do."

"We gonna do it?"

Bud's face was made of granite.

"We ain gonna do it, Bud. Now let me in."

He shoved Bud aside and entered the storage room. Inside, the older prisoner was sitting in the dim light of a dying, hissing lightbulb. Sam's appearance lit up his face. Sam sat down across from him and pulled out his cigarettes.

"Want one?"

The German took one and put it in his mouth. As Sam leaned forward to light it, he introduced himself:

"Hannes Kröger."

"Samuel Harris."

Sam lit his own cigarette.

"That boy that's with ya, how old is he?"

"Nineteen."

"Hm, not too bad. I thought he was younger n that."

He paused.

"I mean, I seen some *really* young German kids out there."

The man named Hannes Kröger just shrugged.

"Hungry?" Without awaiting a response, Sam handed him half of the bread he had gotten from the kitchen. Hannes Kröger halved the half he received and put it in his pocket.

"No, no, go 'head and eat it all. I got some for ya buddy, too."

The door opened and Ray entered with the German kid. Sam could not give him his ration just yet, for Bud was standing in the door, keenly observant. So Sam left the room and walked back down the hall with Ray.

"Thanks, man." Ray nodded, but Sam added: "Some folks here'd say he wasn worth ya time."

"Like who?"

"Rhees wants me n Bud to kill them po' devils."

"They not prisoners?"

"Yeah, they are."

"I thought we spose to take care of prisoners."

"Yeah, but Bud and me weren't spose to *take* prisoners in the first place. Ya shoot em righ when ya see em, then it's fine. Then it's called *combat.* But ya hesitate for jus one moment, then ya got prisoners on ya hands. Rhees is mad as hell."

"Oh, screw him." Sam arched an eyebrow at Ray for his explicit disagreement with their lieutenant. "Look, I'm a medic. And I *know* we're spose to follow rules. Like the Brits do. They got this whole big thing goin on with prisoners over there, ya know, on the road to Caen."

"How d'ya know that?"

"Yesterday, when I's down there to pick up some

meds, I saw that huge place where they coop em all up. Thousands of Krauts. Like cattle. They said they was gonna walk them all to some camp."

"That so?" asked Sam keenly. "Where's that at?"

"Man," Ray shook his head in resignation. "Ya better do what Rhees tole ya to. That's a good thirty-mile drive, ya gonna get in trouble if ya waste that much fuel."

"Where's that at?" Sam insisted.

Ray looked into Sam's face and saw that it was undaunted by the prospect of trouble. So Ray shrugged:

"Fine. Let me show ya. I got a map in here."

JANUARNACHT

Die raue Felswand schimmerte feucht. Wolfi konnte nicht wegsehen. Er hatte Durst. Er zog Max' Jacke aus, denn hier unten war es wärmer als in der eisigen Wohnung. Im Gegenteil, es war muffig und begann schon zu riechen. Wenn jetzt noch irgendein Baby seine Hosen voll schiss, oder jemand kotzte, dann würde die Luft in dem dicht gepackten Keller unerträglich, das wusste Wolfi. Und sein Mund war so trocken. Je länger er die Tropfen ansah, die zwischen den Furchen der bröckligen Wand hinunter krochen, desto ekelhafter fühlte sich seine Zunge an, die trocken an seinem Gaumen klebte. Die Leute waren recht still, weil man die Flieger schon hören konnte. Da war es immer ganz still. Oft saß man stundenlang hier unten, und hörte man keine Flieger, dann wurden die Leute gesprächig, und der dunkle Raum klang wie ein Kinosaal, bevor der Film losgeht. Aber die Flieger brummten jetzt schon, also flüsterte man nur. Man hörte nur ab und zu eine Mutter zischen, weil die Kleinsten nichts begriffen. Die wollten krabbeln, spielen, ihre Geschwister an den Haaren ziehen. Ein Tropfen perlte von der Wand ab und landete auf Wolfis Nase. Da hielt er es nicht mehr aus. Er lehnte sich nach hinten, verdrehte seinen Hals, und leckte. Schmeckte salzig.

Die anderen Mütter nahmen sich doch auch einen Moment Zeit, ein bisschen für die lange Nacht im

Luftschutzkeller zu packen. Nur seine Mutter ... Wenn die die Sirenen aufheulen hörte, wenn Onkel Baldrian mit noch so besonnener Stimme die Luftlagemeldungen im Radio verlas, verlor sie sofort die Nerven und zerrte blind, panisch, und völlig ungerüstet ihre Kinder mit sich in die Felsengänge. Den Onkel Friedrich hatte sie diesmal sogar oben in der Wohnung sitzen lassen. Dem ging nämlich das ständige Gerenne in den Schutzraum in der Zwischenzeit zu sehr auf die Nerven. Er würde warten, bis der Luftschutzwart kam und ihn holte, hatte er gesagt.

Und darum jedenfalls hatte Wolfis Mutter kein Wasser dabei und Wolfi einen Riesendurst.

„Lass des", bremste ihn die Mutter.

„Ich hab an Durscht."

„Des is bestimmt giftig."

„Wieso, is doch bloß a Wasser."

„Ja, Wasser voller Chemikalien", belehrte ihn sein ältester Bruder Bernd, der immer alles wusste. „Wer weiß, was sich da alles löst, wenn das Regenwasser durch den Sandstein hier runter rinnt. Was hier in den Felsenkellern alles im Lauf der Jahrhunderte gebraut und gebeizt und fabriziert worden is."

„Schlegg däi Wand ned", fasste die Mutter Bernds Erklärung effizient zusammen.

„Aber mir ham ja nix zum Trinkn."

„Da, Wolfi", erbarmte sich Frau Kässler und reichte ihm eine Feldflasche.

„Bidde, naa, Frau Kässler, sie ham doch selber bloß die ane Flaschn."

„Eds drink ruhig an Schlugg, Bou", beharrte die Kässlerin.

Mutter nahm Wolfi übel, mit seiner Wandleckerei die Nachbarin zu einem Almosen genötigt zu haben. Selbst solch einen kleinen Gefallen angemessen zu erwidern war dieser Tage schwierig.

„Wie viel Uhr isn?", flüsterte Bernd.

„Fast acht", konnte ein Nachbar Auskunft geben, weil der nämlich eine ganz moderne Uhr besaß, mit leuchtenden Phosphormarkierungen.

„Oh, kann mer die a im Dunkeln lesn?", animierte sich Wolfi.

„Freili, da, schau's dir nur an."

Der ältere Nachbar verdrehte sein Handgelenk, um Wolfi die Uhr genauer bestaunen zu lassen.

„Ham Sie so weit gute Feiertag ghabt, Frau Wächter?" fragte nun Frau Kässler.

„So gut's halt geht", gab Mutter zurück. „Ich bin ned amol bis Middernacht aufbliebn vorgestern."

„Sylvester war a no nie meins", bestätigte Frau Kässler. „Und a Feierwerch kriegn mer ja fast jede

Wochn kostenlos von die Ami," sagte sie lakonisch.

„I bin fei bis Middernacht aufbliebn", brüstete sich Wolfi.

„Wieso, du hast doch bei mir gschlafn", wunderte sich Mutter.

„Der Maxi had mi aufgweckt!"

„Du, Mama?", ertönte zaghaft die Stimme des mittleren Bruders.

„Ja, Maxi."

„Des sin aber viel Fliecher heit."

Die Wächters, Frau Kässler und der ältere Herr horchten. Das Gebrumm, wenn auch durch die meterdicke Felsendecke gedämpft, war bedenklich nahe.

„Aber Bombn falln ja no kane."

„Des sin ja a no ned die Bomber. Die setzn erst amol die Tannabäum."

Mutter horchte auf die Flieger. Wolfi nutzte den Moment, sich noch einmal zur Wand zu drehen und noch ein wenig von dem salzigen Nass zu lecken. Seine Zungenspitze berührte die Wand. Doch in dem Moment rückte die Wand von ihm weg. Als er es noch einmal versuchte, stieß der spröde Fels ihm gegen die Nasenspitze. Der Boden erzitterte. Wolfi purzelte auf den Schoß seiner Mutter. Eine Kinderstimme quietschte, Erwachsene stöhnten. Der ganze Keller rüttelte. Die

Bilder vor Wolfis Augen bebten unscharf, wie ein wackeliger alter Film. Die Menschen, die dicht an dicht entlang der Wand aufgereiht waren, schüttelte es durcheinander, sie fielen auf die Knie, kauerten, hielten sich auf allen Vieren. Die Mütter griffen nach ihren Kindern, krümmten sich über sie wie menschliche Kokons. Wolfi bekam Angst. Heute Nacht war wie keine andere. Staub und Sandsteinbrösel rieselten von der Decke.

„Mama, bricht der Keller eds zam?", schrie er, und wartete auf eine von Mutters üblichen beschwichtigenden Antworten im Getöse. Ein *Freili ned* oder ein *Ach, Gschmarri*. Aber diesmal sagte sie nichts dergleichen. Wolfi wimmerte. Mutter fasste ihn, presste ihn gegen ihren weichen Mamabusen, rollte sich über ihn, als ob sie eine einstürzende Felsendecke mit ihrem Rücken aufhalten könnte. Mit ihrem anderen Arm hielt sie den Max. Bernd kauerte ihr gegenüber, den Kopf eingezogen, seine Hand schützend auf dem Rücken seiner Mutter.

Dann stand der Boden wieder still, doch das Brummen der Flieger dröhnte weiter.

„Herrgott, steh uns bei!", schrie Frau Kässler, ihre sonst so kratzbürstige Hausmeisterinnenstimme brüchig, außer sich.

Der nächste Treffer. Das Licht flackerte aus. Die Säuglinge schrien nun ohne Unterlass. Die Erwachsenen ächzten. Mutters Fingernägel kerbten sich in Wolfis Haut. Wolfi sah die Phosphorstriche auf der Armbanduhr des älteren Herrn. Bei jedem neuen Beben malten sie zittrige grünliche Streifen in die Schwärze.

„Eds is alles aus", hörte er Frau Kässler.

♦

„Wolfi", schüttelte ihn Mutter. „Wolfi, bist du wach?"

War er wach? Wolfi wusste es nicht so recht. Das Licht war wieder an. Als die Bomber endlich von der Altstadt abließen und seine Mutter sich aufrappelte, blieb Wolfi einfach eingerollt wie ein Embryo auf dem Felsboden liegen.

„Es is vorbei."

Wolfis Arme und Beine waren eingeschlafen und bitzelten, er konnte sich nicht regen.

„Bleib ruhig sitzn, wir könna eds eh no ned raus."

„I will gar ned raus. I wills gar ned sehn", machte Frau Kässler dumpf.

„Und i hab ned amol unser Kartenheftla dabei", bemerkte Mutter, was ihre Gedanken verriet: Sie zweifelte daran, ob ihre Wohnung noch stand. Und sie hatte noch nicht mal die Lebensmittelmarken mitgenommen. Ihre Augen flimmerten ins Leere, während sie weiter in Gedanken ihre Lage sondierte.

„Bernd!", schluchzte sie in plötzlicher, grässlicher Verzweiflung. „Der Onkel!" Mutters Körper versteifte sich, sie sprang auf die Füße, als könnte sie den Onkel im Keller ausmachen.

„Mama", versuchte Bernd sie zu beruhigen. Er zog an ihrer Hand, bedeutete ihr, sich wieder zu setzen. „Der Luftschutzwart hat ihn bestimmt abgholt. Aber finden werden wir ihn eds ned, es sin ja Tausende von Menschen hier unten."

Max suchte Bernds Blick. *Der Angriff war dieses Mal rasch gekommen.* Ob der Luftschutzwart überhaupt Zeit gehabt hatte, seine gewohnte Runde zu machen, und ob der sture Onkel dessen Anweisungen gefolgt war...

Ein ihnen unbekannter Luftschutzwart erschien. Er war schmutzig, benebelt, fassungslos.

„Könna mir raus?" fragte eine Stimme, ohne Hoffnung auf eine positive Antwort.

„Naa, is alles dicht. Die Ausgänge sin alle verschüttet. Mir gehn durchn Stadtgraben raus, aber des dauert a weng. Sind ja an die zwanzigtausend Leut hier herunten, die müssn alle durch den einen Gang. I sag euch scho, wenn mir dran sind."

Als ihre Sektion evakuiert wurde, musste Mutter Wolfi tragen, denn es graute schon der Morgen und Wolfi war zwar noch nicht eingeschlafen, aber völlig erschöpft. Außerdem traute Mutter der ermatteten Ruhe der anderen Menschen ringsum nicht. Bräche eine Panik aus, würde ihr Kleinster zertrampelt. Also trug sie ihn lieber.

„Gib mir den Wolfi, Mama", bot Bernd an. Sie übergab den Jüngsten ihrem ältesten Sohn und hob dann den noch schwereren Max auf. Max, stolze neun Jahre alt, duldete normalerweise nicht mal eine flüchtige Berührung seiner Mutter. Nun aber ließ er sich tragen wie ein Kleinkind, schlang seine Arme um ihren Hals, schmiegte sein verstaubtes Gesicht an ihre Schulter.

Der Gang, der tief unter der Altstadt bis zum Stadtgraben führte, gehörte nicht zu den mittelalterlichen Felsengängen. Den hatten sie eigens für den Luftschutz gebaut. Statt des urigen Burgsandsteins waren die Wände hier aus banalem Backstein, weiß getüncht, und so niedrig, dass die Erwachsenen sich bücken mussten. So schmal, dass man nur im Gänsemarsch voranschlurfen konnte. Jedes Straucheln, jedes Zaudern verursachte einen Stau, der einen Lindwurm aus hunderten verstörten und übermüdeten Menschen in misslichen Körperhaltungen stecken bleiben ließ. Die Babies hatten das Weinen aufgegeben, blickten mit ihren großen Augen matt und starr in die Tiefe des Ganges.

Wolfi spürte einen eisigen Hauch, in dem sich frischer Sauerstoff mit kratzigem Rauch vermischte. *Der Ausgang*. Mutter und Bernd konnten sich endlich voll aufrichten, Wolfi und Max wurden auf den Boden herabgelassen. Der Stadtgraben war nachtschwarz, doch auf den Gesichtern schimmerte es rötlich. Der Schein kam von jenseits der Stadtmauer. Die Nacht war erfüllt von Knistern, Knacken, und dem Rauschen fallender Holzbalken. Heizkessel explodierten. Tausende Menschen standen hilflos, wortlos in der Januarnacht herum. Manche hatten Koffer. Andere trugen nicht einmal einen Mantel. Der übliche Drang, nach einem Luftangriff sofort nach Hause zu hasten, nach dem Rechten zu sehen, ließ alle unruhig umher watscheln. Doch war jedem klar: In die Altstadt kam heute Nacht keiner mehr rein.

Bernd übernahm das Ruder. Er begann nach Norden zu marschieren, bergan, von wo aus man vielleicht die Altstadt überblicken konnte. Seine Mutter und Brüder folgten ihm taub. Auch außerhalb des Mauerrings brannte es vielerorts.

„Bernd", sagte Mutter.

„Ich will bloß schauen, ob man was sehn kann."

Selbst die Kaiserburg loderte orangerot gegen den Nachthimmel.

„Bernd."

Bernd ging rastlos weiter, reckte den Hals, wollte einen Blick über die Stadtmauern werfen, das Ausmaß der Zerstörung innerhalb des Mauerrings erfassen. Wo ihre Wohnung war. Wo der alte Onkel Friedrich vielleicht immer noch stur in seinem Ohrensessel saß.

„Bernd, da brauchmer ned schaun, es is alles kaputt. Die Altstadt is wech."

Endlich blieb Bernd stehen, all seiner Kraft entleert. Ihm schwand die Männlichkeit, die ihn durch die Nacht getrieben hatte, er schrumpfte wieder zu einem der

Kinder. Mutter hielt alle drei an sich gedrückt.

„Buam. Meine Buam. Was machmern eds?"

Decision

The bell went, the shift was over. During the day, Sam worked like a machine, his mind abuzz, his body dull, mechanical, repetitive. The shrill sound brought him back to reality, and the first thing Sam became aware of was the thin layer of dry sawdust coating his throat. He left the work-hall and made towards the water fountain in the hallway. He bent down. No water came out.

"Damn it. Again?"

"Gotta push harder, and a lil to the left," a fellow worker behind him advised. Everybody was familiar with the frequent malfunctions of the damned fountain and hence knew how to troubleshoot it.

The foreman came and bent his flaxen head down to the fountain for white people – which was the actual fountain, and not just a little bowl connected to the main plumbing with a rusty pipe. He drank and walked away again.

"Rattle it a lil," recommended another voice. A line was forming behind Sam, everyone wanted to wash down the sawdust. No one as much as glanced over to the fully functional, idle main fountain right next to their problem.

"Ain workin," Sam concluded, straightened up and walked away. To hell with it, it was only a ten-minute walk home. He heard the others launch into a keen analysis of the fountain failure.

When he arrived at his mother's house, he poured almost a whole pitcher full of water down his parched throat before he dropped onto his chair across from his mother. He had spent all day planning this conversation in his mind:

"I'm goin back to Europe, mother," was all that came out.

The steady creak of her rocking chair squealed out of its rhythm.

"What was that, son?"

"I enlisted again. Got ma assignment in the mail las night. I'm headed back to Germany."

There was a silence while her mind worked through his words. Jason was still, too.

"I considered maself lucky to get at leas one of my boys back whole. And now ya wantin to go *back o'er there*?"

She resumed rocking, and the moan of her chair matched her voice. Which was peculiar, Sam mused, because when she was cheerful, so was the squeaking of her chair on the old floor. Jason did not look at Sam, pretended to be completely absorbed by his task – threading a bit of tattered yarn into the eye of a needle with with his six and a half fingers. Why did Jason always have to attempt tasks that made his damn fingers stand out? He could be doing things that he was able to do as well as anybody else. For example, Hester could really use some help bringing in the firewood, and if Sam didn't have to break some important news to his mother, that's what he would be doing right now. But no, Jason was always doing things that made his mangled fingers stand out.

"Well, mother...."

"Close that doo', Hester, will ya?"

"I'm gonna be in an out the parlor at leas five mo'e times, Nana," Hester justified his method, which consisted of slamming open the front door and letting the cold air whisk in while he was hauling in load after load of firewood. He did that on purpose. Whoever wasn't hauling wood should at least suffer the same frigid temperatures that he was exposed to.

"Dear Lord," his mother continued her lament, "this one came home whole, and now he's wantin to go back o'er there."

"Mother, look. The war is long over. There's no...."

"Ya got that needle threaded for me, Jason? I'd do it maself if I could see."

"Ya see well 'nough to do ya needlework all day long."

"The eye of that needle is jus gettin too small for ma ole eyes."

"There it is, mother."

"Bless ya heart. Havin to do that for ya ole blind mother with ya bad hand."

His mother's habit of starting conversations and then not listening to the answer was a perpetual source of vexation for Sam, but on this particular night, it saved him the trouble of having to sustain a cohesive argument.

Jason was crippled by more than two mangled hands. In forty-five, he had been in Germany, just like Sam. Like Sam, he had rolled down those scarred German streets, horror just behind them, and triumph just ahead, under the dejected blue-eyed glances of the defeated – who perceived *them* as conquerors. As masters. Like Sam, he had handed out candy to throngs of disheveled freckled German moppets. Like Sam, he was free to walk into any place he wanted. Late in the war, very late, a pocket of German resistance in some remote village took his squadron by surprise and a few fingers off Jason's hands. But he had already tasted victory. The war had already clouded his judgement, had already emboldened him. So when he was back home, Jason left the house one afternoon to walk downtown with his Purple Heart on his uniformed chest. And the next time Sam saw his brother, he was in the hospital. His brain was concussed and his jaw broken, as was his spirit. Just as his attackers had intended.

Sam did not walk around town in his uniform. But that did not mean he hadn't also felt what Jason had felt.

In fact, it was the main reason why Sam had enlisted again, why he volunteered to be deployed back to the place he had so luckily escaped from unscathed six years ago.

"Why, Sam? Why ya goin back over there?" his mother retrieved the thread of the conversation at the same time as that of her needlework.

Because I felt like a person over there.

"It's good money," Sam offered, just to feed the conversation.

"Ya ain makin 'nough at the mill?" Jason's tone was reproachful, implying that he would be *happy* to work at the mill. Sam knew, however, that Jason had never even applied there. Sam was quite sure they would have hired Jason, even with a maimed hand. Business was booming, they always needed people for all kinds of jobs. But Jason did not want to work at the mill in any capacity. Before the war, he had aspired to be a professional pianist. He had landed some promising engagement in Charleston, had already bought a suit and a bus ticket – when he was drafted.

Sam sighed. He'd spent too many years in this house, in this town, at this mill. With his nit-picking mother, his wallowing brother, his abrasive brother-in-law. His life was slowly seeping away.

It was time to go.

ENTSCHEIDUNG

„Über so was redmer, wenn der Papa hamkommt", wimmelte Mutter sie ab, ohne dabei von ihrer Wäsche abzulassen, die sie gerade nass und schwer aus dem Zuber hievte.

Auffordernd, und nur für seine Brüder sichtbar, drehte Bernd die Augen aus den Höhlen. Gerade vor ein paar Minuten hatten sie darüber einen brüderlichen Kriegsrat gehalten. *Man müsse halt mal Klartext mit ihr reden*, hatte Bernd verlangt. *Bernd habe leicht reden, weil er ja nun nur noch am Wochenende zu Hause war*, hatte Max gemeint. Aber Recht hatte Bernd schon, sie konnten nicht ihr ganzes Leben auf einen unbestimmten, in aller Wahrscheinlichkeit nie eintretenden Zeitpunkt vertrösten, an dem wie durch ein Wunder ihr in Russland vermisster Vater wieder auftauchte. Der Kleinste, Wolfi, fasste sich ein Herz:

„Du, Mama?"

„Mh."

„Und wenn der Papa denn kommt, wird's dann recht viel anders?"

„Na freili. Alles wird anders."

Sie walkte die Tücher noch fester und schaffte es tatsächlich, sie fast bis auf den letzten Tropfen auszuwringen. Ihre Fingerknöchel waren abwechselnd weiß von dem Druck und rot von der Anstrengung.

„Dann kehrt wieder a Ordnung ein. Und du kriegst die Hosen viel öfter stramm zogn, wenn wieder a Mo im Haus is."

„Des kommt drauf an, in welchem Zustand er heim kommt", bemerkte Max trocken.

Mutter ließ eines der Tücher pfeifend gegen das Holzbrett peitschen, um es aus dem Knoten zu lösen, den sie beim Auswringen gezwirbelt hatte. Ungeachtet dieses Warnsignals fuhr Max fort:

„Die ham ja alle an Padscher, die im Krieg warn. Und die im Krieg *und* in Gfangenschaft warn, die ham gleich an doppelten Hau."

„Max", bremste Bernd seinen Bruder ab. Weitere Handtücher peitschten scharf gegen das Brett und wurden dann rasch und stramm mit Holzklammern auf die Leine gespannt, die im Zickzack quer durch die Küche hing.

„Jeder. Brauchst bloß unsere Lehrer amol anschaun. Der Hölzl, zum Beispiel...."

„Dei Vadder is aber ned der Hölzl", barst es aus Mutter. Ihre Stimme klang so hart wie die Tücher, die gegen das Brett pfiffen.

„Außerdem hat der Hölzl schon vor dem Krieg gesponnen", lenkte Bernd das Gespräch.

„Langt amoi oaner mit her?", mischte sich ein neuer,

bayerischer Tonfall ins Gespräch, gemächlicher und unbekümmerter als das emotional geladene Raspeln der Exilfranken, weil Theresa gerade von draußen herein kam.

Die beiden jüngeren Brüder sprangen beflissen auf, um sowohl dem Gespräch als auch dem Mühsal des Waschtags zu entkommen. Die Aufgaben, die Theresa ihnen auftrug, lagen den Kindern viel mehr, denn sie verrichtete die ‚echten' Arbeiten hier auf ihrem Hof – nämlich die bäuerlichen Pflichten. Theresa herrschte über den Winklerischen Hof, seit ihr Mann Ludwig anno dreiundvierzig blutjung und frisch verheiratet an die Front musste und erst vier Jahre später von einem Kameraden heimgebracht wurde, und zwar in einer Urne.

Seit Waltraud im Januar 1945 mit noch drei weiteren hungrigen Mäulern hier erschienen war, nahm sie sich des Haushalts und Theresas neugeborener Tochter Brigitte an, damit Theresa sich ganz ihrem Hof und der Landwirtschaft widmen konnte. Die Buben gingen zur Hand, so gut jeder konnte. Sowie die bayerischen Städte in Schutt und Asche versanken, kamen noch mehr Frauen und Kinder auf den Hof, aus München, aus Ingolstadt. Wolfis umtriebiges Wesen machte ihn, damals sechs, zum natürlichen Rudelsführer aller noch kleineren Knirpse. Die kleine Brigitte schleppte er mit sich herum wie eine Puppe, bis sie laufen konnte und ihm wie ein Schatten auf Schritt und Tritt folgte. Wolfi war stolz auf sein gelehriges Mündel. Mit drei Jahren war sie schon eine brauchbare Steinschleuderschützin.

Die Frauen hatten derweil zu viel Mühe mit dem Überleben, um sich all zu große Gedanken um ihren Nachwuchs zu machen. Sie glaubten die kleinen Gören und Bengel von Wolfi mehr oder minder betreut. Schließlich sah und hörte man oft den ganzen Tag nichts von den Kindern, und indessen wurden Hopfentriebe um Drähte gewunden, im Herbst die Reben geerntet, nebenher Gemüse angebaut, Eier eingesammelt, Marmelade eingeweckt, der Haushalt gemacht, Brotsuppen gekocht. Man überlebte. Die anderen Familien gingen einige Monate nach Kriegsende wieder weg. Waltraud blieb. Jahr für Jahr, absichtslos, mechanisch ihr Tagessoll verrichtend. Mit sechzehn hatte Bernd genug. Ein entfernter Verwandter in Nürnberg wurde angezapft und Bernd kam dort unter, um zur höheren Schule zu gehen. Nur am Wochenende kam er nach Manching und beobachtete mit wachsendem Unbehagen, wie seine kleinen Brüder wie Raubkatzen durch die Landschaft streunten. Wolfi war nun elf. Max schon fünfzehn. *Wäre doch höchste Zeit, in die Stadt zurückzukehren*, schlug Bernd immer wieder vor und fand seine Mutter gelähmt, gefangen in der Überzeugung, sie müsse für größere Entscheidungen die Rückkehr ihres verschollenen Mannes abwarten.

Heute folgte Bernd Theresa nicht in die Scheune, wie seine Brüder, sondern blieb am Küchentisch sitzen. Seine Mutter aber wollte das Gespräch, das unvollendet im Raum hing, nicht fortfahren:

„Eds geh halt a der Theresa a weng zur Hand."

„Des machen der Wolfi und der Max schon. Mutter."

‚Mutter' sagte Bernd ganz selten. Waltraud hielt inne, sah ihm ins ernste Gesicht und konnte dem Gespräch nicht weiter ausweichen. Sie ließ von ihren nassen Handtüchern ab und wandte sich ihrem ältesten Sohn zu.

„Es wird wirklich Zeit, dass der Max und der Bernd wieder in die Stadt kommen. Die verkümmern hier."

„Wie meinstn des."

„Die lernen nix Gescheites. Streunen nur rum. Machen den ganzen Tag nur Blödsinn."

„In der Stadt wär's doch aa ned besser. In die Trümmer."

„Zumindest gibt's da echte Schulen."

„Es steht doch bloß no a aanzigs Schulhaus. Und des betreibns in Schichten."

„Mutter. Glaubst du wirklich, dass aus deinen Kindern hier zwischen den Gockeln und den Säuen was wird? Wir sind keine Bauern. Wir sind hier nur zu Gast."

Jetzt setzte sie sich sogar zu ihm. Mit ihrem Finger fuhr sie rastlos eines der Astlöcher in der Tischplatte nach.

„I möcherd ja selber gern zrück, aber des geht erst, wenn der Papa wieder da is."

Der Tisch bebte unter Bernds Faust, die in plötzlicher,

frustrierter Wut darauf hernieder fuhr. Waltrauds Finger hüpften vom Astloch weg und zog sich erschrocken in ihre Schürze zurück, wo sie unruhig den steifen Stoff zu kneten anfingen.

„Hör halt auf damit. Hör endli auf mit dem Gschmarri."

In Bernds Zorn zitterten fast Tränen. „Irgendwann müssen wirs doch mal laut sagen. Der kommt nimmer heim. *Der Papa is tot. Schon lang tot.*"

Waltrauds Gesicht war steinern, die Finger zwirbelten den Schürzenzipfel. Eine dicke Fliege betonte mit ihrem Gebrumm die Eisesstille in der Küche. Bernd fuhr schließlich fort:

„Wir müssen doch irgendwann weitermachen, auch ohne ihn. Gehn wir doch alle zurück nach Nürnberg, Mutter. Wenn ihr hier weiter auf ihn wartet, versauert ihr nur."

„Und wovon solln mern leben?", fragte Waltraud brüchig. Bernd fasste ihre Hände, ermutigt. Mutter nahm eine mögliche Heimkehr in die Stadt so ernst, dass ihr sogar schon ein Hindernis einfiel.

„Ja, des... wollt ich mit dir besprechen. Ich wüsst nämlich was."

Waltrauds Finger lösten sich nun aus der Schürze. Sie wischte sich die Hände daran ab, als wären sie schwitzig.

„Der Zeitschriftenladen in den Merrell Barracks. Den

hätte ich ja bloß zeitweise in den Ferien führen sollen, aber es schaut so aus, als hätten die Amis niemand anderen dafür. Weil sie mich nämlich gefragt haben, ob ich weiter machen könnte."

„Ja, aber der Unterricht geht ja wieder los, da kannst du ja ned den ganzn Tag in der SS-Kaserne stehn."

„Ja eben", bestätigte Bernd, ohne die Wortwahl seiner Mutter zu korrigieren. Die Kaserne auf der Frankenstrasse blieb im unverbesserlichen Volksmund die SS-Kaserne, auch wenn schon längst amerikanische Truppen darin stationiert waren.

Bernd sah seine Mutter auffordernd an: Sie solle doch endlich begreifen. Da fiel der Groschen. Waltraud wich mit ihrem Oberkörper etwas zurück wie vor einem seltsamen Geruch. Die welligen Falten auf ihrer Stirn rückten zusammen:

„Du meinst …. ich? Aber ich kann doch gar ka Englisch."

„Mehr als die meisten Frauen in deinem Alter. Außerdem musst ja ned viel reden, du kassierst halt, verwaltest den Bestand und am Monatsende musst du mit dem Sergeant abrechnen, da helfe ich dir schon."

Waltrauds Stirnfalten arbeiteten. Bernd beobachtete ihr Mienenspiel genau, hoffnungsvoll: „Und beim Metzger Ahrend wird eine Wohnung frei, die Zieglers ziehn nämlich irgendwohin ins Ruhrgebiet."

„Und was kostn des Miete da?"

Bernds Blut strömte ihm warm in die Backen vor Freude, dass seine Mutter seinem Gedankengang so willig folgte.

„Fünfzig Mark. Des kriegst leicht zusammen mit dem *Stars and Stripes*."

„Mit wem?"

„So heißt er doch, der Laden."

„Ach so. Und wovon sollmern leben?"

„Mittagessen kriegen die Buben günstig in der Schule. Und für Abendessen bleibt schon genug übrig. Und weit is es ja ned, da fährst mit meinem alten Fahrrad hin, brauchst keine Straßenbahn zahlen und nix."

Ein schreckliches Getöse zerriss das Gespräch. Waltraud fuhr auf. Vom Fenster aus sahen sie und Bernd die Bescherung: ein splitterndes Loch im Gewächshausdach. Durch die trüben, grünschmutzigen Scheiben erahnten sie den Schaden im Innern: zerbrochene Blumentöpfe, geknickte Tomatensträuche.

„Sagamal, spinnt ihr?!"

Die unverkennbar strauchelnden Schritte von Wolfi sausten davon, gefolgt von den flinken, leichten Mädchenfüßen der kleinen Brigitte.

„Wir wissn, dass ihr des wart! Ich hab dacht, ihr helft der Theresa! Kommt sofort her, ihr Teufelsbraten!", brüllte Waltraud durch das halb geöffnete Fenster.

„Siehst du, was ich mein, Mama?", fragte ruhig die junge Männerstimme neben ihr. Waltraud hielt inne und sah Bernd an. Ihr Ausdruck veränderte sich plötzlich, ihre Wut wich schmerzlicher Zärtlichkeit.

„Du hast eds grad gschaut und klungen wie der Vadder. Genau wie dei Vadder."

Ihre Augen füllten sich feucht. Bernd stand auf. Er nahm sie in den Arm, und sie ließ ihn gewähren. Sie vergrub ihr Gesicht in seinem Hemd, während ein Schluchzen sie schüttelte.

„Ich vermiss ihn fei gscheid, Bernd. Und der Wolfi und der Max, die bräuchten ihn so."

Bernd drückte sie und zwinkerte über ihre Schulter hinweg eine Träne aus seinen eigenen Augen. Er war doch jetzt der Mann im Haus. Sie sollte sich an ihm anlehnen können. Und darum seinen Schmerz möglichst nicht sehen.

„Des weiß ich doch. Aber der Papa würd nicht wollen, dass wir hier vor uns hin vegetieren, so Nebendarsteller im Leben von jemand anders, und ned auf unseren eigenen Beinen stehen."

„Hast ja Recht, Bernd." Sie wischte sich mit dem Handrücken die Augen und schniefte, suchte in ihrer Schürzentasche nach ihrem Taschentuch.

„Hast ja Recht."

Weird Tales

"How much is that one?" Sam waved a copy of 'Weird Tales' under the lady's nose, hastily, because he was somewhat embarrassed by its cover, which featured purple, half-clad female Martians.

"Twenty-five cents," the cashier responded matter-of-factly. And, pointing it out quite impatiently with her index finger, she added: "Steht doch da, right here."

Of course Sam had seen the price of one quarter printed on the cover. But he had assumed there would be a mark-up, given the fact that it had been shipped here all the way across the Atlantic Ocean. He tried to explain his reasoning, but found no receptive ears. The lady was eying him warily, impatiently waiting for him to either purchase the item or put it back on the shelf.

"All right," Sam said, pulling a quarter from his pocket.

"Good-bye," she dispatched him as she took the money. But Sam was not done shopping. He actually had not come here to buy this bizarre pulp magazine. He had been hovering around another section of the store, but a pair of rather unfriendly and keenly observant eyes had kept him from picking up the volume he actually wanted. Now the soldier who had been observing him had left the store. What was this unpleasant fellow's name name again, Tucker or something? Now that he was unobserved, Sam slowly paced back to the shelf with the classics.

"Ma'am? What 'bout that one?"

Cumbersomely, reluctantly, the cashier wound her way out of the bulwark, consisting of her cash register, a wall of cardboard boxes and stacks of books, from behind which she normally reigned over the store. She came wobbling over to Sam. Whereas his purchase of naked aliens had been business as usual, the book he was holding up to her now was not exactly a bestseller. With a frown, she snatched the copy of 'Walden' out of Sam's hand and flipped through the first couple of pages to find the penciled-in price.

"Two fifty."

"All right."

When Sam hopped the concrete stairs out of the building with the elastic bounce of someone who has his afternoon entertainment all planned out, he almost stepped on a little hand that was resting on the bottom step. A child was loitering there in the faint sunlight. He was idle, on the verge of boredom. As the boy lifted his glance to him, Sam felt a bout of instant kinship. The kid's blue-eyed, curious gaze was full of friendly mischief.

"Hey there," Sam greeted him. "Watch your fingers there, lil man, people are tryin to get in an outa the store." The boy smiled, obviously clueless as to what Sam had said. So Sam repeated: "Fingers. Your fingers."

„Ah," understood the boy, wiggling his fingers to indicate he got the message. As Sam walked back towards the main building, the boy followed him.

"Want a magazine?" Sam asked, holding up his newly purchased copy of 'Weird Tales'. He wasn't sure why he was offering it to the child. He just knew he liked his presence and that he himself didn't feel like reading about interstellar vixens, anyway – now that he had a Thoreau in his pocket.

The child's eyes lit up in exquisite pleasure.

"Sank you. Sank you!" he exclaimed, charmingly unable to produce a 'th', and with such excitement that it garnered the attention of the newsagent behind the window as they were passing under it. She opened the window, and her facial expression left no doubt how much she disapproved of the transaction that had just taken place. She hollered a command in German, which made the boy frown in misery. Sam understood he had been ordered to return the magazine.

"No, no, it's okay. I gave it to him. I actually got it *for* him," Sam lied. The woman scowled as the boy took advantage of this opportunity to take off as fast as a weasel and avoid confiscation of his precious gift.

"My son," she explained to Sam. "Ten years old. Sis magazine ..." Sam's blood thinned a little with mortification as he realized both how very inappropriate the publication was for a young kid – and that he was facing the child's mother.

"I'm sorry, ma'am. Next time I'll get him, uh, Mickey Mouse or sumthin… more suitable."

"No next time! You give him nuhssing!" she insisted.

Sam shrugged and walked back to his quarters.

Mittsommerabends

Der Juliabend glitzerte auf dem Wasser. Die Sonne döste ruhig und wärmend auf Wolfis Bauch. Er kniff die Augen zusammen. Die Flusswellen tanzten funkelnden zwischen seinen Wimpern. Sein Körper wippte sanft, glitt ruhig unter den zerfurchten Schatten hindurch, die die Bäume von links und rechts auf ihn warfen. Der Sandstein der Ufermauern hatte den ganzen herrlichen Tag über die Sommersonne gesammelt und gab sie nun sanft glühend zurück. Blütenduft paffte in süßen Schwaden über den Mief von Entenfedern und grün-abgestandenem Pegnitzwasser. Die Altstadt zog vorbei. Es gab von allem etwas: Vom Schicksal verschonte Fachwerkbauten, dazwischen Ruinen, dann klaffte wieder ein Stück Ödland, wo kaputte Drahtzäune sinnlos über Sandberge und Geröllhaufen wachten. Dann kamen aber auch lärmende Baustellen, aus denen banal und eckig moderne Wohnklötze wuchsen. An Wolfis behaglichem Blick schwammen Fensterläden vorbei, Vorfahrtsschilder, ins Leere gähnende Rohre, Scherben, Kieshaufen. Wolfis Stadt eben. Nürnberg.

So, dachte Wolfi müde, *müsste ich einfach liegen bleiben können*. Rücklings auf dem alten Lasterreifenschlauch die Pegnitz hinabtreibend, ohne Zeitgefühl, im brüder-, mutter- und vor allem lehrerfreien Raum, zufrieden, für den Moment jedenfalls. In ein paar Stunden würde sein Magen wieder rumoren und anstelle des sanften, sonnigen Nichts würde ihn dann wieder der Hunger durch die Straßen treiben, ruhelos und zunehmend übellaunig. Wolfi verlagerte intuitiv sein Gewicht nach vorne, denn er wusste mit dem Instinkt eines Pegnitzbibers, wir der Fluss verlief, wo die fast meterhohe Stufe war, die seinen Schlauch mit einen Satz in die Tiefe würde platschen lassen. Der Schlauch rutschte, stürzte, und Wolfi ließ sich routiniert nach hinten plumpsen, um den Reifen aus dem Sog des Strudels zu manövrieren. Er wurde kaum nass dabei. Vorbei am Spital. Nur noch ein kleines Stückchen weiter, sagte er sich, denn er hatte eigentlich keine Lust, kilometerweit nach Hause laufen zu müssen. Das Problem war nur, fiel ihm siedend heiß ein, er hatte heute noch nichts Brauchbares gefunden!

Da! Da glitzerte etwas im Wasser. Und es war nicht die Sonne. Wolfi beugte sich nach vorne, zwinkerte angestrengt die Augen zusammen. Sein Schlauch trieb zu schnell, also schnappte er nach einem tief hängenden Ast und sein schwimmender Untersatz begann um die eigene Achse zu kreiseln. Da war doch was im Wasser. Relativ groß sogar. Zum Glück. Mamas Provision vom Zeitschriftenladen reichte gerade so für die Miete, wenn es gut lief, aber ohne Wolfis und Maxis Geschäfte mit den Wertstoffhändlern würde es dann doch zu knapp. Und was da gerade in der Pegnitz flimmerte, versprach ein schönes, großes Trumm Metall zu sein. Wolfi sprang ab, watete zum Ufer, hievte seinen Reifen an Land und arbeitete sich im brusttiefen Wasser zurück zu der Fundstelle. Er tauchte danach, doch das Ding rührte sich kaum. Tatsächlich, es war etwas Schweres! Er würde vielleicht sogar Max brauchen, um es zu bergen. Aber wenn er es nun unbeaufsichtigt ließ… womöglich hatten ihm andere Streuner sogar dabei zugesehen, wie er so eifrig im Wasser stocherte, und würden ihm seine Beute vor der Nase weg schnappen, während er Verstärkung holte! Hm. Vielleicht ging es doch auch ohne Max. Wolfi tauchte drei, fünf, zehn Mal. Endlich löste sich etwas aus dem Flussbettschlamm. Er bekam einen Teil gut zu fassen, es ging vorwärts! Stück für Stück zerrte und schob Wolfi das Ungetüm Richtung Ufer. Als er es von dort aus mit großer Mühe die Uferböschung hinan manövrierte, wurde ihm klar: Das war kein üblicher Altstadtschrott, kein verrostetes Rohr, kein alter Heizkessel…

„Ach du liebe Scheiße, is des a Maschinengewehr?"

Wolfi fuhr herum. Sein Bruder Max kam auf dem Hosenboden die Böschung heruntergerutscht.

„Schaut ganz so aus", bestätigte Wolfi, mit vor Anstrengung und Triumph glühenden Wangen.

„Glaubst du, der Hagermann gibt uns da was dafür?"

Max rümpfte nachdenklich seine sommersprossige Nase.

„Naa, des is doch nix fürn Hagermann."

„Für wen denn dann?"

„Na, wenn des Ding noch geht…"

„Is doch wurscht obs geht, wer willn heutzutag a Maschinengwehr?"

„Ich wüsst scho wen."

Deal

"Wow, not bad, kid!"

Shane Tucker strutted into the bookstore storage room in perfect coolness, while Sam watched the scene unfold with growing unease.

"Where on earth did you get this, boys?"

"Pegnitz," the older one declared. The younger boy, the one whom Sam had given his science fiction magazine, pointed to his own chest, claiming credit for the find.

"And you hauled it out yourselves? You're something else."

"Now, listen, kids," said Sam, not nearly as delighted at the sight of a seemingly operational machine gun in the storage room as the other GI. He spoke very slowly, because he wanted the children to understand: "If you find stuff like this, leave it alone. Hear me? Leave – it – alone. Or let a grown-up know. Ja? Grown-up, understand? Big person. Do you hear me? Tell your dad."

"No dad," said the older one matter-of-factly.

"How much you asking for it?" Shane wanted to know.

"Tuck....," Sam tried to reign him in.

"Shut up, boy," Shane snarled. Sam's skin was crawling with an eerie sense that this was no situation in which a freshly desegregated black soldier should find himself. Yet there he was, standing in the poorly lit storage room with ginger-haired, freckled Shane Tucker, in front of a piece of heavy weaponry that two German children had hauled out of the river. Sam had just happened to be in the store at the same time as Shane when little Wolfi tugged his sleeve and motioned him to follow. Sam, instinctively answering the boy's gesture to follow, and Shane, just plain curious, had then both trailed the boy to the newsagent's storage room.

Sam's mind was racing. Should he report the incident? But how would that make him look? Tell the kids to get rid of it? No, they were just kids. They really should not be handling this thing any more than they already had. While Sam was pondering the situation, Shane repeated:

"How much, boys?" The children shrugged at first, then the prospect of making a deal triggered the younger one's business sense:

„Also des Metall... zwei Mark." He held up two little fingers.

"You mean the metal would fetch two Deutschmarks? Where, at the scrap yard? But this is not just a pile of scrap. This thing seems to *work*."

Shane stepped closer and began to inspect. The gun was rusty, but showed no sign of mechanical damage. At the end of the war, people had dumped all sorts of fully functional weaponry into the rivers and lakes, for fear of being found armed. Of course this thing still worked.

"I love it," Shane admired the gun.

"Ten," the older one now dared ask.

"Deal," said Shane instantly.

"Tuck...," Sam tried to intervene again.

"Did I not tell you to shut up," Shane said, in a tone that was so condescending it sounded almost affable. He reached for the wallet in his back pocket.

"Well, I ain got nuthin to do with this," said Sam and left the room. He meant to get the hell out of here, back to the safety of his daily routine. But as he passed the glass door to the *Stars and Stripes* store, he saw the storekeeper, the boys' mother, sitting at the counter. She was hacking away at a mechanical calculator. He could not help himself, he entered.

"Hey, ma'am? Mrs...."

"Wächter. Wächter is my name," she informed him. Sam felt stupid; he'd been a regular customer for over a month and just now learned her name.

"I need to talk to you. Your sons..."

"What did sey do?" she wanted to know, her voice rising with the instant alarm of a seasoned mother of rascals.

"They... it's not ... I mean it *is*.... they jus sold a functional machine gun to one of the GIs."

Frau Wächter's sigh was silent.

"For ten Deutschmarks."

"Ten?" she asked. Her tone gave Sam to understand that there was a real conflict of interest between her conscience and the prospect of ten additional Deutschmarks in the family purse.

"It ain none of ma business, but.... Never mind. It actually really ain none of ma business."

She was not going to do anything about it. Sam could tell. *Ten marks*, for God's sake.

SACHSCHÄDEN

Die Juli-Inventur war haarig. Waltraud schwitzte das ganze Wochenende darüber, unterstützt von Bernd, Max und sogar von Wolfi. Der Bestand stimmte nämlich nicht. In der Kasse waren 345 Dollar und 55 Cent, und exakt in diesem Wert waren auch Bücher und Zeitschriften über den Ladentisch gegangen – Waltraud war akribisch. Aber der tatsächliche Bestand stimmte damit nicht überein. Es fehlten Waren im Wert von fast zehn Dollar. Sechs Stunden dauerte die Inventur, vier weitere Stunden die erste Überprüfung, bei der Waltraud noch hoffte, sie würde nur ein paar simple Rechenfehler berichtigen müssen. Doch die fünfzehn Dollar fehlten immer noch. Auf Bernds Drängen hin unternahmen Waltraud und Bernd ohne die Kleinen noch einen dritten Durchgang, bei dem sie nicht nur die Werte aufaddierten, sondern auch nachforschten, welche Waren genau abhanden gekommen waren. Nicht, dass Waltraud etwas hätte tun können. Auf einen reinen Verdacht hin konnte sie, die deutsche Buchhändlerin, wohl kaum einen ehrbaren Angehörigen der U.S. Army des Diebstahls bezichtigen. Aber *wissen* wollte sie es, um in Zukunft ein schärferes Auge auf diese Kunden zu haben. Sollte sich zum Beispiel herausstellen, dass Hemmingway, Melville oder Thackeray fehlten, dann war für den Schwund im Bücherbestand wohl der dünne Schwarze mit der Nickelbrille verantwortlich. Wären es jedoch billige Wochenhefte, dann fielen ihr ein paar andere Verdächtige ein, zum Beispiel der sommersprossige Rothaarige. Ansonsten war Waltrauds Kundschaft gemischt und unstetig, sie konnte niemandem sonst konkrete Lesemuster nachweisen. Nach ein paar weiteren mühsamen Stunden am Sonntag stand der Befund fest: die Diskrepanz im Lagerbestand lag bei etwa dreißig Schundheften, und der Rest war nicht auszumachen.

Erschöpft, mit geschwollenen Augenlidern und schmerzendem Rücken kehrte Waltraud dann am späten Sonntagnachmittag in die Wohnung heim, nur um verdrossen festzustellen, dass das Wochenende vorbei war, ohne dass Wäsche gewaschen oder die Wohnung sauber gemacht worden war. Zwei ihrer drei Söhne kamen allabendlich drecksteif nach Hause, und ihr Ältester, in vollster Blüte seiner Manneskraft, legte größten Wert auf blitzsaubere, gepresste Hemden, wenn er auf den Fluren der Uni an den jungen Damen vorbei spazierte.

Also.

Waltraud seufzte, heizte Wasser, lud ihre alte Bottichwaschmaschine in der Küche, füllte den Putzeimer, zerrte den Besen aus Abstellkammer. Ihr Rücken bettelte um Erbarmen. Half ja nichts. Ihr Körper war wund, ihr Herz schwer, ihr Kopf schwirrte. Wutig schrubbte sie die Dielen, als wären die an ihrem Unglück schuld. *Zehn Dollar*. Fast vierzig Mark. Fast die Miete, die sie morgen für die dreckige Bude hier dem Metzger würde zahlen müssen. So viel Geld.

Waltraud hielt inne, denn sie schwitzte nun aus allen Poren. Die schweren dunkelroten Vorhänge, die eigentlich die pralle Sonne draußen halten sollten, sperrten die stickig drückende Hitze des Tages nun in der kleinen Wohnung ein. Waltraud richtete sich stöhnend auf, um die Gardinen aufzuziehen und ein bisschen von der Abendbrise herein zu lassen. Als sie den Stoff packte, bemerkte sie ein kleines kreisrundes Loch.

„Auch des noch."

Sie schüttelte den Stoff. Motten? Bitte nicht. Wenn die auch in die Kleiderschränke gerieten! Sie hatten doch kein Geld. Waltraud suchte nach weiteren Schäden. Da, tatsächlich. Noch ein Loch. Und da noch eins. Waltraud wurde stutzig. Die Löcher waren alle exakt auf der gleichen Höhe. Waltraud zog den Vorhang ganz auf. Er wies mehr als ein Dutzend identischer runder Löcher auf, und zwar so ungefähr auf Brusthöhe, in regelmäßigen Abstanden von etwa zwanzig Zentimetern.

„Ja sagamal, was isn des?"

Sie schob den Vorhang wieder zurück. Sowie er sich in seine gewohnten Falten legte, reihten sich die Löcher perfekt auf. Waltraud konnte regelrecht durch einen kleinen Tunnel hindurchsehen. Wer hatte nur ihren Vorhang so durchbohrt?

„Wolfi!", entfuhr es Waltraud, noch ehe sie wusste, wie ihr Teufelsbraten diese Bescherung bewerkstelligt hatte. Ratlos wendete sie den gefalteten Vorhang von einer Seite zur anderen, inspizierte den Schaden von allen Seiten. Da sah sie es. In der Wand, direkt hinter dem Vorhang war die Tapete zerfetzt, der Putz geplatzt, klaffte ein tiefes Loch genau auf Höhe des Vorhangschadens. Ein *Einschussloch*.

Die Wohnungstür schabte über den Boden.

„Wolfi!!!"

Seine Schritte in der Diele waren unbekümmert und arglos.

„Komm sofort her!"

Wolfi steckte seinen schmutzigen Kopf ins Wohnzimmer.

„*Hierher.*"

Wolfi sah, wo seine Mutter stand, und ihm dämmerte, was ihm nun blühte. Instinktiv zog er den Kopf ein, genug Beweis für Waltraud, dass sie den Schuldigen richtig identifiziert hatte.

„Was isn des, bitte?"

„Äh, was?", fragte Wolfi und reckte dabei unschuldig den Hals, als müsste er erst mal sehen, was seine Mutter denn meinte. „Meinst du des?"

„Ja, *des.*"

„Äh... schaut aus wie a Loch. Des war vielleicht scho länger da."

„Wolfi!!!", donnerte Waltraud. „Du sagst mir eds sofort, was in Gotts Namen du da scho wieder angstellt hast!"

Wolfi zuckte, und gab auf:

„Ich hab's ned gwollt."

„Was hast du ned gwolllt?"

„Der Max hat gsacht, die wär ned gladen."

„*Geladen*!?"

„Und dann had's an Mordsschlag tan. Aber is ja zum Glück bloß in die Wand gangen."

„Ihr habt hier drin *gschossen*?", begriff Waltraud mit wachsendem Entsetzen.

„Hat aber kanner ghört. Des war heut früh, die Nachbarn warn alle in der Kirch."

„Und mit was habt ihr gschossen?"

„Mit ner altn Luger."

„Woher habt ihr die ghabt?"

„Aus am Trümmerhaufn."

„Und wo is die eds?"

„Im Küchnschrank."

Waltraud fegte in die Küche, gefolgt von Wolfi, dessen Interesse an seinem Fundstück noch größer war als seine Zerknirschung. Waltraud fand das Gesuchte sorgfältig zwischen Geschirrtücher gebettet.

„Wenn du mir no amol so a Trumm ins Haus bringst,

Kerl ...", knurrte Waltraud und ließ ihre Drohung offen im Raum stehen. Nicht nur, weil sie so besser wirkte. Sondern auch, weil sie nicht so recht wusste, wie man den Bengel denn bestrafen sollte. Er besaß nichts, was man ihm wegnehmen konnte. Einen Stubenarrest konnte sie schlecht durchsetzen, weil sie den ganzen Tag arbeitete. Also machte sie offene Drohungen.

„Versprochen. Mach i nimmer, Mama", nickte Wolfi kooperativ und sah auf einmal sehr klein und niedlich aus.

„Allmächtiger", entfuhr es Waltraud, während ihre Wut in mütterliche Sorge umschlug. Sie presste sein kleines Gesicht an ihren Bauch. „Ihr hättet euch gegnseitig erschießn könna! Hast selber Angst ghabt, als die losgangen is, oder, Wolfi?"

„Bin scho erschrockn, Mama", gab er zu und Waltraud drückte ihn noch fester an sich. Ihr Wackerla, ihr kleiner, unbeaufsichtigter Vrecker!

„Und an Wahnsinnsschlag hat des tan", fügte Wolfi hinzu. In seinen Augen funkelten schon wieder Schabernack und Vergnügen. Waltraud befreite sich frustriert aus der Umarmung. Nichts machte Wolfi glücklicher als gefährliche oder grob fahrlässige Aktionen. Das würde Waltraud ihm wohl nie austreiben können. Und so lange sie so viel schuften musste, konnte sie auch nichts anderes tun als hoffen, dass ihre Bengel jeden Abend heil aus der Trümmerwüste nach Hause kämen.

Die Waffe lag schwer in ihrer Hand. Wolfi starrte

darauf.

„Soll i die in die Pegnitz schmeißn, Mama?", fragte er und streckte schon die Hand danach aus.

„Na, na, na, naaa", machte Waltraud und hielt die Pistole an ihre Brust. „Du fasst mir des Ding nimmer an. Ich kümmer mi scho drum. Da, mach du di lieber nützlich, kehr amol die Küchn zam", verwies sie ihn auf den Besen, der noch gegen die Anrichte lehnte. Wolfi tat, wie ihm geheißen, Waltraud legte die Waffe in ihre Handtasche und wandte sich wieder der Wäsche zu. Das Reisig des Besens kratzte unbeholfen über die Fliesen, die Wäsche im Bottich schwappte. In dem geschäftigen Schweigen erriet Wolfi Waltrauds Gedanken:

„Der Rothaarige tät's der bestimmt abkaufn. Der mit die Sommersprossn."

„Halt du dei Goschn!", herrschte ihn Waltraud an, bei genau diesem Einfall ertappt, und setzte laut ratternd die Zentrifuge in Gang.

BAMBERG

Sam stared at the rushing, gurgling waters of the Regnitz. He inhaled the sweet, lazy scent that came drifting from the pink flowers, letting himself get lost in a moment so still and ageless that he forgot why he had come here. Time had warped the timberframe of the houses on the crisp green of the riverbank. It had taken them centuries to settle snugly into the perfect position in the soft soil. Little boats were bobbing on the water right by the back doors. The crates on the windowsills were overflowing with masses of blazing flowers.

Just sitting here in the sweet, serene beauty of Bamberg was a perplexing mental exercise to Sam. Almost six years after the war, Nürnberg was still a carcass of molten steel and splintered wood. Little ones went about their childhood pursuits amidst piles of rubble in complete normalcy. And in this sense, Nürnberg was like any other place Sam had seen back in forty-five. As his armored vehicle had rolled over the scorched, smoking remains of the Third Reich, it had not really occurred to him that these heaps of sweltering rubble had once stood tall and proud. That the wide-eyed, terrified people that his approaching tank sent scurrying squirrel-like in all directions – had once gone about their business on these streets in placid innocence. All the miserable ruins he had seen ... were once just like this town of Bamberg. Some quaint, some grand, but all used to be whole and beautiful.

When Sam moved, he felt the 'Pocket Guide to Germany' in his back pocket. He took it out. This little manual for conquerors had been handed to him back in 44 when he first set foot in Germany. He remembered why he had come to Bamberg. Between the yellowed pages of the booklet was another, smaller scrap of paper, which he had also been given eight years ago. It stated a name and an address in remarkably confident, sure-stroked cursive, especially considering the fact that the man who had written it down didn't know whether he would live or die the next minute.

Johannes Kröger

Obere Sandstrasse 8 in Bamberg

Sam crossed the Untere Brücke one more time. He searched his outdated pocket guide for phrases to ask for directions. He should have bought a map.

As usual, it was a child that dared break through the barrier that stood between him and the locals. That invisible wall between the conqueror and the defeated still seemed insurmountable to many adults. Children had no notion that it even existed. This one here was a typical specimen: snot-nosed, keen-eyed and undaunted, running about on scrawny, agile legs that stuck out from worn old leather shorts. The boy addressed him in

German. Sam did not need to understand his words to know he wanted some chocolate or gum. Sam had none on him, which he tried to communicate along with his regrets. The boy understood and skittered away.

"Wait, buddy."

The boy turned back. Sam wanted to test his pocket guide on him. He opened the booklet and tried to assemble chunks of language:

„Fayr-TSAI-oong... VO IST....?"

That can't be right, thought Sam even as he said it. It just looked and sounded too funny. „Uh, VO IST Obere Sandstraße?"

The boy looked at him in mild fascination. Sam leafed through his guide and found the phrase 'Do you understand?'

„Fer-SHTAY-en zee?"

The boy's mouth widened into a broad grin. He said something and motioned Sam to follow him.

„DAN-kuh", Sam said. It only took a few minutes to get there. Although the street-signs were written in unfamiliar, Gothic lettering, Sam was able to decipher *Obere Standstraße*. There it was; the storefront of a beautiful old pharmacy. He thanked the boy again, unable to reward him with any goodies, but the child's good humor was undampened by the lack of compensation. He hopped away as happily as he had crossed Sam's path. Before Sam entered the pharmacy, he examined the entrance. The brass sign next to the door confirmed that Johannes Kröger was indeed the owner. Sam felt strangely excited, as if he was about to reunite with a long-lost friend. The German soldier had stuffed the paper into his hand in Normandy in 1944, right before he and his companion had been swallowed up by a thick cloud of dust that was rising from an enormous marching column of German prisoners. Sam had kept the crumpled paper all these years. Looking at a map of Franconia in the briefing room the other day, Sam had realized that Bamberg was not far from Nürnberg. His next free Saturday, Sam had taken the train to Bamberg, and here he was.

He entered.

„Grüß Gott," the man in the white coat started to say… and then stopped short. His short-sighted eyes behind the round horn-rimmed spectacles widened. He pushed his glasses up the bridge of his nose as if that could sharpen his vision.

"Samuel Harris?"

"Yes. Oh man, ya remember me," confirmed Sam in surprise and delight.

"Samuel Harris!" Kröger repeated, now with certainty. He edged around the corner of his counter, opening his arms as if to hug Sam, but then he checked his enthusiasm and instead gave him a vigorous, two-fisted handshake.

"Samuel Harris. For Pete's sake, how is it that *Samuel Harris* is standing in my pharmacy?"

Sam marveled at Kröger's distinct, rather good British accent. Well, it was into British hands that Sam had delivered the man eight years ago.

"I was deployed back over here, an I thought I'd just... I dunno ... check on ya," Sam shrugged. Johannes Kröger was beaming.

"Mathilde!!!" he shouted over his shoulder. "You must meet my wife", he explained. "Mathilde!"

A woman emerged from the back room of the pharmacy. Strangely, seeing her felt like a reunion, too, for she looked exactly like she did in the photograph in Kröger's wallet that Sam remembered so well. Kröger explained Sam's presence in rapid, breathless German sentences. Sam caught the words *Normandie* and *Engländer*. Her face lit up, and her handshake, though less forceful than her husband's, was no less sincere.

Soon later he was sitting in their living room upstairs, being served the best of what they had, from cigars to real bean coffee. Sam tried to decline most of it, but was urged so eagerly that any further refusal would have amounted to an insult.

"May I pour you some more coffee, Mr. Harris?"

Sam fought off a strange sense of danger that crept up his spine as Mrs. Kröger came so very close to him. White women were not supposed to offer him stuff, let alone wait on him the way she was doing. An attractive white woman was not supposed to smile at him, with the husband sitting right there.

"No, thank ya so much, ma'am."

"Oh please, Mr. Harris, you need a little more coffee for your cake." Ignoring his refusal, she refilled his cup to the rim.

Kröger, in the meantime, was happily prattling away in the hilariously British accent that he had taken away from more than two years in British captivity.

"And what about the kid?" Sam then asked.

The question arrested Kröger's jolly chatter. His expression changed instantly, a melancholy shadow passed over the cheerfulness.

"If you mean Ludwig Winkler, I'm sorry to say that he is deceased."

"What!? But... y'all were prisoners, outa combat ... what else could possibly....?"

"It's a long story," said Kröger, whose expression suggested that this story better be told on another occasion.

"His po' lil woman," Sam thought aloud. The photograph of the sweet innocent creature that was young Winkler's wife suddenly appeared before him as if he had just pulled it out of Winkler's dirty wallet. He saw her very clearly. The girl widow.

"Yes, and he left her with a little child, too. Mathilde and I check on them whenever we can. They are doing fine. Farmers, you know. The only sure way to feed a family in this new Germany. She's fine."

Kröger looked into his cup as he pondered his own words and then said: "You know, come to think of it, I am sure she would love to meet you so that she can thank you, too."

"What's there to thank. He didn make it home."

"But he got a lot closer to home. Ludwig lived to know that he had a daughter. And as his friend, I can tell you that the two years in England were the most important years of his short life." He put down his cup before he added: "And that he owed to you."

Sam shrugged awkwardly.

"I know you had orders to kill us, Mr. Harris. Ludwig and I both understood what you did for us."

Sam shrugged again.

"And I have often wondered what consequences this act of courage had for you and your comrade."

Hannes Kröger looked at him intently.

"Well, my officer … didn like it, that much is fo' sure."

"Did you get into hot water?"

"A lil bit. I'll tell ya all 'bout it the day ya tell me how

Ludwig died."

"Well, that means we must meet again", said Hannes Kröger with a smile.

On the train ride home, Sam's new book lay closed in his lap. He felt strangely different than this morning. He was no longer just a soldier in a foreign land. He was no longer a nobody walking amongst nameless faces. Now he had people whose fates mattered to him, and who took a vivid interest in his.

Begegnung

„Also dann, Frau Winkler..."

„Auf Wiedersehen, Herr Stengele."

„Also dann..."

Der Besucher stand in beflissener Haltung und mit gelüpftem Hut in Theresas Küche, wenig geneigt zu gehen. Er hoffte wohl, im allgemeinen Gewimmel der neu eintreffenden Besucher vielleicht doch auch noch zu Tee und Kuchen eingeladen zu werden. Während Theresa die Wächters begrüßte, griff Hannes ein:

„Herr Stengele, brechen Sie lieber geschwind auf, da braut sich was zusammen", sagte er mit einer Geste auf den wolkenschweren Himmel.

„Ja, ich geh wohl besser. Also dann, Frau Winkler..."

„Das wird gleich wie aus Eimern losschütten." Hannes schob den zudringlichen Besucher nun sogar ein wenig und schloss rasch die Tür, sobald Stengele endlich über die Schwelle war.

„Was warn des für a Dialekt?", wunderte sich Waltraud Wächter.

„Schlesisch", gab Theresa Auskunft, mit den Tellern klirrend.

„Ah...", verstand Waltraud.

„So geht das hier den ganzen Tag zu", erläuterte Hannes. „Wie die Freier um Penelope schwirren sie, die Vertriebenen, ist ja klar. Saubere junge Witwe mit ordentlichem Hof. Und in den Städten hocken die Leute zu zwölft in Zwei-Zimmer-Wohnungen."

„Des is klar. Da tät i a schaun, ob i ned a Landpartie machn kann", witzelte Waltraud.

„Wer isn Penelope?", fragte Theresa, während sie an ihrem recht fest geratenen Kuchen säbelte. Sie war beim Backen sparsam mit der Butter.

„Das war die Frau vom Odysseus, der zwanzig Jahre gebraucht hat, um von Troja heimzukommen, während bei ihr daheim die Freier saßen und sie alle heiraten wollten."

„Mei Odysseus kommt aber nimmer hoam", sagte Theresa hart, und ihr Messer, das soeben den Kuchen besiegt hatte, klirrte hart auf den Teller. Sie prüfte das Porzellan nach Kratzern.

„Ja, um so mehr Grund für deine Freier, sich Hoffnungen zu machen. Wenn du die los haben willst, musst du Klartext mit denen reden, Theresa."

„Mach i doch."

„Machst eben ned," sagte Waltraud.

„Oder aber", fügte Hannes bedächtiger hinzu, „du suchst dir einen Tüchtigen aus, machst einen Pachtvertrag mit ihm, überlässt ihm den Hof und gehst mit der Brigitte fort. Du musst ja nicht heiraten, um einen Hof zu übergeben."

„Eds geht des wieder los", seufzte Theresa.

„Ja, bis du mal ernsthaft darüber nachdenkst."

„Die Stadt is koa guater Ort für a Kind."

„Wer sagt denn das?"

Theresa blickte schief zu Waltraud.

„Na, *i* sag des ned", wehrte die sich gegen den stummen Vorwurf.

„Dass der Wolfi a schußfähigs Maschinengewehr ausm Fluss zogn und an an Ami verkauft hoat, des sagt doch ois. Des wär hier am Land ned passiert."

„Ja gut. Aber er geht eds aa täglich zur Schul und lernt was. Und der Max, der hat sogar scho a Lehrstell in Aussicht."

Max hob fragend die Augenbrauen.

„Hab ich des?"

„Die Brigitte is eds sechs, eds musst scho langsam amol über ihr Schulbildung nachdenkn."

„Als obs hier koa Volksschul gäb in Manching."

„Ja, und wie lang mussna da laufn bis nach Manching, die Klanne? A Stund?"

„Na, ned soo lang."

„A dreiviertel Stund", präzisierte Wolfi.

„Und zwar ganz allein!", fügte Hannes hinzu.

Theresa verteilte die endlich zerlegten Kuchenstücke, Waltraud goss Tee ein. Im allgemeinen Klimpern, Schlurfen und Schmatzen machte sich jeder so seine Gedanken.

Es klopfte.

„Zefix, ned no aner."

„Mach gar ned auf. Mir sin ned da", schlug Waltraud vor.

Hannes jedoch erhob sich mit einem Blick auf seine Armbanduhr. „Drei Uhr genau."

Und er öffnete die Tür, als wäre er der Hausherr.

"Like clockwork, my friend. Come on in."

"Good afternoon."

Ein hochgewachsener Mann trat ein. Mit einer Scheu, die gar nicht zu seiner Statur passte, duckte er sich unter dem Türrahmen durch. Es hatte tatsächlich zu regnen begonnen und der Fremde wusste nicht so recht, was er mit seinem triefnassen Hut tun sollte. Er war dunkelhäutig, was sogleich jeden Verdacht ausschloss, dass er ein Vertriebener auf Brautschau sein könnte. Theresa zuckte unmerklich zusammen. Das steckte ihr noch so in den Knochen, vom Kriegsende. Dunkle Haut war ihr gleichbedeutend mit Amerikanern, und damit mit rumpelnden Panzern, Eroberung und Angst. Waltraud hingegen zwinkerte erkennend.

"Oh, Frau Wächter", erkannte freudig auch der Fremde, von seiner Verlegenheit im Nu erlöst.

„Ihr kennt euch?", fragte Hannes baff.

„Von der Kaserne," erläuterte Waltraud.

„Sapperlott. Na, dann geht die Vorstellung ja umso schneller. Also, das hier ist der Samuel Harris. Theresa, das ist er. Er hat uns damals in der Normandie das Leben gerettet, mir und dem Ludwig. Und jetzt ist er in der ehemaligen SS-Kaserne in Nürnberg stationiert. Und daher kennt ihr zwei euch also schon?"

„Ja freili, der kafft mer doch n ganzn Laden leer", bestätigte Waltraud und besah ihren ewig unentschlossenen, zauderhaften Dauerkunden mit ganz neuen Augen.

Der Amerikaner verstand nicht viel von dem deutschen Gespräch, aber lächelte offen und nickte freundlich zu jedem Satz, der gesagt wurde. Theresas Schrecken war indessen in Ehrfurcht umgeschlagen. Den Namen hatte sie schon oft gehört, hatte sich von Hannes dutzende Male erzählen lassen, was ihm und ihrem Ludwig damals in Saint Lô widerfahren war.

"It's a pleasure to meet you, ma'am."

Und vor ihr stand da nun also der Mann, der damals für zwei wildfremde Feinde Kopf und Kragen riskiert hatte, aus Fleisch und Blut, so groß, dass er sich unter der Küchenlampe ducken musste, seine Stimme so volltönend, dass der ganze Raum mitschwang, als er sprach, seine vom Regen noch feuchte Haut so dunkel, dass sie im Halblicht der Küche schimmerte.

"Mr. Harris", brachte Theresa schließlich über die Lippen und näherte sich ihm. Sie streckte ihm schüchtern die Hand entgegen.

"Sank you."

Er griff zögernd danach, und weil sich ihr Händedruck so gut anfühlte – zart und doch aufrichtig und fest – nahm er sich ein Herz und packte sie innig.

"Sank you", wiederholte sie. Hinter Theresa erschien nun eine ältere Frau, vom Leben und Kummer verwittert, aber eindeutig als Ludwigs Mutter erkennbar. Sie hielt sich im Hintergrund, nickte jedoch die Worte ihrer Schwiegertochter bestätigend.

"I'm so sorry, ma'am, to hear that he didn make it home."

Hannes wollte übersetzen, merkte aber, dass es nicht nötig war. Theresas Augen schwammen ein klein wenig. An einem verregneten Herbstnachmittag voll Kindergeschrei, ungebetenen und geladenen Besuchern und trockenem Sandkuchen so plötzlich, so wuchtig von der Vergangenheit überrollt zu werden – war ein bisschen viel. Ludwigs Mutter schlurfte zurück an den Herd, machte sich an Tellern zu schaffen. Hannes zweifelte fast daran, ob das mit der ‚Überraschung' so eine gute Idee gewesen war.

„Kuchen, Mr. Harris?"

"Want some cake?", übersetzte Waltraud eilig, wollte zeigen, wie versiert sie schon im Umgang mit den Besatzern war.

„Ya, DAN-kuh", akzeptierte Sam. Er wurde zu einem Stuhl gewiesen, auf den er sich sehr vorsichtig setzte, obwohl der massivhölzerne Bauernstubenstuhl alles andere als fragil war.

„Also, so ein Zufall", sagte Waltraud kopfschüttelnd, während sie Sam Tee einschenkte, "sat you know Hannes and Ludwig."

„Ick gesehen *Sie*, auch", sagte Sam, für alle in der Runde unerwartet. Seine Worte waren an Theresa gerichtet und ganz offenbar im Voraus überlegt. Sie hielt inne.

„Foto. Ludwig gehabt ein Foto. Von *Sie*."

„Ach ja. Stimmt, er hat damals unsere Geldbeutel konfisziert", erinnerte sich Hannes. "So you remember, huh?"

"As if it was yesterday. I also remember *your* wife's picture. Cause I's thinkin to maself how lucky ya both were to have such fine ladies. I spent that whole night thinkin 'bout how they needed ya to cum back home."

Hannes nickte. Theresa öffnete mit einem Knack ein Glas ihrer wohl gehüteten Marmelade, um Sams Kuchen zu versüßen.

Gnädige Herren

A heap of white fabric came flying over the rail of his bed and landed on the page Sam was reading. It was a shirt. A nice one.

"Put it on!"

Sam tossed it back down. He enjoyed throwing things down from his bed, the only advantage that sleeping on the top bunk offered.

"Hey."

The shirt came back up.

"Cut it out. I got ma own shirt."

"Then put ya own shirt *on*," said Greg. Sam leaned over the edge of his bed. Both Greg and Carl were standing underneath, grinning up at him.

"It is said of Sam Harris that he's never been out before," said Carl melodramatically.

"Well, that ain true. I been all over Bavaria."

Carl caught his dress shirt, which came sailing down from Sam's bunk again, and folded it over his arm.

"Well, you haven't gone out with us all winter."

"Cause we been stuck at the damn border camp in the middle of nowhere."

"And now we're back here, where the fun is."

"I went downtown once. That was 'nough."

Most of the other soldiers of his rank were much younger than himself, draftees on their life's first adventure. Their idea of fun on a Friday night starkly differed from his.

"You went with the wrong people to the wrong places."

"That may well be", said Sam, turning back onto his side towards his book.

"Who'd ya go with, Herman?" Greg wanted to know, unrelenting. Carl laughed when Sam's response was no more than a grunt.

"Let *us* show ya 'round. Ya missin out," said Greg.

Sam turned his page.

"Put ya peepers on and let's go. Ya gonna like it."

Sam stuck his head over the rail again.

"No hookers, no endin up unconscious in a ditch...."

"None of that," promised Carl.

Sam swung his legs over the rail.

Half an hour later they were in a cab headed downtown. It was dark already. Sam liked the early winter night-falls here. But it was also mighty cold. Shivering on the back bench, he produced his knitted cap and gloves from his inner coat pocket. He loved those things. Of course, he'd never owned a woollen cap and gloves in Georgia. Greg laughed when Sam pulled the cap way down over his ears. But he was not here to impress anyone. Let Carl and Greg freeze the tips of their ears off under their spiffy fedoras.

Sam was surprised to find the Hauptmarkt transformed. Usually, the market square was a muddy open space with scattered produce stands, surrounded by heaps of rubble and construction sites. Almost eight years after the war, the cadaverous old town was nowhere near recovery. Tonight, however, the squalor bordering the square was eclipsed by the panache in the middle: Sam saw row after row of wooden huts with roofs of red-white fabric. Their open fronts were full of dangling, twirling, glistening and gleaming stuff, it was *beautiful*. Tantalizingly sweet aromas were wafting warmly through the icy air. The narrow lanes between the rows were tightly packed with coats, scarves and hats. Everyone's breath was rising in little puffs above the countless heads.

"What is this?"

"Christkindlmarkt."

Sam looked at Carl blankly.

"The Christmas market, goof. Ain't it swell?"

Brass music began to play, measured and solemn, albeit somewhat warped by the cold that gripped the instruments. The grave tunes contrasted oddly with what Sam expected to hear. There was no Rudolph, no Frosty, no Jingle Bells. Sam craned his head to see who was playing. The band had to be somewhere near the beautifully illuminated Frauenkirche, the quaintest of the three churches that dominated the old town. Sam stood and absorbed, did not even notice that Carl had disappeared, until his comrade was back and shoved something into Sam's hands, so hot that it burned his fingers through his gloves.

"What the hell is this?"

"Doan aks, drink!" instructed Greg, who was already taking eager, but careful sips from his mug. An aroma rose into Sam's nostrils, intense, zesty and sweet. It almost made him sneeze. He took a sip, scalding the tip of his tongue. The spices tickled his throat on the way down.

"*Glühwein*," Carl identified it for Sam. "Oh, they're starting. Let's move closer," he said as he began shuffling through the crowded lane towards the glowing Frauenkirche.

"Hey, y'all can't jus shove ya way past all them folks with that hot wine," Sam protested, but then he saw that pretty much everyone was elbowing their way forward, either holding a piping-hot beverage or bread rolls stuffed with greasy roasted sausages and mustard. So he, too, engaged in the general jostle.

They reached an open space right in front of the

church. On a stage that was decorated with fir twigs and lights stood three figures. Two young girls, whose solemn expression contrasted comically with their ludicrous attire of tall crowns and huge flimsy wings, which were clearly made out of cardboard and tin foil. In the middle stood a gentle-looking woman in a light robe. Over her head hovered a poorly constructed wire halo. She began to recite. Her speech was the opposite of her ridiculous garb, for it was commanding and captivating, and effortlessly carried over the sea of hats. There was a whimper. It was coming from about the height of Sam's hip. He looked down – a little child who could not see. Her mother was already holding a baby brother. Sam now noticed that all around him, children were perched on parents' shoulders. They were watching the lady with the lop-sided halo and the crystal-sharp voice in trance-like fascination. Sam realized that whatever she was supposed to be, she was at least as mesmerizing to those children as a real-life Santa was to an American kid. He looked back down at the little girl, who by now was in a state of genuine despair. He dared not budge. *Don't touch that kid*, his instinct said. In fact, *don't even look at her*. Then he heard Carl say:

„Entschuldigung, soll ich...?"

The mother gave an ingratiated nod and before Sam's stunned eyes, Carl lifted the little girl onto his shoulders. The child went from profound misery to sublime bliss in the span of a split second. The mother smiled, then turned her attention back to her youngest. Did not mind one bit that a complete stranger, a *black man*, was handling her child.

Sam gulped down a big swig of his Glühwein.

When the crowd dispersed at the end of the speech, Greg steered them back to the edge of the market square.

"I know a neat place to eat."

The *Café am Hauptmarkt* did look nice indeed. To Sam's regret, the bookstore right next to it was already closed. "All they got is German books," Carl said, pulling him away from the store window. "I already asked."

The golden warmth glowing inside the café shone through its large, arched windows onto the street, contrasting seductively with the glacial night outside. Everything inside looked cozy and inviting, the dark red leather seats, the round fine-wood tables, the chandeliers, the plushy carpet, the bustling waiters, the guests hunched over dainty coffee cups and cream-laden pies.

"What are we waiting for?" urged Carl.

Sam's feet seemed frozen to the pavement.

"It's all righ," said Greg, seizing Sam's arm. "I felt funny, too, the first time."

They entered and immediately got tangled in an excessively heavy scarlet curtain that was draped on a circular rail over the door to keep the cold out. They extricated themselves from the heavy pleats. Sam's glasses fogged up as he entered the warm parlor. A waiter came rushing towards them. Sam's neck grew stiff.

„Tisch für drei, die Herren?"

„Ja, bitte," said Carl with the ease of someone who had never lived under segregation.

We're being seated.

They followed the scurrying waiter to a table in a corner and sat down between a group of elderly ladies and a young family. Two of the old women stared silently.

They consulted the leather-bound menu, and with the help of Sam's Pocket Guide and Carl's expertise in German confectioneries, settled for three *Kännchen Kaffee, Bienenstich, gedeckten Apfelkuchen* and *Eierlikörtorte*.

"What the hell are they staring at?" Carl muttered under his breath, uncomfortable under the unrelenting stares of the elderly women at the next table.

„So, gnädiger Herr, der Bienenstich?"

The waiter skilfully slipped a gold-rimmed plate in front of Sam and then poured coffee into his cup in an audacious trajectory, yet without spilling one drop. Meanwhile, Sam was flipping through his pocket guide.

"What ya lookin for?"

"What's he sayin? GNAY-dig-ER…."

"You woan find that in ya booklet. He said *Gnädiger Herr*. It means sumthin like *milord* or *gracious gentleman*." Greg picked up his plate and leaned back into the soft leather of the seat with a satisfied grin. He fed himself pie in slow relish. "Ya know, Carl, I think ya bein too sensitive," he said to Carl, who was still eying the women, who in turn were still eying them. "Let'em look, they doan hurt us. Sfar as I'm concerned, *gnädiger Herr* sure beats nigger, which is the preferred form of address where I'm from." He laughed. Then, turning serious: "I *love* it here. Makes me sick jus thinkin how fast time's gonna fly by."

Carl was revolving his cup in his hands. He was from Connecticut. Greg was from Mississippi.

"When I get home ... I ain goin back to the ole ways, y'all," said Greg, whose plate was already wiped clean.

"How could you?" Carl shrugged.

"I'm serious, I can't go back." Greg looked at Sam, in search for the empathy of a fellow Southerner, who, unlike Carl, was able to grasp the full meaning of his resolution.

Sam was looking at his Bienenstich.

DER HOF

„Desmoi isser wirkli dabei gwesen, der Sedlmaier."

Ludwigs Mutter ließ den gehäkelten Vorhang wieder fallen, den sie gelüpft hatte, um diskret zum Nachbarhaus zu spähen. Der Sedlmaier war wieder da. Gerade waren er, seine Frau und die vier Kinder im benachbarten Bauernhaus verschwunden.

„So a Erleichtung für die Sedlmaierin", sagte Theresa tonlos. Sie war sich selbst ein wenig böse, dass sie nach all den Jahren noch immer keiner anderen Frau die glückliche Heimkehr eines Ehemanns gönnen konnte.Und dabei war die Rückkehr des kolerischen Gatten vielleicht noch nicht einmal ein Segen für die Familie Sedlmaier, die erstaunlich gut alleine zurechtgekommen war. Die vielen Jahre in Russland hatten ihn bestimmt nicht gerade sanftmütiger gemacht.

„Für uns is es bestimmt koa Erleichterung, dasser wieder do is", kündigte die alte Frau Winkler unheilsschwanger an.

Und tatsächlich dauerte es keine drei Tage, bis sich Bauer Sedlmaier wieder so akklimatisiert hatte, dass er die Zügel in die Hand nahm und sich um all das kümmerte, was seine Frau seiner Ansicht nach so sträflich vernachlässigt hatte. Unter anderem stellte er fest, dass die Winklers, die anno 1941 seinem hochbetagten Vater dessen Hof abgekauft hatten, fast den ganzen Krieg über keine Darlehenszahlungen geleistet hatten ... und *seit* dem Krieg auch nicht regelmäßig. Die gute Frau Sedlmeier hatte der Winklerwitwe gesagt, sie solle halt tun, was sie könne. Und Theresa hatte auch getan, was sie konnte. Und viel war das halt nicht gewesen. Die Sedlmaierin war Pragmatikerin. Im Krieg und in den Hungerjahren danach war es zunächst mal darum gegangen, die ganzen hungrigen Mäuler durchzubringen, die auf beiden Höfen herumschwirrten. Geld war ohnehin nichts mehr wert gewesen. Selbst als die Deutsche Mark dann kam, hatte es die Sedlmaiern nicht übers rustikale Herz gebracht, ihrer jungen Nachbarin allzu großen Druck zu machen.

Herr Sedlmaier sah das allerdings anders. Er nahm es seinem alten Herrn posthum noch äußerst übel, dass er dem jungen Ludwig Winkler den Hof geradezu vom Sterbebett aus verkauft hatte. Das war Theresa sofort klar, als es eines Nachmittags resolut klopfte, sie die Tür öffnete und das Gesicht mit der schwammigen Nase und den gletscherkalten Augen sah. Unter dem Arm hatte er eine Mappe, und der Sedlmaier war nun wirklich kein Papierkrieger. Sedlmaier mit Aktenmappe – das verhieß nichts Gutes.

Als er wieder weg war, weinte Theresa. Weinte wie ein Kind. Frau Winkler hielt den Kopf ihrer Schwiegertochter auf ihrem Schoß. Die kleine Brigitte saß auf dem Boden, gegen die schlotternden Schienbeine ihrer Mutter gelehnt.

„Wie sollin des jemals leisten, was der verlangt?"

„Des koanst ned leistn."

Theresa schluchzte.

„Des isn Ludwig sei Hof!"

„Ich woaß ja, dassd dran hängst. Aber wenn mer ehrlich san: Es war a fixe Idee vom Ludwig, den Hof überhaupt zu kaufn. Des hat der oide Sedlmaier nur mitgmacht, weil ern Ludwig so gern ghabt hat."

„Und drum stinkts ja dem jungen Sedlmaier so, dass mir auf dem Hof sitzn."

„Und abgworfn hat er nie viel und wird er a nie. Gib eam den Hof zrück und lass dir des bissl, was scho getilgt is, auszoin."

„Vüi wird's ja ned sei, nach Abzug der Zinsen. Und was wird aus uns?"

„Mir kenna jederzeit zum Gerd."

„Na, da will i ned hi."

„Des versteh i."

So sehr Theresa Ludwig geliebt hatte, so wenig konnte sie mit seinem älteren Bruder Gerd anfangen. Das wusste sogar seine Mutter.

„Vielleicht", dachte Theresa laut nach, „sollt is wirkli machn wie die Waltraud, und in die Stadt gehn. Di Ami ham angebli Arbeit noch und nöcher."

„Und die Brigitte, die is doch so gscheit. Mir wärs scho recht, wenns koa Bäuerin würd. Wenns in der Stadt aufd Schul geht, wer woaß, was aus ihr no wird. Dass sie si später amoi ned so plagn muss wie unsereins."

Theresa sah ihrer Schwiegermutter ins verbrauchte Gesicht. Sie hatte gar nicht gewusst, dass die ältere Frau Winkler solche Gedanken hegte. Aber Recht hatte sie.

„Und wo du die Waltraud so lang bei dir ghabt hast, die würd di bstimmt a Zeitlang bei sich wohna lassn, bist Fuß gfasst hoast."

New Hire

Sam was walking briskly along the hall. He always took great care to look busy and somewhat hard-pressed to get to his next destination, even if this destination was nothing more than his bunk and a book. That way, bored comrades were less likely to try to recruit him for some stupid or illicit activity. The tread of his boots was echoed by an equally swift, but much lighter ticktock coming towards him from the other end of the hall. A female silhouette turned the corner at the far end of the corridor. When she was close enough for Sam to make out her features, he jumped:

"Frau Winkler!"

When they were only a few yards from each other, both slowed down. The last clomp of his boots and click of her heels echoed in the sudden silence of the hall as they came to a stop, facing each other.

"Hello, Mr. Harris."

"Hello, ma'am. What a mighty nice surprise. On such a dull afternoon."

She smiled, even though Sam was pretty certain that his words had surpassed the scope of her English vocabulary. She was all dressed up, to the extent of a farm widow's possibilities: She had exchanged her shapeless brown garb for a shorter, slimmer skirt and a silk blouse

– Sam presumed she had loaned these clothes from the rather more elegant Mathilde Kröger. She even wore a necklace, and her blonde hair was pulled into a neat bun. At their previous encounter, she had worn two disheveled braids under a loose head-rag. And yet, despite all her efforts, her attempt to look urban failed utterly and endearingly. Her wide-eyed, innocent face clearly betrayed her as a clueless country girl, and she was all the sweeter for it, at least in Sam's eyes. But why was she here in this attire?

"I speak wis the Sergeant," she now explained with an embarrassed grin, pointing to the office at the end of the corridor.

"Jus now? 'Bout what?" Sam asked, intuitively reaching for his back pocket to let his *Pocket Guide* assist in his communication. But he did not have it with him.

"Se Sergeant want... woman... to clean.... clean woman? Putzfrau?" she said, slowly searching for words. Then she laughed: "I must... have better English now."

"Ya jus been hired as a cleaning lady?" Sam gathered. As she nodded eagerly, Sam felt his blood quicken inside his veins.

"Now that's jus wonderful!" Then he bridled himself: "I mean... good for *you*. So ... that means ya cumin here? Ya found someone to take care of the farm?"

She smiled at him blankly.

"Ya cumin here? To live?" he asked, slowing down. She nodded.

"With Frau Wächter?" A nod.

"And the farm?" Another nod.

"I mean, who's gonna work the farm?"

She shook her head in apology. Sam gave up. He would inquire further details from Frau Wächter.

"Well, it was good to see ya, Frau Winkler."

He stretched out his hand. He felt no danger. She seized it just as tightly as she had at their first encounter, a firm squeeze of wordless kinship and gratitude. They remained thus, just a second longer than a casual handshake should have taken. When Theresa let go, Sam saw the whites of her eyes glisten, but she held her tears. How strange it was to be a living symbol of loss to another person. But that's what Sam was to her, a walking reminder of her boy-husband who had come home in an urn.

She stilted away in her unaccustomed high-heeled shoes, and he continued on his way, slowly, forgetting to resume his busy gait from before. He was completely absorbed in his encounter … and the implications! If Frau Winkler had indeed picked up a job at the barracks, he would now see her *all the time*.

"Now, what was that?"

A stark voice startled him from his musings. Shane

Tucker stood there, idly, for he was always idle, his expression a mixture of amusement and revulsion.

"Chasing after those *Fräuleins* already?"

"I ain chasin no one. I was greetin an acquaintance."

"*Acquaintance*?" Shane drawled, savoring Sam's word choice. "Right. You got any more of them pretty *acquaintances*?"

Sam walked on. Shane threw a dirty, menacing laugh after him.

"You know the only reason those Nazi brides would even deign to look at a nigger is because of the American dollars he's got in his pocket. You're aware of that, right?"

Sam walked on, did not turn back, because he wasn't sure what he would do if he looked into Tucker's driveling face once more.

"You know, *at home* they would take care of such excesses."

A split second later, Sam saw a bright red smudge dance in the blur before his eyes. It was blood, blood on Shane Tucker's bewildered face. *I hit him*, Sam gathered, though he had no awareness of it. Holding his own fist, Sam took a couple of confused steps backwards. He realized that his hand was hurting from the blow of which he had no conscious recollection. Now he also heard Shane groan in disbelief. Sam's adrenaline rushed in with a few seconds' delay, and with it came regret. What the hell had he just done?

"Man," he just said. His first instinct had been to say "Sorry, man", but Shane's words were still echoing in his head, and he would not apologize.

Shane's moan grew louder as he shook off his surprise and sought an audience to witness this outrage, this egregious thing that had just happened to him. Shane looked almost satisfied through the blood and the stupidity on his face. Doors opened on the hallway. The incident had occurred right outside of the Commandant's office, and so Frau Kellermann, his secretary, was the first to stick her head in the corridor.

"Ach, du lieber Gott. What's going on here?"

"Pretty obvious, ain't it," panted Tucker.

"Lieutenant Colonel!" Frau Kellermann called out, seeking a higher authority than herself to deal with the situation. Others had now joined the scene, curiosity on every face ... and almost imperceptible amusement on only the black soldiers' faces. Tucker, whose intention had been to get his superior's, but not necessarily his comrades' attention, unsuccessfully tried to dispel them with angry gestures while holding his hand to his nose. Lieutenant Colonel Vaughn emerged from his office, with the natural calm that had earned him his high position, and viewed the scene, without the stern anger that Shane was hoping to reap from the incident. Vaughn dispersed the crowd with one flick of his hand.

"Can we sort this out quickly?" Vaughn asked, with an expression that made it clear that he would not tolerate any childish bullshit.

"Yes, sir. I jus lost ma temper and hit Sergeant Tucker in the face. I'm sorry."

"Unprovoked?"

"Entirely unprovoked, sir," Shane interjected, now wiping his face with a handkerchief that Frau Kellermann had provided. Vaughn looked at Sam to see if he was going to challenge Shane's statement, but Sam just stood still, looking into his superior's eyes steadily, awaiting the consequence, showing neither contrition, nor making any attempts to justify himself.

"Do you need to see the nurse, Tucker?" said Vaughn coolly.

"No, sir, I'm okay."

"Then go and clean yourself up. And you..."

"PFC Samuel Harris, sir."

"Harris, you follow me into my office."

Once inside, they quickly crossed the secretary's room and entered Vaughn's office, where he immediately shut the white-washed office door with the textured-glass pane, much to Frau Kellermann's disappointment.

"Have a seat, Harris." He walked over to his filing cabinet. "A man does not usually bloody another one's nose 'entirely unprovoked'. Tell me what happened." He opened the upper drawer of his cabinet, found the section with the letter 'H'. Sam waited for him to turn back around before he answered:

"Sergeant Tucker insulted the young lady that jus left ya office."

"How?"

"I'd rather not repeat it."

"And that enraged you so much that you were willing to risk your first disciplinary action, not even a month into your deployment here," Vaughn said, almost distractedly as his finger followed a passage in Sam's file.

"It was a gut reaction, sir. Had I thought 'bout it first, I woulda found a better way to express ma... indignation."

"How come you landed in Normandy with the 320th Barrage Balloon Battalion in 44, fought with it all the way into Germany in forty-five and never made it beyond private first class?" This was an unnecessary question, since Vaughn had his finger right on the spot in Sam's file that explained it. But Vaughn wanted to hear Sam say it.

"I was demoted, sir."

"Were you, now."

"I defied a superior's orders, appropriated a military vehicle for unauthorized use, and abandoned ma assigned post, sir," Sam quoted from his own file.

"What the hell were you trying to do?"

Sam remained silent, because that was what he knew to do. But then he took another look at Vaughn's face. His frank eyes and open-ended questions reminded him of Hannes Kröger.

"I took the car and left ma post, sir, so I wouldn....." Sam paused.

"I'm not going to pull it out of your nose, Harris, so tell me the whole story now or don't tell me at all."

"I'd been aksed to kill two unarmed German prisoners. An instead, I took'em to a place where the Brits were processin prisoners."

"Were they subsequently processed as British POWs?"

"Yes. And I'd do it 'gain, sir."

"Name of the superior who ordered you to kill the prisoners?" asked Vaughn, now armed with a pen.

"Thomas Rhees, sergeant at the time. It wasn a direct order, though. He jus... he made it clear to us."

"Ah, here he is," Vaughn said as he found Rhees's name in the file. "He was the one who initiated the disciplinary action that led to your demotion. Would you be willing to make a detailed statement on this incident if it came to it, Harris?"

Sam paused for a second.

"Yes, sir, I would."

"Good. And the next time you feel like punching someone, do what you just did now. Go to the right authority with your grievance."

"Thank you, sir."

Sam left the office, almost floating by Frau Kellermann's desk, who was quite surprised, and just a little disappointed, to see him leave the Lieutenant Colonel's office in such good spirits.

Vaughn liked him.

GESCHÄFTE

„Gib des her!"

Das ohrenbetäubende Gezanke brachte Waltraud nicht aus der Ruhe. Wohl aber das klitzekleine ratschende Geräusch, das auf den Schlagabtausch der Kinder folgte.

„Was war des?", fragte sie, während sie wie ein Pfeil von ihrem Tresen hochfuhr.

„Nix." Gemeinsam ertappt, wurden die beiden Streithähne augenblicklich die trautesten Komplizen.

Wolfi schwebte nämlich eigentlich im Glück, seit seine geliebte Brigitte aus Manching zu ihm gezogen war. Die riesige Trümmerwüste, die er seinen Abenteuerspielplatz nannte, zeigte er ihr bis in den letzten baufälligen Winkel, in all ihrem einsturzgefährdeten Charme; gemeinsam schwelgten die beiden in den Aromen heimtückischer toxischer Ausdünstungen und im Zauber explosiver Fundstücke. Eigentlich war es Waltraud ja lieber, wenn die Kinder sich hier in der Sicherheit der Kaserne beschäftigten, und gerade wegen der Gefahren der Altstadt duldete Lieutenant Colonel Vaughn die Kinder auch auf dem Gelände – doch heute gingen ihr die beiden Teufelsbraten doch sehr auf die Nerven:

„Sagt die Wahrheit. Habt ihr da grad a Heftle

zerrissen?"

„Hammer ned."

„Zeig mir, was du da grad ghabt hast."

Wolfi rückte es heraus: der aktuelle *U.S. News and World Report*. Waltraud musste das Heft erst durchblättern, um den Schaden zu finden. Da, von einer Seite im Politikteil war ein Eck abgerissen.

„Und so soll ich des eds noch verkaufn? Die Kunden wolln doch ka zerfetzte Zeitschrift!"

Brigitte und Wolfi blickten mit zerknirscht-großen Kinderaugen zu Waltraud herauf.

„Und was wolltn ihr überhaupt mit so aner Zeitung? Ich hab dacht, ihr streitet über a Micki-Maus Heftle."

Kopfschüttelnd schlurfte Waltraud zurück zu ihrem Tresen, richtete auf dem Weg noch ein paar schiefe Bücherstapel und glättete hängende Zeitschriften auf den Rondells. Brigitte und Wolfi setzten sich in ein Eck und nahmen sehr leise, sehr gesittet und sehr vorsichtig ein paar *Mickey-Mouse*-Hefte vom Regal, um sie zu lesen.

„Spielt halt draußn. Ihr seid doch sonst immer n ganzen Tag bloß auf der Wöhrder Wiesn."

Doch die Kinder blieben wie angewurzelt sitzen. Gegen Mittag wollte Waltraud eigentlich essen, doch sie traute dem Frieden nicht.

„Geht ihr mit mir zum Metzger? Ich hol a Wurstbrot."

„Nein, danke."

„Ich will euch aber eigentlich ned allein lassen. Ihr macht mir bloß wieder was kaputt."

„Geh du ruhig, Waltraud, i muss eds eh hier putzn", sagte Theresa, die zum wilden Gebimmel der Ladenklingel ihren Putzwagen über die Schwelle hievte.

„Ah, gut. Passt du mir kurz auf die zwa Vrecker auf?"

„Aber sicher." Theresa hebelte ihren schweren Mopp aus dem Eimer und begann den Boden zu schrubben.

„I bin glei wieder da. Mogst du aa was vom Metzger?", verabschiedete sich Waltraud. Theresa lehnte dankend ab.

Die Kinder blieben still sitzen.

„Ihr verstehts des doch eh ned", kommentierte Theresa die Tatsache, dass die Kinder, die nur mit Mühe und Not überhaupt lesen konnten, in englische Comic-Hefte starrten.

„Doch, mit der Zeit versteht mers scho", behauptete Wolfi.

„Na ja, schaden konns ja ned. Englisch muss ma kenna, wenn ma was werdn will heitzutag."

Die Türklingel ging erneut. Diesmal schossen die Kinder wie Pfeile hoch.

"Sam! I got it", rief Wolfi eifrig. Theresa zuckte herum, aber grüßte nicht, sondern beobachtete verblüfft, wie ihre Tochter und Wolfi wie Hündchen an Samuel Harris hoch hüpften. Wolfi wedelte mit einem schon etwas ramponierten *U.S. News and World Report*.

"Great. Good job, guys."

Er griff in seine Hosentasche, gab Wolfi das Geld für die Zeitschrift und belohnte die Kinder mit bunten Bonbons.

„Neccos!", begeisterte sich Wolfi. „Die sin die allerbesten, Brigitte, schau." Sam lachte, die Freude der Kinder sichtlich genießend. Dann hockte er sich zu ihnen hinunter, schielte hinüber zur verwaisten Verkaufstheke und fragte leise:

"Ya mom out?"

"Yes."

"Got the other thing I wanted, too?"

"Yes!", triumphierte Wolfi. Aus dem Innenfutter seiner alten, von zwei Generationen älterer Brüder abgetragenen Jacke zog er ein kleines dunkelblaues Buch hervor.

"Great. How much was it?"

„Zwei Mark fünfzig."

"Here's two *dollars* fifty", entlohnte ihn Sam mit dem vierfachen Wert. Wolfi steckte hastig und dankbar die zehn Vierteldollarmünzen in seine Hosentasche. Sam richtete sich auf und nahm erst jetzt wahr, dass auf der anderen Seite des Ladenraums noch jemand stand.

"Oh", erschrak er. "Mrs. Winkler. How do ya do?"

"How do you do?", gab sie schüchtern zurück. Aus ihrem still stehenden Mopp sickerte das Wasser auf den Boden. Sie strich sich verschämt über die verschwitzte Stirn und das zerzauste Haar, das bei all dem Bücken und Wringen aus ihrem grauen Kopftuch hervor gerutscht war.

"How's it goin? Like workin here?"

"Ja, like very", gab sie zurück. Sam trat näher und zeigte ihr, was er gerade in der so geheimnistuerischen Transaktion von den Kindern erstanden hatte.

"The kids always save a copy for me, cuz they sell out fast", erklärte er die Zeitschrift. "And this dictionary here", zeigte er ihr das kleine Buch, "is a whole lot better than that lil pocket guide they gave us. The kids got it for me at... Where d'ya get it, kids?"

„Buchhandlung Jakob", antwortete Wolfi, Brigitte nickte beflissen.

"Soon I'll be able to understand ya much better, ma'am. Besser verstehen." Sam grinste breit und Theresa errötete lächelnd.

„I muss ja auch ... better understand."

"Well, would ya like a dictionary for yaself, ma'am?"

Sam fischte eifrig nach seinem Geldbeutel und gab

Wolfi noch drei Dollarscheine. "Get her one, too."

"No, no", wehrte Theresa verlegen ab, doch Wolfi wollte sich bei der hervorragenden Rendite den Auftrag freilich nicht entgehen lassen.

"Hey", sagte Sam nun beschwörend zu allen dreien. "Let's not talk to Frau Wächter 'bout our little deals here, okay? Nix sagen Mama."

„Niemals", bestätigte Wolfi sofort. Klar, Waltraud würde das alles natürlich sofort unterbinden. Theresa nickte sanft. So ein Wörterbuch wäre schon nicht schlecht. Dann kehrte sie zu ihrem Mopp zurück, unter dem sich zwischenzeitlich eine nasse Lache gebildet hatte.

The Road to Augsburg

"Watch out, man, that's farmland."

"So?"

"So... I doan think the farmer would 'preciate ya tearin into it."

In response, Herman pulled even further to the right. The tank tilted slightly. Sam could feel the dirt splatter and quake as the tracks ripped through it. There were too many like Herman, GIs who somehow perceived their surroundings as a mere scenery, unrelated to real people's factual reality. As far as Herman was concerned, this field was just there for him to plough through; there was no real-life farmer who just lost a few rows of freshly sown of barley to his vandalism.

"Take a left here," grunted Sam, before Herman could miss their turn and barrel right down the main street of the next village. Herman kept starting conversations, and Sam kept letting them run aground. He was irritated. As a matter of fact, he was continuously irritated out here at the border camp. Well, at least this was their last day. How he loathed this boring existence, mindlessly rolling down country roads and village streets along the Iron Curtain. As the devil always finds work for idle hands, the troops were tormenting the locals with their raucuous noise, their disregard for civilian property and all sorts of other inappropriate off-duty behaviors. Last night, one of Herman's buddies had harvested a whole bunch of spring flowers from someone's window crate to present to a waitress at one of the bars. Around here, the GIs' watering holes were much fewer and far less elaborate than in Nürnberg. Most of the bars were, in fact, barns that the owner had re-dedicated to a more lucrative use. But they were no less rowdy and randy. In short, Sam could not wait to return to Nürnberg. His luggage could not even hold enough books to carry him through the month-long tedium of the border tours.

Eventually, and without further incident, they made it back to their border camp near Zwiesel.

"What took you so long?" asked the logistics officer, without waiting for an answer. "Hurry up and grab your stuff, you're gonna need to catch a ride to Ausgburg."

"Augsburg?" barked Herman. "Why ain we goin home?"

"You missed your ride home. You're going with these guys to Augsburg, and from there to Nürnberg on Monday."

"Why didn they wait for us?" Herman was aggravated. It was *Friday night*. "Augsburg is dead. What are we spose to do there all weekend?"

Sam looked at the map to see exactly where Augsburg was. His eye caught a little town that lay right on their route. Manching. He'd been there before! That's where the Winklers were from. He felt an urge to visit that place again. Theresa Winkler lived in Nürnberg now. But Ludwig was buried there. No, he wasn't buried.

"What do people do with urns?" Sam asked Herman when they sat on the bus.

"Huh?" The contextless question distracted Herman from his disappointment.

"When they cremate people, what do they do with the urns?"

"I dunno. What the hell makes ya think of that righ now?"

"Jus curious."

Sam decided that he would find out.

"Drop me off righ here," Sam asked the bus driver when they passed the town sign of Manching.

"Hey. Where ya headed?" Herman wanted to know, tucking Sam's sleeve as he got up to wrench his bag from the shelf overhead.

"Nowhere ya'd wanna go."

"Cum on, tell me. Ya know a good place round here, doan ya?"

"Not really."

"What ya wantin to get off for, then?" Herman insisted, desperate to save his Friday night from utter boredom.

"I'm headed to a graveyard," Sam said to shut him up. "I wanna find a graveyard." Herman let go of his sleeve.

"You are a *weird* fella, ya know that?"

"What are we spose to tell them in Augsburg?" the driver enquired, not quite comfortable letting a comrade off the bus in the middle of nowhere, even off-duty.

"Jus tell'em I'm gonna be there tomorrow."

The driver shook his head disapprovingly, but without too much consequence. None of his business, after all. Sam got off, the bus roared away. And there he stood on the road with his bag. This was a small town. A hunchbacked old woman was taking care of the flowers in her front yard in an excruciatingly slow, arthritic effort.

„Entschuldigung, hat Manching ein Friedhof?" Sam asked.

„Na freili, zwoa, an katholischn und an evangelischn," the woman informed him, unintimidated by the stranger and his American uniform. Sam just understood 'Catholic', and eagerly confirmed:

„Ja, katholischn Friedhof."

„Da, glei di Straß obi. Is ned weit."

„Danke."

Sam walked the short distance in the direction the

woman had indicated and reached the door of a small flower shop across from the cemetery just as the owner was about to shut for the night. Sam entered and looked around, keenly watched by the florist who did not know what to make of her unusual customer. Sam realized that he had no clue what to get. The customary wreaths of garish silk flowers which one stuck onto Georgian graves were not for sale here.

„Entschuldigung, Fräulein, was... kaufen für Grab?" he asked, proud of himself for remembering the word for 'tomb', which he had looked up on the bus, along with 'cemetery'.

„Na, a Kerzn halt. Oder a Blumengsteck."

„*Caredsn*?"

„Kerze. Da, so oane. Die macht a Zehnerl."

„*Tsaynarl*?"

„Zehn Pfennig."

„Aah," Sam understood and happily produced the copper coin.

„Kerse," he repeated to himself.

He left the shop, which was immediately locked behind him. He continued on through the gates of the cemetery. A sign indicated the opening times: He had a mere half hour before the cemetery would close for the night.

The tombs were aligned in neat rows. Some were marked by simple wooden crosses with little slated roofs, others by massive, heavy marble slates that were almost the size of the coffin underneath. In the middle of the cemetery stood several long rows of concrete. This was not only ugly, but also bore an undignified resemblance to a wall of lockers at a high school. Sam realized: Those had to be the urn graves! He decided to pace along the concrete walls and find Ludwig's name.

He walked the length of the first wall. When he turned the corner, he found that he was not the only late visitor here. A woman was crouching before one of the urn graves at the bottom, next to a child who was small enough to stand up in front of it. Sam's heartbeat picked up, he almost ran the few steps until he was right behind them. When his tall frame blocked the evening sun on her back, the woman turned around.

„Guten Abend. Ich bringen ein Kerse," Sam explained to Theresa.

„Is die für mein Papa?" Brigitte crowed happily, not in the least surprised to see a soldier from the barracks one hundred kilometers away in her hometown's graveyard.

Sam adored this little tow-headed girl. Her hair was blandly bobbed just below the tips of her ears, never kempt, and her stubborn ears invariably stuck out between the streaky blonde strands. The upward bend of her nose-tip spelled trouble, her chirpy eyes promised fun. She spent most of her days in a pair of shabby leather shorts, most likely handed down from Waltraud's boys, and wisely so, because a skirt would not survive Brigitte's adventures for even a day. Today, however, she was wearing one. Her legs stuck out under the hem like twigs, bruised and scraped in various places.

„Ja, is für dein Papa," confirmed Sam.

Meanwhile, her mother's glance remained fixed on Sam in doe-eyed bewilderment, quite unable to make sense of Samuel Harris's sudden appearance by her late husband's gravesite. Theresa's hand mechanically accepted the candle Sam was holding out to her.

Since she remained suspended in baffled immobility, Sam stooped down beside her. He opened the little glass-paned casing next to Ludwig's name plaque, a contraption that German resourcefulness had produced for the sole purpose of protecting those fat red memorial candles from the elements. Sam produced his matches, Theresa held the wick of the candle to the flickering spark, shielding it from the draft with her other hand. As the shimmer of the flame danced in Theresa's quiet eyes, her loveliness rolled over Sam like a wave. He pushed his mouth right onto her unsuspecting lips, while the fire ate up the match and began to lick his fingertips. The burn jerked him back to reality. He flinched and looked at Theresa, anxious to see the effect of his sudden surge of passion. She was kneeling in the dirt in the exact same position, except that her pale cheeks were now flushed. She was still holding the lit candle, whose flame was dancing happily on the wick.

She turned to put the candle inside the case before the evening breeze could snuff it.

"I'm sorry," said Sam, but was not. He stayed right where he was, quietly, very close to her, unable to let go of that moment. The child stood by and watched, in her usual serene curiosity, finding the encounter between her mother and the man from the barracks neither strange nor upsetting.

„Was machen Sie denn überhaupt hier?" Theresa finally found words.

„Ich bringen ein Kerse. We missed our ride back to Nürnberg and had to go through Augsburg. I saw that Manching was on the way, so I thought I could pay a visit to Ludwig's grave. Ludwigs Grab. So here I am."

He accompanied his slow, over-enunciated explanation with ample gestures, trying to describe his detour to Augsburg and his intentions in coming here. Theresa nodded, and her lips formed a sweet, friendly smile which Sam could hardly resist kissing again.

„Da." Brigitte had picked up his matchbox from the ground.

„Danke, sweetheart," said Sam and Theresa's smile opened fully; she understood what Sam called her daughter and liked it.

"She is, she truly is a sweetheart," Sam repeated.

„Ham Sie Hunger? Ham Sie hait Abend Ausgang?"

„Ja."

„Der Friedhof macht glei zu. Closed."

"Yeah, I know," Sam said, checking his watch.

„Wolln Sie vielleicht mit uns bei maner Schwiegermutter Abend essen?" When he knitted his brow, she attempted her question in English: "Eat dinner in se house of Ludwig's mosser? You want?"

"Yes."

He followed Theresa out the cemetery gate, which an edgy groundskeeper was impatient to lock.

As they walked, he reiterated the strange events of the past few moments. He had kissed that woman and reaped no indignation or panic, but a shy smile and an invitation to supper. He floated behind mother and daughter in a sort of trance. How sweet, how modest, how quietly wonderful was this woman, how adorable and feisty her child, who was a perfect blend of her mellow mother and her candid father. Sam was walking towards the former home of a dead man whose widow he had just kissed, and felt no more guilt towards Ludwig than an archaeologist feels towards a pharaoh whose treasures he just unearthed in a desert. Sam Harris felt more like an heir than a rival, full of fascination and appreciation for the erstwhile owner of Theresa's heart, dazzled by his own good fortune. His gait was jubilant, oblivious to how very inappropriate the past five minutes had been, how many army rules, even state laws, not to mention cultural taboos he had just violated. Such unnerving thoughts were tucked away safely under a fluffy, heavenly daze.

During the mile-long walk to her brother-in-law's farm, Theresa explained the family situation. Constrained by the limits of her English and Sam's German, the conversation was arduous and comical at the same time. But by the time they reached Mother Winkler's house, Sam had gathered that the elderly woman, whom life had robbed of her husband and her younger son, had been residing in a small hut on her older son's land since Theresa had moved to the city.

The front door sprang open in impatient expectation before they even reached it. That is, what Frau Winkler had expected was the return of Theresa and Brigitte. She gazed at Sam in wonder. Theresa explained his presence in a rapid cascade of gritty Bavarian that Sam could not follow, but he could tell that her tone was resolute and tolerated no further inquiries. So Frau Winkler held out her hand to him.

„Ja, i erinner mich scho no. Grüß Gott."

Sam nodded and shook her hand.

„Wollns a Suppn?"

„Na freili, an Hunger hat er. Und mir zwoa a," Theresa accepted for him, and within moments, Sam found himself at a sturdy kitchen table spooning soup from a white bowl with rustic blue florets. The spoon he was using was as old as the house. The soup was piping hot, sparsely sprinkled with tiny noodles and some peas, but the grease drops twirling on the surface were large and abundant. He imitated little Brigitte's technique of soaking her crust of bread in the soup. Somehow the simple meal tasted utterly delicious. The women were talking, without trying to involve him in the conversation, but constantly and smiling at him and checking the soup level in his bowl. Sam could have sat here forever.

But the meal ended, and he knew he had to be on his way now. He inquired if there was a hostel where he could spend the night before taking a train to Augsburg early the next morning. Once they grasped what he was asking, both women stared at him as if his request was a shocking extravagance.

„Na! Sie kenna doch hier bleibn," insisted the mother.

"You can…," Theresa began translating.

"Sleep here!" Brigitte blurted out, thrilled to beat her mother to the right words.

"You're a smart lil thing." In a bout of affection, Sam leaned forward and tousled her hair, and in doing so displaced the hair clip that kept it out of her eyes. He carefully placed it back. The two women watched him quietly. His mind returned to their suggestion:

"Spend the night here? I dunno… Ya sure that's all

righ?"

"Ja, very all right," Theresa said, eager to dispel his reservations. So it was decided. The dinner table was cleared and wiped, and they played a few rounds of a card game, the rules of which were too complex to fathom by sheer observation. Any attempt to give instructions would have far exceeded either one's command of the other language. Sam simply pulled Brigitte's chair close to his and let her play his hand for him. The women played with almost comical seriouness and stunningly swift moves.

At half past eight, Theresa motioned him to follow her into the back of the small house. It smelt of moldy timber and countryside. She led him into a small bedroom and began to pull white linen out of an ancient wooden wardrobe. It had been folded so neatly and pressed so firmly that the linen was stiff, unfolding almost like sheets of paper. She shook out a bedsheet with vigor, then flung it over a bed, which was at least half a foot too short for Sam.

"Ya lil girl is wonderful."

Theresa smiled as she tightened the sheet around the mattress and tried to smooth out the meticulous creases where it had been folded. The linen had a peculiar smell, clean and dusty at the same time.

"Ja, Brigitte is smart. Smart girl. And only eight."

"Eight? She is ... quite small."

Theresa shrugged: "Not so good food."

"Eight," a bright voice crowed proudly behind them. „Alt gnug für die Kommunion."

"Old enough for Holy Communion?" Sam figured.

"Yes. Her friends in se school. Kommunion. Sis year."

"And I *not*," added Brigitte in a tone of profound discontent. She puckered her chapped lips into a pout.

"She must wait. Next year."

"Why?"

"She has no dress. I must wait for more money. Next year. So." She looked around the room. „Brauchen Sie sonst no was?"

"No. Thank you so much."

„Gute Nacht."

"Good night, Frau Winkler."

He was not the least bit tired yet. But that was okay. He had much to ruminate.

KUMMER

„Na, also eds fläicht ihr aber raus!", wurde Ahrend laut. „Eds fläicht ihr aber werkli!"

Wolfi, sonst nicht schüchtern, fegte hinter Wallis Hosenbeine wie ein verschrecktes Kätzchen.

„Bitte, Herr Ahrend, eds regens Ehner doch ned so auf. Zwei Tag Aufschub..."

„Es sin aber kanne zwei Tag, des wissens doch selber. Heut hammer den siebten. Und letzts Monat wars der sechzehnte, bis endlich amol zahlt habn."

Waltrauds angespannte, auf Verteidigung stehende Schultern erschlafften. Ihre Augen wurden feucht, was sogar den vom Leben gegerbten Metzger Ahrend veranlasste, seinen groben Ton zu mäßigen. Etwas sanfter fügte er hinzu: „Naa, beim besten Willn, Frau Wächter. Ich hab scho viel Geduld mit Ehner ghabt, weger die Bubn und allm, aber i muss aa selber schaun, wo i bleib. Und schauns amal, wie viel Leut drin sin in der Wohnung. Acht?"

„Naa, bloß sechs", korrigierte Waltraud schwach.

„Kann da kaner a weng zur Miete beitragn?"

„Na, doch, aber die Frau Winkler hat ja grad erst angfangen bei der SS-Kasern. Sobald die ihrn erstn Zahltag hat..."

„Zwei Tag hams gsagt, Frau Wächter?"

„Ja, ganz bestimmt", stürzte sich Waltraud auf das Fünkchen Hoffnung und versprach etwas, was sie nicht würde halten können.

„Also, des is eds des allerletzte Mal, dass ich Ehner entgegnkomm, Frau Wächter. Und des Theater dou, des mach i ned jedn Monat mit. Im April will i die Miete dann am ersten ham, oder sie fläign wirkli raus."

„Dankschön, Herr Ahrend. Dankschön."

„Passt scho. Mei Geld will i ham", brummte er und stapfte den Flur entlang von dannen. Waltraud, Brigitte, Wolfi, Max und Bernd standen wie eingefroren, bis die Wohnungstür mürrisch ins Schloss geworfen wurde und die schweren Schritte des Metzgers auf den schiefen Treppenhausstufen knarzten.

„Und was is denn in zwei Tagen, Mama, dass du dann auf einmal bezahlen kannst?", atmete Bernd aus.

„Nix", sagte sie schulterzuckend und sank erst einmal entkräftet an den Küchentisch, wo sich noch die Kartoffelschalen türmten. Ahrend kam immer zur Essenszeit, um möglichst viele Familienmitglieder zusammen abzufangen.

„Wo isn überhaupt die Theresa?"

„Däi macht Überstundn. Da war heit a Fest in der Offizierskantine, dou muss no aufräumen."

„Und die hat wohl übermorgn Zahltag?"

„Na, erst am Monatsende."

„Warum hast du denn dann dem Ahrend versprochen, dass die Miete übermorgen bezahlt wird?"

„Was hätt i'n machn solln?"

In der Stille, die sich nun schwer über die Familie senkte, schälte Max weiter Kartoffeln. Wolfi und Brigitte spielten gedankenverloren mit den Schalen. In ihrer Kinderwelt gab es keine anhaltenden, nagenden Sorgen. Der böse, brüllende Herr Ahrend war wieder weg, für Wolfi war das so gut, als hätte sich damit auch das Problem erledigt. Bernd stand an den Küchenschrank gelehnt, grübelte nach. Aber Bernd kam ja kaum selbst über die Runden, saß den ganzen Tag in der Universitätsbibliothek, weil er sich kein einziges eigenes Lehrbuch leisten konnte. Er aß so viele Kartoffeln, dass ihm schon beim Geruch von kochendem Salzwasser, so wie er auch jetzt in der mütterlichen Küche hing, ein bisschen übel wurde. Er hatte seine Mutter gedrängt, vom Winklerhof wegzuziehen, und jetzt saß sogar die Winklerin selbst mit ihrer Tochter in der kleinen Wohnung in Nürnberg. Und allesamt waren sie zwei Tage vom Rauswurf entfernt.

„Ich such mir Arbeit", tat Bernd kund.

„Wie willstn des schaffen, mit die Vorlesungen."

„Scheiß auf die Vorlesungen. Ich mein, ich such mir eine richtige Arbeit. Ich schmeiß des Studium."

„Naa", erhob sich Waltraud mit neuer Energie, „des

kommt ja überhaupt ned in Frag. Dass du dei ganzes Studium aufgibst, weils bei uns manchmal a weng knapp wird."

„A weng knapp", schnaubte Bernd.

„Naa, Bernd, werkli. Du bist a so a feiner Kerl", sagte sie mit wässrigen Augen, und musste sich auf die Zehenspitzen stellen, um ihrem Ältesten übers pomadenstarrende Haar zu streichen. „Aber des machmer ned. Mir findn a bessere Lösung, als dass du dei Zukunft wechschmeißt."

Sie griff nach einer neuen Kartoffel, aber kam nicht zu Werke. Die Kartoffel drehte sich ein paar Mal ungeschält in ihren Fingern und klatschte dann mutlos auf den Tisch. Waltrauds Schultern bebten.

„Mama."

„Was soll i'n machn? Was mach i'n bloß?"

Das Weinen seiner Mutter holte Wolfi in den Ernst der Lage zurück. Und schenkte ihm einen Einfall.

„Du, Mama, waßt du noch, wie du gsacht hast, du willst nie wieder a Waffe hier sehn?"

„Wolfi, mir habn jetzt grad andere Probleme", bremste ihn Max.

„Und i wollt aa brav sein und auf dich hörn, aber dann... Und waßt noch, wie der Tucker dir fünf Mark gebn hat für die alte Luger?"

Waltraud blickte auf. Wolfi druckste, dann rückte er heraus:

„I hab a Panzerfaust in der Abstellkammer, hinterm Bügelbrett."

„A was?!"

„I wollts erst net hambringa, aber ... ich hab halt no nie so a gute gfunden ghabt."

„So a verrosts alts Ding aus der Pegnitz?"

„Naa, ebn ned. Däi da hab i aus am zerbombtn Haus raus. Überhaupt ned verrostet. Wie neu."

„Zeig amol her", schniefte Waltraud, stand auf und wischte ihr Gesicht mit der Schürze.

„Versprich, dass du ned sauer bist, Mama."

„I bin ned sauer", gelobte Waltraud. Bernd und Max standen ganz ruhig.

THE WHITE LITTLE DRESS

Underneath Sam whirled the usual flurry of activity. Mud was being hosed off tank tracks, metal was being scrubbed, bearings were being oiled. It was Friday again, and everyone was eager to finish up here and get ready for their night out. The group of soldiers working right underneath Sam thought he was lending a hand outside in the courtyard. And the guys outside believed he was busy inside the hangar. But Sam was working neither inside nor outside. He was suspended in one of the large camouflage nets just under the ceiling, a good twenty feet above the hangar floor, cozy as if he was lounging in a hammock, out of sight, out of mind. He was reading Oliver Twist, and quite shocked how deep this old book dug into his own wounds. For God's sake, wasn't this supposed to be a children's story? Each blow that fate dealt to the orphan boy stirred real, red-hot anger in Sam. He found himself crumpling the corners of pages or tossing the book on the floor at the end of a chapter. At first, reading had been a way to avoid unpleasant company. The constant pressure of socializing was best relieved by holding a book in front of your face. Within a few weeks, Sam had successfully built a reputation as a book worm and a bore, and people left him alone most of the time. Yet the new pastime had turned into an addiction. It had him climb up goddamn hangar ducts and lay in flimsy nylon nets at dizzying heights, just so he could dodge cleaning duty and devour another chapter.

He was almost through. His impatience grew and his pace accelerated, he was reading voraciously, at the same time dreading the moment he would turn the last page. That was always an awfully empty moment, reaching that last page of a great book, when the characters left a void in Sam as if they were real people.

Suddenly Sam realized that the hangar around him was still.

"Damn."

He scrambled up, almost capsizing his makeshift hammock, and wriggled his way back to the duct he had used to clamber up here. He slowly slid down, clamping both hands and feet around the duct, the book tucked into the back of his belt. When his feet touched the floor, he noticed a shadow in the hangar door. Greg was looking at him with the calm, curious gaze of someone who has been watching for a while.

"Ya ain gonna tell on me, buddy, are ya?" Sam said to him in the most casual tone he could muster.

"No worries. Great idea, actually. Ya mind if I use the technique some time?"

"Be ma guest. Kinda rickety up there, though. Gotta have a good head fo' heights."

They made their way across the yard. It was windy. Little spring flowers pushed their yellow heads out between the gravel.

"Why ya avoidin everybody, anyways."

"I ain avoidin anyone. Jus been readin."

Greg slowed down some.

"People startin to talk 'bout you, man."

"Sayin what, that I'm a wet rag?"

"How cum you doan like anybody here?"

"I like a lot of folks here."

Their boots crunched over the gravel. Greg eyed him sideways.

"All righ, I'll be social and cum 'long tonigh, you pest."

♦

When they hopped out of the cab downtown, the stores were still open. As soon as they stepped onto the sidewalk, Sam spotted a small shop. It looked as if it had been around for a long time, with twirling Art Noveau lettering across the window. Behind the glass was a group of eerily faceless, child-sized manikins that were dressed up to look like tiny brides.

"What the hell is that? They marryin off their lil children now?" laughed Herman behind Sam.

"To who, though?" wondered Greg.

"To us!" Greg and Herman barked a dirty laugh while Sam deciphered the handwritten sign between the creepy manikins:

Alles für die Heilige Kommunion.

"I think that's the kinof dress the lil girls wear fo' their First Communion," Sam conjectured.

"Oh, is that what that is?" said Herman.

"Y'all go 'head," Sam said, sending his comrades on their way. "I woan be long."

"Cum on, man, ya said ya was gonna cum with us tonigh," Greg complained.

"I still am. Jus gimme a minute."

"I know ya. Ya gonna slip away again. What business ya got in that store, anyway?"

Eventually, the others walked ahead. Sam pulled his dictionary out of his pocket, armed himself with a few words, and entered.

A little later he caught up with Greg and Herman, panting. He had a folded paper bag under his arm.

"'What ya got in there?" Greg wanted to know.

"Nuthin."

"Cum on. We lost the rest of our party cuz we's

walking slowly to let ya catch up," Herman insisted.

"Nunya business," Sam insisted, clutching the bag tightly. He would have to carry it around with him all night. Just a few more minutes further down the road, the battered, yet neat and bourgeois German townscape gave way to an entirely different kind of scenery. The raunchy, garish street life along the Frauentormauer existed only for the American GIs. American coin had converted traditional German guesthouses into night clubs and bars. Local stouts and ales had been scratched from the menus to make room for rum and Coke. German records had been pulled off the jukeboxes and replaced with Patti Page and Nat King Cole. Monstrous tail-fins and countless cabs were cruising slowly along the streets. Taxi doors were banging, the deep and roaring laughter of male voices was punctuated by the giddy giggles of the girls. Sam was drifting along in this wild bustle, still clutching the bag with Brigitte's Holy Communion gear. The paper became soft and mushy in his sweaty grip.

"Wanna get a drink?"

"Sure," confirmed Sam, who was getting dizzy in this sea of sounds and movement.

Herman pulled open a dark, narrow door which Sam had not even noticed, for it was tucked quietly between two far more eye-catching, blazingly lit windows. Right behind the door, crooked stairs plunged steeply into the unknown. Sam followed in the dim light of a few colorful light-bulbs. Down in the basement, the smoke was so dense that every breath equaled drawing on a cigarette. Sam's eyes watered instantly. He worried about the content of his paper bag and the vile stench it would absorb down here. He could not very well gift a little child with a Holy Communion dress that reeked of Sodom and Gomorrah.

His discomfort grew further as he glanced around. In the neon-colored nicotine swaths, he perceived nothing but white GIs. German girls were whirring around them like moths. The keening voice of Kitty Wells was wailing from the jukebox.

"Herman, let's get out of this honkatonk."

"What's wrong with it?"

"Look around ya, man."

"It's fine."

Herman nudged Sam towards a table and plopped down on a seat, taking up a remarkable amount of space, as if his body had suddenly widened by a few inches. Greg sat down, as well, though with less aplomb. Sam remained standing.

„Frollein!" Herman beckoned the waitress. "Cum on, man, sit ya ass down now."

A scurrying waitress arrived.

„Die Herren?"

"Rum an Coke for everyone. Ma treat," Herman said. The waitress noted the order with a hectic nod, scribbling on her pad. Sam saw a set of resolute, thick fingers appear over the edge of her scrawny shoulder. The hand pulled on her, not yanking, but with strength.

It was a GI. When she turned to face him, he started talking to her. In the brouhaha of the drunken chatter and the music, his lips moved soundlessly to Sam, but the agitation of the already nervous waitress grew visibly. She helplessly arched her eyebrows at Herman and company, silently pleading with them to resolve the dilemma. Sam took the hint.

"Cum on, Herman."

"Cum on what?" Herman said stubbornly.

The complaining party now dropped all subtlety; the GI stepped out from behind the waitress's back.

"Just so y'all know: in 'bout ten minutes, my whole platoon will be here. You wanna be out of here well before then."

"There's plenty of room," Herman replied comfortably, waving his hand around the empty seats. "I'm really thirsty, Frollein," he prodded the waitress, who was still lingering, in the hope that her problematic customers might withdraw voluntarily.

"Herman," Sam sighed.

Two more white soldiers joined the first one, standing

as tall and broad-shouldered as they could. Herman got up, easily towering over all three of their slick heads.

"I drink wherever I goddamn well please, gentlemen."

"You better not get too uppity. They're gonna put you back in your place when you get home."

"'Specially," added the sluggish drunken voice of another, "if you dare get near any of our women back home the way you're feeling up them Frolleins here."

"Herman," Sam repeated, trying to steer his companion away from the rising heat. Almost to his relieve, the men that came barging into the pub now were not the rest of the platoon, but MP.

"Any trouble, gentlemen?" asked their commander, instantly sensing it.

"Just trying to get these guys to understand they need to go to their own place," said the soldier who had first accosted them, in almost congenial certainty that the military police would side with him.

"We doan want any trouble," Sam muttered vaguely, more than ready to leave.

"Sure we doan. All we want is a drink," said Herman, heavily plopping back down on his seat. "Here."

"Herman, cum on. We doan wanna end up in a fight," Greg now finally joined Sam's cause.

"Well, we ain pickin none. It's them. Look athem. They still in some kinof blood-rage. I reckon that's from mowin down all 'em Gooks in Korea."

"God, and he hasn't even had anything to drink yet," Sam whispered to Greg.

"You're leaving now, with us," the MP decided the matter.

"Ya can't make me."

"I'm outa here," Sam finally broke his affiliation with Herman and Greg. He climbed the steep stairs out of this hell-hole of a pub, his neck hair bristling with the ugly comments that were thrown after him.

"Now here's a nigger who's got some sense."

"Oh, ya fuckin wimp! Ya stay in the fuckin barracks with your fuckin books next time," roared Herman.

Right on, thought Sam. Atop the stairs, he forced the heavy door open, his paper bag still wedged under his arm. There he was, back among the honking and blinking, squealing and flashing. He had walked but a few steps when a figure emerged from a shady entrance-way:

"Good evening, sir."

From the Lucky Strike that was dangling from the corner of her glaring red mouth and the silk stockings under her pettycoated skirt, Sam could tell that this was not her first encounter with an American.

„Entschuldigung, aber…", he tried to fend her off.

"Oh," she meowed in delight and endearment, "Sie sprechen ja Deutsch."

„Ick habe leider keine Dseit, wirklich ned," Sam said, trying to veer his way around her, but with an agile little swivel of her daringly high heels, she blocked his way again.

„Was ham Sie denn da?" she asked, pointing at his bag, with a expectant twinkle in her eyes and a twitch of her nose, like a dog in front of a butcher shop. What was in there? Canned food? Chocolate bars? Cigarettes or gum? Clothes or make-up?

„Eine kleine Kommunionkleid."

„Ein was?"

This time, Sam was quick enough and managed to walk himself clear of the Veronika. As he turned his eyes back on the road, he saw them – the rest of the platoon, just as the fellow in the bar had announced, trooping down the street towards their destination. When they beheld him and the Veronika, they collectively crossed the street, causing some frantic braking maneuvers and angry honking on the part of the motorists.

Sam's pace was hurried and his mind deflated with self-reproach, rage and twirling thoughts of how he could have handled the situation better. *Idiot*, he scolded himself, for going out with Herman in the first place. *Weakling*, for not being able to control that fool. *Coward*, for slinking out of that bar, leaving Greg behind, and cowering to the injustice of the while situation. *Hypocrite*, for walking past that poor whore and not giving her some money and telling her to go home for the night.

Sam walked and walked. When he looked up, he realized his oblivious march had taken him into the heart of Wöhrd. He looked at his hands. He was clutching the bag so tightly that the paper had almost disintegrated in his clammy grip. He drifted down Nunnenbeckstraße until he found the place he had unconsciously been seeking all along.

Sam took off his glasses, wiped his face with his sleeve in front of house number forty-six. Then he rang the doorbell with the grimy, handwritten label that read "Wächter".

A buzzer crackled, and he was so surprised that someone actually answered that by the time he gingerly pushed the doorknob, the hissing signal had stopped and the door was locked again. He rang the bell once more, this time ready to shove his shoulder against the heavy door as soon as he heard the buzzing sound. The hallway was dark and in it hung all kinds of smells. From the wooden stairs, a strong, biting tang of floor polish; from the floors above, a slightly sickening, stale odor of steamed cabbage; from the basement, the pungent stench of motor oil. The aroma was not exactly pleasant, but it smelled soothingly of simple, lived family life.

Sam made his way up the slick, freshly polished stairs, holding on to the wooden handrail. On the third floor, a door stood open, with a gangly tall figure in its frame.

Sam recognized him as Frau Wächter's oldest son. What was his name again? Before Frau Wächter took over the bookstore, he had run it for a few weeks. Sam remembered him as a lot more talkative than his mother, much more at ease with the English language.

He blinked into the dim staircase until Sam was close enough.

"Ah," he said. "Harris, right?" he remembered.

"I wish I had that kinof memory. Ya name was…"

"Bernd. Bernd Wächter." He stretched out a hand as if the presence of U.S. military on a Friday night in his smelly staircase was a matter of course. "So you are the GI who is friends with Hannes Kröger?"

"Friends… well, I haven't had the pleasure but a couple o times. But, yeah."

"Come on in", Bernd said, stepping aside without even knowing the purpose of Sam's visit. He liked the young man, a tall, calmer version of little Wolfi.

„Mama! Besuch!"

Frau Wächter appeared from a door in the narrow hallway, which had to be door to the kitchen, judging by the way she was wiping her hands on her apron. "Mr.

Harris", she mouthed, a good deal more baffled than her son. At this utterance, another door flung open with a crash, and two little beings came bolting out at hip-height. Wolfi and Brigitte impacted with Sam's midriff, knocking the breath out of him, then both clung to his waist as if he was a life-long friend.

„Eds lasst halt den Mr. Harris erst amol reikomma. Entschuldigens bitte", said Frau Wächter, trying to remove the little rascals that were dangling from Sam.

„Nein, nein, ist okay", Sam laughed, his lungs vibrating with relief. The dingy, murky bar was light-years away. *This* was where he needed to be.

„Ick bringe ... ", he began, at the same time realizing that he had not prepared this time. Otherwise, he would have looked up the word *present* or *surprise* before ringing the bell.

"… a gift?" he asked, arching his eyebrows at Bernd, who was the most likely to be able to help him out.

„*Gift*! " shrieked Brigitte, aghast. „Warum bringa Sie a Gift?"

„Ein Geschenk hat er," Bernd clarified. „*Gift* means poison," he explained to Sam.

"Oh, no sweetheart", Sam laughed. "As if I'd ever bring sumthin bad near you. Nein, nein, *Geschenk*."

„Für wen denn?"

„Für dich", he said as he produced the bag, the effect

of which was not very grand, since he had been dragging it about town with sweaty hands for a couple of hours.

„Für mi?" whispered Brigitte, eyes as wide as saucers. Sam realized that receiving a present was a most uncommon event in the life of that little girl. She opened the top of the bag with ginger, almost wary fingers, and peered inside. At the sight of the pearly shiny fabric, her eyes grew even larger. Wolfi, less reverent than her, yanked it out.

„A Kleid!" Wolfi identified.

„A Kommunionkleidle!" said Frau Wächter, clasping her hands in front of her bosom. „Ällmächt, und was für a scheens."

Brigitte yelped again, grabbed the little white dress and held it up against her scrawny body. As she twirled and hopped about the room in unadulterated bliss, Sam captured the glances of everyone in the room: Wolfi was bouncing around in selfless, vicarious joy, Frau Wächter watched both of them with a tenderness that contrasted strangely and touchingly with her hardened features, and Bernd was observing Sam, with a quietly analytical, yet approving glance.

"Try it on, sweetheart", Sam encouraged Brigitte. She scurried into the bedroom whence she had come dashing earlier.

„Ja, Frau Winkler is not home yet," Frau Wächter now said, shrugging. „But she should come in.…" She twisted her neck towards the wall clock in the kitchen behind her. „Fifteen minutes. Do you want to wait here?" She motioned towards her kitchen table.

„If I ain botherin…"

„No bother at all," said Bernd, ushering Sam into the room. The half-finished bottle of beer and the book on the table told Sam that Bernd was spending his Friday night here, in his mother's kitchen. Sam presumed that Bernd lacked the financial means for a more lavish form of entertainment.

He sat down, was offered a beer, which he declined. They sat in awkward silence for a moment. Sam glanced at the clock — only one minute had ticked by. He could not sit here mutely for fourteen more minutes. So he started a conversation:

"What ya readin?"

"Oh", said Bernd, and looked ever so slightly uncomfortable when he saw that Sam was trying to decipher the title of his book. It was Marx's *Kommunistisches Manifest*.

"Are ya Communist?"

"No, not at all, actually. I plan to vote FDP in the fall."

"Then why ya readin this?"

"Because I need to know what I'm talking about. This book is more about social injustice than anything else," explained Bernd, waving a dismissive hand across the cover. Sam eyed the book with the guarded, yet intrigued fascination of someone observing a copperhead snake.

"Marx," Sam said as he picked it up and turned the book in his hands. "Ya reckon he ever knew how much trouble he'd be? How'd he cum up with that stuff, anyhow."

"Marx spent some time in Manchester. He saw the mines and the mills. People working 16-hour shifts for a pittance. *Kids* working 16-hour days. The terrible injustice of unrestrained profiteering."

"Oh, I know all 'bout that," said Sam eagerly, referencing his literary forages into 19th-century Britain that made him toss his library books in anger.

"So, this experience set his brilliant mind in motion, and he created a philosophy to break this circle of greed and oppression. That's all he wanted. It's not his fault that people abuse the idea and create a new kind of hell."

"Well, I wish I knew 'nough German to read it maself," said Sam, dropping the book back on the table with a shrug.

"Oh, I can get you an English copy," Bernd offered.

"Man," Sam huffed as if he had just been offered illegal booze, "It'll get me into trouble."

"Trouble? For reading a hundred-year-old book by a man who is long dead?"

"Fo' readin Stalinist stuff."

"What I'm trying to tell you is, this is not *Stalinist*."

"Marxist, then. Same thing."

"Noo," Bernd laughed in slight exasperation.

"And where d'ya reckon ya'd get me an English copy?" Sam said, gingerly taking another step towards certain trouble.

"Easy. Should I bring it to the bookstore Monday night?"

"I'd rather cum pick it up from *you*."

"Man, aren't you paranoid," Bernd chuckled.

The door clicked and there stood Theresa, in each hand a shopping net, stretched dangerously thin by the weight of their contents. The straps were plowing deep red welts into the delicate skin of Theresa's fingers. She looked at their visitor in surprise and restrained delight.

"Good evening, Frau Winkler. We're waitin for lil Brigitte to try sumthin on."

„Ja, wie lang braucht sie denn noch?" wondered Bernd. Before Theresa could respond, the bedroom door opened, and from it emerged, no, *floated*, Brigitte in an ankle-long white dress, with a pretty wide collar and a broad white belt.

„Wie ein klein Prinzessin," Sam acclaimed.

„Ein*e* klein*e* Prinzessin," Brigitte corrected his

grammar, giving a kittenish twirl of her skirt.

„Na, des geht ned," Theresa refused Sam's gift, perplexed and overwhelmed.

"Cum on, Frau Winkler, she spose to have her Holy Communion this year, same time as all her lil friends. She ain gotta wait til next year."

Sam reached into the paper bag, found a little box and opened it carefully.

"Cum o'r here, sweetheart."

He carefully removed its contents, a wreath of white silk flowers that was laced with long satin bands, and placed it on Brigitte's unruly hair.

"Perfect."

„Des is doch ois zu teier."

"Nickt teuer. Deutschmark is schleckt und der Dollar ist gut. Let'er have her Holy Communion. She wants it."

"Mr. Harris...."

"I ain Mr. Harris in here," he told her with emphasis.

KOMMUNION

Waltraud hisste und zischte, ohne Erfolg. Wolfi war einfach nicht in der Lage, auf der harten Kirchenbank still zu sitzen. Der pubertierende Max wiederum war zu zynisch, um den fremd und seltsam anmutenden Ritualen der katholischen Kirche gebührenden Respekt zu erweisen, und Bernd war nach langer Überredung zwar anwesend, drückte aber mit jeder atheistischen Faser seines flegelhaft lümmelnden Körpers aus, was er von Weihrauch und Marienanbetung hielt.

„Eds reiß di halt zam. A Stund wirst es ja wohl aushaltn", gebot Waltraud, die aus dem Schämen gar nicht mehr herauskam. Doch Theresa schien das nicht zu stören. Hannes und Mathilde waren aus Bamberg da, ihre Schwiegermutter und Schwager aus Manching angereist, und deswegen war sie schon seit dem Vortag hoch beschäftigt, buk, wusch, und polierte, als ob sie in Waltrauds kleiner Wohnung ein paar Dutzend Staatsgäste erwartete.

Nun, da der Einzug der Kommunionskinder schon vom Glockengeläut eingebimmelt wurde, setzte Theresa sich zum ersten Mal seit fünf Uhr morgens hin, war allerdings kaum ruhiger als Wolfi. Sie drehte sich unentwegt um, strich sich Rock und Haare glatt, spähte nervös. Da. Endlich rieb die schwere, jahrhundertealte Holzpforte der Bartholomäuskirche stöhnend über die etwas zu dicke rote Fußmatte, und eine Silhouette erschien im Torrahmen, überstürzt und zaghaft zugleich. Der Neuankömmling tastete mit dem Blick die versammelte Gemeinde ab, erkannte seine Gesellschaft und machte sich eilig auf zu ihnen. Sein Versuch, flink und unauffällig zu huschen, scheiterte kläglich – was bei einer Körpergröße von einem Meter neunzig und einer Hautfarbe von Ebenholz unvermeidbar war. Die Gemeinde starrte, erst glotzäugig auf Sam, dann neugierig auf die Winklerin, die Wächters und die Krögers, zu denen Sam sich nun auf die Kirchenbank gleiten ließ. Hannes, der ganz außen saß, drückte ihm zum Gruß herzlich beide Hände. Die Hälse in den umliegenden Bänken verdrehten sich noch ein wenig weiter.

„Ich hoff bloß, es kriegt keiner eine Genickstarre", kommentierte Bernd hörbar, bevor seine Worte in Waltrauds verzweifeltem Zischen untergingen.

"So sorry", entschuldigte Sam seine Verspätung.

"It's okay."

"I couldn get out any sooner."

"It's okay."

Das Hauptportal öffnete sich erneut, und das Erscheinen der kleinen Hauptpersonen wandte die Aufmerksamkeit der Gemeinde von Sam und seiner Gesellschaft ab. Glückselig und stolz marschierten die Kinder ein, Jungen rechts, Mädchen links, die langen Kommunionkerzen wippten schief in schwitzigen kleinen Griffen. Sam strahlte mit den Vätern um die Wette. Theresa sonnte ihre Seele in Sams zärtlichem Blick auf ihr Kind.

„Die Ärmsten", raunte Wolfi beim Anblick der steifen Hemden und streng gescheitelten Schöpfe, „hoffentlich springt wenigstens was Gscheites raus für die." Waltrauds wütendes Hissen war deutlich lauter als Wolfis frecher Kommentar. Aber zum Schweigen brachte es ihn doch.

„Mr. Harris, Sie komma doch nu auf an Kuachn mit", befahl die alte Frau Winkler mehr, als sie ihn einlud, und erwies damit ihrer Schwiegertochter nichtsahnend den Gefallen, dass Theresa ihn nicht selbst einzuladen brauchte.

„Kuchen, oh, immer", nahm Sam gefällig an. „Wunderbare Kommunion, sweetheart", gratulierte er Brigitte. Die strahlte.

„Eds hält des Negerunwesen scho bei uns in Wöhrd Einzug", driftete eine keifende Stimme zu ihnen. Waltraud grabschte beschwichtigend Bernds Arm, noch bevor der vor Wut aufzucken konnte.

„Na, bitte ned. Da machmer eds ka Szene draus. Es is der Brigitte ihr Kommunion heut."

Bernd beherrschte sich mühsam. Brigitte hatte entweder nicht gehört, oder gar nicht begriffen. Sie glühte vor Glück und in der ungewohnten Aufmerksamkeit.

„Woar i die Hübscheste in meim Kleid?", fragte sie Sam kokett.

"Prettiest. Was she the prettiest?", beantwortete Max das Fragezeichen auf Sams Gesicht.

"Why do ya even aks? Course you were the prettiest, ma sweetheart."

"Easy with the flattery, man", bremste ihn Bernd.

"What?"

"Vanity is the last thing a German girl needs in this day and age", belehrte ihn Bernd, den der lange, aufreibend katholische Gottesdienst unmutig gemacht hatte.

"*You* take it easy. She's eight years old. She's runnin 'round in leather shorts all year. A lil compliment woan hurt her."

"I guess", gab Bernd nach.

"I'm almos through with yo lil book, by the way," fügte Sam mit einem vielsagenden Blick hinzu. Bernds Augenbrauen hoben sich erheitert.

"Are you."

"What book?", stieg Hannes in das Gespräch ein.

„Kommunistisches Manifest."

„Bernd", rügte Hannes, „das lohnt sich doch nicht. Das bringt den armen Kerl doch bloß in Teufels Küche…"

"Devil's kitchen", interpretierte Sam lachend, "I like that word." Bernd grinste breit. Hannes schüttelte unbilligend den Kopf.

Sie waren bei der Metzgerei Ahrend angekommen. Der Metzger, etwas milder gestimmt, seit Waltraud endlich regelmäßig die Miete bezahlte, grüßte durchs Ladenfenster.

Oben in der Wohnung machten sich die Frauen augenblicklich ans Werk. In die Wohnungsluft, die sonst eher nach staubmuffigen Gardinen und verkochtem Kohl roch, stieg nun das köstliche Aroma von Kirschkuchen und Bohnenkaffee.

„Was hoatsn eds da scho wieda?", bemerkte Theresa, misstrauisch geworden ob der ungewöhnlichen Ruhe der Kinder. Brigitte saß in tiefster Ehrfurcht auf dem Bett im Schlafzimmer, Wolfi ihr gegenüber. Brigitte hielt eine nagelneue Schildkröt-Puppe, ein Baby in einem süßen blauen Hemdchen und schneeweißen Schühchen.

„Vom Sam", erklärte sie, ohne den Blick davon abzuwenden.

„Mr. Harris, wirkli....", machte Theresa vorwurfsvoll.

„Sie heißt Paulina, sagt der Sam."

Theresa war peinlich berührt, wollte das teure Geschenk nicht annehmen, aber auch nicht das unbändige Glück im Gesicht ihrer Tochter trüben.

"No mo'e *Geschenke*, I promise", lachte Sam.

Wolfi und Brigitte spielten ungefähr zehn Minuten auf dem Bett mit der Puppe. Dann hielt es sie nicht länger in der Stube, beide wollten zurück in ihre speckigen Lederhosen und in dem herrlichen Frühlingstag herumräubern. Mit Paulina im Schlepptau, natürlich.

„Machs ned kaputt, di neie Puppn!"

„Die kriegt sie so leicht nicht kaputt, die is doch original Schildkröt", sagte Hannes und erinnerte Theresa damit an die Unsumme, die Sam vermutlich dafür ausgegeben hatte.

„Aber Brigitte, es is doch dei eigene Kommunion", protestierte ihre Großmutter.

„Lass sie gehn, Mutter", sagte Theresa. „Es sin andre Zeiten. Die Kinder heitzutag wissn doch goar ned, was a Fest is. Und es is ja a kaum a Fest, mit zehn Leit in am engen Wohnzimmer. Des war halt früher ois anders."

„Als obs bei solchen Festen *überhaupt* um die Hauptperson ginge", merkte Bernd an und stand auf. „Feiern kann man auch ohne Kommunionskinder. Also, in diesem Sinne: Ein Toast auf den edlen Spender, ohne dessen großzügige Bereitstellung eines angemessenen Gewandes eine Einführung in das Haus des Herrn völlig undenkbar gewesen wäre", spottete er und erhob die Kaffeetasse, als wäre sie ein Champagnerglas.

Waltraud wollte gerade entnervt eingreifen, als Theresa sagte:

„Du hasts gut, Bernd. Du scherst di koan Deut drum, was die Leit von dir denken. Ich wünscht, mir wär des a ois gleich. Aber des kommt bei mir scho a no. Langsam."

Hannes beobachtete Sams aufmerksamen Blick. Man konnte regelrecht zusehen, wie sein Gehirn fiebrig arbeitete, wie er gierig alles in sich aufsaugte und versuchte, dem abwechselnd auf fränkisch, Studentenhochdeutsch und oberbayrisch geführten Gespräch zu folgen.

„Was macht das Deutsch, Sam?", fragte er ihn also.

„A bissl besser jede Tag."

„Das find ich ganz wunderbar, dass Sie sich so bemühen", lobte ihn Mathilde Kröger.

„Ich lerne mit das Buch und mit die Leute", sagte Sam mit einer Geste in den Raum.

„Mit *dem* Buch und mit *den* Leuten", verbesserte Hannes freundlich.

"Oh, doan even bother", wehrte Sam lachend ab, "that grammar is way 'bove ma ignorant head. I doan even put endins on ma *English* words."

"Well, you *will* put them on your German words."

"Ya got any idea what ma schoolin was like? It ain like them nice schools for white folks, ya know. What I know, I learned by maself."

Das rege plätschernde Gespräch versiegte abrupt. Löffelchen klimperten unangenehm berührt in den Kaffeetassen.

"Let me tell you something, Sam Harris", sagte

Hannes, und rückte dabei wichtig seinen Stuhl zurecht, "These boys here go to school in shifts. How many years of orderly schooling do you think our Max here has gotten, between the war, and the hunger and the destruction? Bernd is going to university after a childhood spent literally in fire and brimstone. The circumstances have not exactly been favorable for the education of these youngsters. But even though we cannot offer them the childhood they deserve, we have great expectations for them. They are our pride, our hope, our future. You should have great expectations for yourself and your remarkable intellect."

"Problem is I was never anybody's pride, or hope, or future."

"But you are", widersprach Hannes mit Selbstverständlichkeit.

Es war wieder still im Raum, und Sam schabte mit dem winzigen Kuchengäbelchen angestrengt Krümel von seinem ebenso zierlichen Porzellanteller. In ihm herrschte ein Sturm, den die anderen sich nur vage vorstellen konnten. Er überspielte die Schwere seiner Empfindungen mit einem spöttischen:

"And ya reckon I should start by puttin endins on ma German words?"

Bernd mischte sich ins Gespräch, erregt, in jugendlichem Zorn über die Ungerechtigkeit der Welt: "You start by thinking better of yourself. You just called yourself ignorant! The racists have done a great job over there. You actually *believe* you are a lesser man than others."

Da, das Wort war gefallen. Sams inneres Toben brach aus ihm heraus: "First of all, that's rich, a lecture 'bout racism from a *Kraut*", schappte er, obwohl er wusste, dass er beiden Männern damit Unrecht tat. "Second, what d'ya know 'bout us, kid? Been almos a hundred years since Emancipation, and where am I? I still have nuthin. I still am nuthin. I still can't have what I want."

"What you *want*", wiederholte Bernd bedächtig. "And why can't you?"

Bernd sah sich kurz um, ehe er fortfuhr. Die Frauen waren alle drei in Waltrauds Schlafzimmer und hängten dort sorgsam Brigittes Kommunionskleid auf, das das Mädchen achtlos über einen Stuhl geworfen hatte. Bernd senkte seine Stimme:

"You *go* for her."

"What are you talking about?", fragte Hannes verständnislos.

"Theresa", sagte Bernd. Hannes Augen weiteten sich, überrascht, dann erfreut, dann besorgt. Sam saß still, in seinem Kopf wüteten immer noch die Gedanken.

"People wouldn understand. I'd cause her nuthin but trouble."

"Enough people would understand", beharrte Bernd.

"Yeah? And where are they? Cuz outside of this

apartment, I doan see them."

Hannes schaltete sich wieder ein, nachdenklich:

"They are hiding. It was the same under Hitler. I thought I was the only one who saw how wrong everything was. I felt so lonely, sometimes I thought I was losing my bloody mind. But once Hitler was dead, and the war was lost, they all came out of their little foxholes. I asked myself: Now where the bloody hell have all these intelligent people been all that time? And I realized: I had spent the past twelve years in hiding myself! Nowadays we live in the rubble, we don't always have enough to eat, we can't even put our little girls in nice dresses for their Holy Communion. But Sam, I am *alive*. Just look at this one", sagte Hannes und wies dabei auf Bernd. "What a beautiful mind, what a force of nature he is. No new Hitler will rise as long as there are enough Bernds. And the universities are full of them. And they are all loud, and they will not be silenced."

„No an Kuachen?"

Die Frauen waren zurück.

„Wenn noch genug da ist, gern", bat Hannes.

„Des war aber a leidenschaftliche Red", bemerkte Theresa, scheinbar lakonisch, den Teller mit den letzten paar Stück Kirschkuchen auf den Tisch scheppernd. „Wenn i bloß mehr als die Hälft verstandn hätt."

„Wenn du die Hälfte verstanden hast, ist das schon mehr als genug. Du hörst ja erst seit ein paar Monaten

Englisch."

„Also, wenn ihr rausfindn wollts, was die ganzn GI so denkn, dann soll halt die Waltraud amol aufpassen, wer was kauft im Laden", schlug Theresa vor. „Ich trau mi wettn, dass die Waltraud in den ganzn Barrracks am besten woaß, was so in die Köpf vorgeht. Weil sie nämlich woaß, wer was liest."

Bernd machte eine anerkennende Schnute. Er dachte, Theresa wüsste entweder gar nicht, worum ihr Gespräch ging, oder es wäre ihr gleichgültig. Sam starrte seine Angebetete an wie vom Donner gerührt.

BOOK CLUB

Sam was sitting in the main office on one of the uncomfortable chairs that were lined up along the wall. Frau Kellermann was hacking away at her typewriter. Flies were buzzing around, wretchedly failing to find the way out through the slightly opened windows. The flowers on the window sill behind Frau Kellermann needed watering. Sam felt like a high school kid waiting to be called into the principal's office. And he was similarly nervous. He was exhausted, too, because since Sunday afternoon, his mind had been reeling with the same irrepressible thoughts.

He was thinking about Carl, who picked up white little children who were complete stangers to him without the slightest hesitation, without the slightest fear that anything might go wrong. He thought about Greg, whose eyes almost watered up when he talked about going home to Mississippi and the 'ole ways' he could not tolerate any more. He thought about Herman, who was a drunken philanderer with a pea-sized brain, yet who would rather get in a fist-fight than cede a mediocre bar to white dominance.

And then he thought about himself.

No matter how his thoughts meandered, he always arrived at the conclusion that the best thing he had ever done in his life was transgress. Back then in Normandy, when Rhees gave him an order, and he did the opposite.

When he did what was *right*. It had gotten him into trouble. But it had connected him with the Krögers, the Wächters and the Winklers.

Except for this one bout of courage, he had spent his life tiptoeing around the obstacles and the walls of hatred and bigotry. He needed to transgress, but not like Herman. And not the way he had responded to Shane Tucker. Quite apart from the fact that he was not cut out to physically stand up to his adversaries. He was lucky Tuck was such a chicken. Shit, all a raging redneck had to do in a bar fight with him was knock off Sam's glasses to incapacitate him. No, he needed be very smart about it. Like in Normandy. And he didn't need to do it alone. He remembered what Hannes had said about his experience in Nazi Germany: *I felt so lonely, sometimes I thought I was losing my bloody mind*. Like-minded enlightened Germans had left each other in desperate isolation by going into intellectual hiding. His kindred spirits needed to come out of their shells, but how?

That led his thoughts to Theresa. *That woman*. And her almost incidental comment as she was clattering with the dishes. He had fallen in love with her humble sweetness, her lovely face, her firm and slender body. But she was more than she let on. She, whose schooling had been hardly any better than Sam's, who had had no other instruction in English than a little dictionary and listening to the GIs' bullshit around the barracks – had understood everything that Hannes had uttered in his rapid, cultured British accent, and then casually suggested an ingenius way to identify Sam's hidden soulmates.

♦

"*Book* club?" echoed Captain Perry, in a tone as if Sam had requested permission to start a swinger club. Or worse, some kind of Soviet Worker's Council. Why did Vaughn have to refer him to the next lower rung in the hierarchy? Vaughn could have just signed Sam's request, and Perry would never have known that there even was a book club.

"Yes sir. We'd like to use meeting room five on Monday nights."

"And who is 'we'?"

"Maself and a few others, sir," said Sam vaguely. He was going to recruit members after he obtained permission to start the club.

"What kind of books are you going to read, Harris?"

"Jus... literature, sir."

"Like what? Examples."

"Like... Charles Dickens," Sam named the least compromising author he could cite off the top of his head.

"Dickens?" said Vaughn, perplexed.

"Jus… classics, ya know."

"Okay," exhaled Perry, skeptical, but finding no grounds to deny the request. He took the form and signed it.

"There's your club. Room 5, you said?"

"Yes, sir."

"Check with Frau Kellermann if it's available on Monday nights."

"I already did, sir. Thank you, sir."

Sam retreated quickly, as if he feared that Perry might change his mind if he did not get out of his sight fast enough. He almost skipped the way to the *Stars and Stripes* bookstore.

„So, ich hab Buchclub jetzt. Perry gesagt ja. Kannst du geben das zu andere Soldaten?"

Waltraud took the stack of carbon-copied flyers.

„Und wem soll i die gebn?"

„Alle wer kauft was. Naa, warte. Wer nur Junk kauft, kriegt nicht."

„Also, no amal: jedm, der was Brauchbars kauft, geb i a so a Einladung."

„Genau. Danke," he said and turned to dash away busily.

„Ja, Moment, und wohl bloß die Farbign?"

Sam paused. Then he shook his head:

„Na. *Alle*, wer gute Bücher kauft."

♦

Monday rolled around. The company finished their exercise on the *Große Straße* late. Sam almost ran back into the west building, straight to meeting room five. There had been no time to plan for any refreshments, or even think of a topic for this first session. Striding down the corridor, he feverishly thought about how he would start the meeting, how he was going to describe the purpose of the club, what book he would suggest for their first reading. Words were floating in his head, all awkward and odd.

When he arrived at room five, he was greeted only by a row of scattered chairs, which the officers had not bothered to push back after their meeting earlier in the afternoon. Good, no one was here yet. That gave Sam another moment to gather his thoughts. He pushed the tables up against the walls, formed a circle with a dozen chairs, sat down on one of them and started to think. When he finally felt he knew what to say, the clock in the room said ten after seven.

"Where is everybody?" Sam muttered to himself. He removed four chairs from the circle. Sat down again.

The door opened. Sam jumped to his feet.

A large angular object appeared. It banged against the door-frame a couple of times before it was finally sufficiently aligned to pop through the door into the room. The wet mops wiggled, the bottles of cleaner quivered in their holders. It was a cleaning cart.

"Mr. Harris?" asked a confused Theresa when she beheld him sitting lonely in the middle of the room.

"That late already?"

„Halb acht."

"I booked this room for our club. No one showed."

„Hm," said Theresa. She abandoned her cart and sat down next to Sam in the vacant circle of chairs.

„Musst halt no mehr Werbung machen."

„Werbung?"

„Mehr Leit sagn, dass kommen solln."

"Ah so. Well, Walli handed out at leas fifty flyers."

„So geht des ned. Du musst die Leit persönli einladen."

"Hm."

They sat in silence for a moment.

„Na guat, i muass weiter machn," Theresa said, making a move to get up and start cleaning the room. Sam grabbed the strings of her apron.

„Frau Winkler."

She allowed him to pull her back.

"I wanna apologize for that terrible kiss at the cemetery."

She laughed. Emboldened by her reaction, he pulled her closer.

"No, really, it was terrible. I should have done a lot better."

This time it was no awkward, impulsive peck on her face. It was a slow, deliberate, much more mutual, much more genuine kiss. He found her an astoundingly good kisser for a Catholic farm girl, and Sam knew with whom she had learned this skill. He shivered, not only with the tremor of sensual adventure, not just with the warmth of budding love — but also with the thrill of a forbidden deed.

„Du, i muss sauber machn," she eventually said, writhing out of his grip.

"Doan ya like it?" he said, a little deflated. She grinned.

„Like it? Du bist lustig. I hab bloß Angst, dass oaner kimmt."

"Okay."

„Gehnmer vielleicht am Wochenend wo spaziern?"

„Spazieren. Ja," he agreed, while his groin wildly

protested the notion of adjourning their romance by five more days. His reason, however, acknowledged the prudence of her suggestion.

She stood up, straightened her apron and grabbed a broom from her cart.

„Diese alten Ferkel," she commented as she swept up the clutter the officers had left on the floor. Sam could not resist laying his hand on her buttocks and pressing another little kiss on her cheek before he left the room.

♦

Sam passed the next few days heeding Theresa's advice and trying to coax comrades into joining his club face-to-face. They were a little puzzled by the fact that the recluse whose face was continuously hidden behind a book now was all over them, striking up conversations, ambushing them in the halls, in the cafeteria, while scrubbing tank tracks or floors.

"What are you up to?" Shane Tucker assailed him one afternoon, waving a copy of the flyer in Sam's face with irritated vehemence.

"Ya know how to read, I spose."

"I didn't ask what your stupid flyer says, I asked what you're *up to*."

"Readin."

"Yeah, right."

Shane took off.

Monday came, and with it, six people. Carl was perched on the very edge of his chair with an air of genuine expectation.

Herman was there, too, folding his flyer into a paper boat – sheer boredom had brought him. Greg had come to do Sam a favor. There were two others whom Sam only knew from the bookstore, one black, one white. Last, intentionally late by five minutes, Shane Tucker made his entrance, filling the room with his vociferous presence and nudging Sam out of his fragile poise. Sam was angry at himself for being so easily unnerved. As he began to speak, he realized that he had never addressed a group larger than two or three people outside of his own family.

"Okay, evryone, thanks for cumin."

Sam's ideas, so razor-sharp in his mind, did not find nearly as clear an articulation:

"So basically, I jus wanted to start a group with people, ya know, who like to read. I really like to read...."

Greg huffed: "Do ya really?"

"And I know there's many of us that like to read so I reckoned we could... ya know. Jus talk 'bout stuff we all read." Sam cringed with embarrassment at how dim this sounded. Shane exacerbated his sense of clumsiness:

"That sounds so familiar... Wait... Oh yeah, it sounds exactly like a high school English class."

"Cept we get to chose what we wanna read n talk 'bout. Now, I personally like books 'bout injustice. And ignorance."

"You doan need no book to learn 'bout injustice and ignorance. That's all around us," Herman puffed.

"That's why I wanna read 'bout it."

"I really liked *Not Without Laughter*," Carl interjected. The tight muscles in Sam's neck melted in gratitude. *Someone* was taking this seriously. "Have you read it?"

"No."

"It's a book from the Thirties, you know, the Harlem Renaissance."

Sam, Greg and Herman did *not* know. Carl saw the question mark on their faces and added: "New York Negro literature. And since we are mostly black in this group here....," Carl said, ascertaining his statement with a glance around the tight circle of chairs.

"And not by coincidence, I reckon," drawled Shane.

Unperturbed, Carl continued: "We could maybe read some books from that era, and discuss how it concerns us today. The question is, how do we get enough copies?"

Sam nodded with eager interest, baffled by the existence of such a thing as 'negro literature'.

"Frau Wächter, ya know, the lady who runs the bookstore. We jus let her know what we want, and she'll order it."

"So, are we even welcome here?" said Shane tartly with a gesture that included the other white man, who flinched and pushed his black-rimmed glasses back up the bridge of his steep nose.

"Well, Tucker, if the reason ya're here is to sniff 'round and fin' out what we're *up to*, ya gonna be mighty bored, cause we ain up to nuthin in particular. If ya wanna read books and talk, be our guest."

"Well, if I may add something. My name is Whitson Clarke, and as it happens, I am an avid reader of the *Harlem Renaissance*," said the other white man, distancing himself from Shane. "And I think it would be a perfect starting point."

"Oh great, we got a nerd, too," Tucker continued to torpedo the meeting.

"Shall we start with Langston Hughes, then? We could, of course, do *Not Without Laughter*, as Carl suggested, or we could start out with some short stories, to get talking faster," Whitson suggested. Sam painfully felt the gulf of literacy between him, the founder of this book club, and some of its members, who threw around names and terms he had never heard before.

"Would ya write down some titles, so I can get 'em to Frau Wächter?" Sam asked. "And since it's gonna take a few weeks til they ship, why doan we start by talkin 'bout sumthin we already read."

"Yes, some classic that everybody knows, maybe," Whitson Clarke said. Carl nodded his head in agreement. Shane was slouching in his chair in defiant disinterest. Herman chuckled, Greg frowned, both for the same reason: The likelihood that they would be familiar with *any* book that would be suggested was close to nil.

"Well, Sam you started this club. What have you been reading lately?"

"May sound stupid, but I really like Oliver Twist."

"That ain't stupid at all. Nineteenth-century England or twentieth-century America. In some ways, not as different as we'd like to think," said Carl.

"Oliver Twist – I seen that movie!" exclaimed Greg happily. "Wasn't it at the movies couple years back?"

"It sure was," confirmed Whitson.

"Oh yeah. I know what y'all are talkin 'bout." Greg was grinning, clearly relieved to be able to participate in the discussion.

Sam smiled. *He'd done it*. He had a little group of people with whom to share his feverish thoughts. He would no longer feel this dreadful loneliness in the barracks. Shane's chair squealed impatiently as he pushed it back.

"Now, excuse me, but I know better uses for my free time than listen to some blathering nuts."

Sam rolled his eyes comically as Shane left the room, and the others chuckled.

EIN FREMDER

Die Julisonne brannte. Theresa zog ihren Strohhut tiefer über ihr Gesicht.

"Joy", sagte sie.

„Freude", spielte Sam zurück.

„Gut. Und sadness?"

"Since I met ya, I forgot what that word even means."

"Come on."

„Somethin *traurig*."

„Traurigkeit."

"How many more?"

„Noch...", Theresa blätterte. „Anderthalb Seitn."

„Naa, heut nimmer", sagte Sam und rollte auf der Decke herum.

„Oh mei", grinste Theresa, „von mir lernst ja koa gscheits Deitsch."

„Warum?"

„*Naa* is koa Wort, und *nimmer* a ned."

„Ja mei."

Er setzte sich ganz auf.

"I got sumthin for ya."

Er zog eine flache, leichte Packung aus seinem Jackenfutter. Theresa nahm sie nicht an, sondern verdrehte nur ein wenig den Hals, um zu sehen, worum es sich handelte.

„Sam...."

„Was?"

Ihre Hand umschloss seine, in der er die Packung Seidenstrümpfe hielt, und schob sie ihm sanft wieder entgegen.

„Schenk mir sowas bitte ned."

„Warum ned?"

„I will ned gsehn werdn in sowas."

„Warum ned? Leute sehn dir schon mit mir."

„Darum gehts ned. Mit dir lass i mi gern sehn. Aber ned mit so teire Sachen. Much money", sagte sie, auf die Strümpfe deutend.

"Ya're worth it a million times over."

„Schenk mir nix", wiederholte sie, nun mit Bestimmtheit. Sam steckte die Strümpfe wieder in sein Jackenfutter, leicht gekränkt.

„Verstehst du des denn ned?"

Doch, Sam verstand schon. Zu viele deutsche Mädchen umflatterten die GIs nur um der Geschenke willen. Es ging um Theresas Ruf.

"Sorry. Ick bin doof", lächelte er schelmisch. "Und du bist sooo smart."

Sie saß und sonnte ihn mit einem zeitlosen, absichtslosen Lächeln. Dann kehrte ihr Blick aber in die Realität zurück.

„Es wird langsam voll hier."

Sam sah sich um. Immer mehr Familien kamen mit Picknickkörben angewalzt. Sie warfen schwungvoll ihre Decken auf die schattigen grünen Flächen aus. Kinder standen im Uferschilf des leicht faulig riechenden Dutzendteichs und bewarfen schnatternde Enten und manchmal auch verliebte Ruderbootfahrer mit Brotkrümeln. Am Wochenende waren die Amis auf der Großen Straße nicht zugange, also konnten die Nürnberger die Sommerfrische genießen. Über allem thronte die gewaltige Fassade der Kongresshalle, die Hitler in seinem Größenwahn dem römischen Kolosseum hatte nachbauen lassen.

Doch als die Menschentrauben am späten Samstagvormittag dichter wurden, wurde es Sam und Theresa doch ein wenig unangenehm, bei all dem Mut, den sie sich eigentlich so fest fassen wollten. Die Blicke der Ewiggestrigen waren giftig, empört. Und was, wenn ein hierher verirrter amerikanischer Kamerad Sam ertappte und ihre Romanze in der Kaserne in die falschen Ohren posaunte? Sie brachen also auf, um sich in die stickige Wohnung zurückzuziehen. Widerwillig. Der Sonnenschein war einfach zu köstlich, die Luft zu sanft, die Wiese zu grün und der Himmel zu blau.

Auf Höhe der Kongresshalle hielt Sam inne.

"Wait."

„Was willstn hier?"

„Nur schauen."

Er erklomm eine Treppe und schritt mit Theresa den Säulengang entlang, und zwar genau so, wie die Erbauer es gewollt hatten: Unter den mächtigen Bögen fühlte man sich winzig, man ging gehetzt, als würde man immer weiter in die scheinbare Endlosigkeit der Säulenreihen gesaugt. Sam und Theresa waren ganz allein. Ihre Schritte hallten. Hier war es auch viel kühler.

„Wo willstn hin?", fragte Theresa.

„Weiß ned", sagte Sam, immer noch gebannt der Krümmung des runden Baus folgend.

„Des ist bestimmt ned erlaubt", warnte Theresa vorsorglich, als Sam fasziniert zum Stehen kam. Eine der schweren Eisentüren in der Fassade stand halb offen. Mit ihrem banalen dunkelgrauen Anstrich brach die Tür die wuchtige Mystik des Säulengangs. Sam ignorierte Theresa und schlüpfte hinein. Im Dunkeln zeichneten sich die nichtssagenden Formen von allerlei Unrat ab. Was genau hier gelagert wurde, konnten sie gar nicht erkennen. Zwei dünne Lichtschächte fielen von beiden Seiten in die Schwärze. Die Tür auf der anderen Seite, die in den Innenhof der Kongresshalle führte, stand ebenfalls offen. Sam folgte dem Licht, Theresa hintendrein. Bald standen sie wieder im Freien.

Dieser riesige Hof, eine Mischung aus Schutthalde, Lagerfläche und Hinterbühne, hätte eigentlich der gigantische Saal der Kongresshalle werden sollen. Sie wanderten die Innenseite des Baus ab. Hier war er zerfurcht, unfertig, aus banalem rotem Backstein. Er passte überhaupt nicht zur Vorderseite, die imposant und schneeweiß in der Sonne strahlte. Unkraut bahnte sich störrisch den Weg durch die Bodenplatten, als läge das Dritte Reich schon im fernen Nebel der Vergangenheit, überwuchert und vergessen.

„Da schau her, und des hätt eigentlich ois tausend Jahr lang halten sollen", kommentierte Theresa spöttisch die Macht der Natur. Sam lachte. Es roch schlecht, nach Baumaterialen, die entweder fertig verarbeitet oder entsorgt hätten werden sollen und die nun in der Julihitze ungesunde Dämpfe abgaben. Nischen und Ecken für ein verstohlenes Liebespaar gab es reichlich. Sam kraxelte emsig über einen Haufen Schutt und Sand.

"Watch out. Pass auf hier."

„Wegen dir schneidmer uns noch die Haxn auf."

Sam und Theresa fanden ein lauschiges Plätzchen hinter einem Haufen schlampig gestapelter Bretter. Sie umschlangen sich gegenseitig die Hüften und versanken in einen langen Sommerkuss.

Ein Scheppern riss die beiden aus ihrer Seligkeit.

"What was that?"

„Wahrscheinli a Streuner. Kinder suchen doch immer Altmetall."

Doch die Stimmen, die sie nun hörten, waren keine krähenden Kinderstimmen. Sie waren auch nicht Deutsch.

"You have it?"

"Yes, sir."

Ein suchendes Rascheln. Sams Augenbrauen hoben sich in ungläubigem Erkennen. Er packte Theresas Hand ganz fest und bedeutete ihr, in seiner Nähe zu bleiben. Er duckte sich und spähte um den Bretterstapel herum. Theresa tat es ihm nach. Da, sehr schmächtig in dem riesigen offenen Raum, der einmal ein gigantischer Saal hätte werden sollen, stand der sommersprossig-bleiche Mann aus den Barracks. Shane Tucker.

"Here it is", übergab er etwas an einen Mann, der trotz der Hitze einen leichten grauen Mantel trug. Seine Hutkrempe verbarg sein Gesicht. Sein Akzent war schwer zu fassen, jedoch nicht amerikanisch.

"Good. When will I hear more?"

"By next week, I've been told. Should we meet here again?"

"No, no. Different location each time. Can you come

on the same weekday and at the same time?"

"Yes, sir. So, where?"

Ein hohles Knacken riss die beiden Männer aus ihrem Gespräch. Die Hutkrempe des Fremden hob sich erschrocken. Sein Blick bohrte sich nun direkt in Sams und Theresas überrumpelte Gesichter. Seine Augen waren stechend blau, seine Züge kantig, irgendwie erbarmungslos. Theresa rutschte von dem Blechrohr, auf das sie versehentlich getreten war, zurück auf festen Boden. Beide Seiten fühlten sich so ertappt, dass sie kurzerhand und wortlos Reißaus nahmen, Tucker und der Fremde geradewegs über den offenen Hof in Richtung Hauptausgang, Sam und Theresa zurück in den dunklen Lagerraum, aus dem sie gekommen waren, und von dort wieder hinaus in den äußeren Säulengang.

"Cum on", rief Sam, packte Theresa an der Hand und zerrte sie mit sich den Gang entlang in Richtung Bayernstraße.

„Sam, hör auf", wehrte sie sich. „Haunmer doch lieber ab."

"No. I wanna see. I wanna see where they headed", beharrte Sam, der nach dem ersten Schreck wild entschlossen war, Tucker weiter zu verfolgen. Theresa blieb nichts anders übrig, als Sam hinterher zu spurten.

„Du woaßt doch gar ned, wo die hinrenna."

"We'll find out."

Sam und Theresa hetzten um die halbe Kongresshalle, ohne die beiden Männer wieder zu erspähen.

„Komm, Sam, die san doch längst weg", keuchte Theresa.

Da rannte ihnen eine flinke, dünne Gestalt geradewegs vor die Füße.

„Wolfi!"

„Oh. Grüßt euch."

„Was machstn du da? Wo is die Brigitte?", schnappte Theresa.

„Mir spieln."

"Wolfi, listen. Grab Brigitte. You gotta do something for me. Shane Tucker is somewhere near here, with a fella in a gray coat. Black hat. Find him. Find out where he's goin."

„Meinst du den Rothaarign von der Kasern?"

"Yeah. Doan let Tucker see ya, though, he knows y'all. Follow that other man. They came out on this side", sagte Sam, in Richtung Dutzendteich deutend.

„Grauer Mantel, schwarzer Hut?", vergewisserte sich Wolfi, in Abenteuerlust schwelgend.

"Ja. Kinof mean face." Sam schnitt eine Grimasse dazu. Wolfi lachte.

„Brigitte!", rief Wolfi hinter sich ins Gebüsch. Die Kleine kam flink herausgekrabbelt. „Schnell, komm mit, wir müssn jemand verfolgen." Die Kinder wetzten glückselig fort. Theresa sah ihnen ein wenig hilflos nach.

"I jus wanna find out who that was. There's sumthin mighty fishy goin on."

„Fischi", lachte Theresa.

„Komisch."

„Ja, ja, i versteh scho."

Sie blickte den Kindern nach, die auf ihren schmutzigen dürren Beinen einem äußerst fragwürdigen Mann nachstellten.

"So, where were we?" Sam drehte sich mit neckischem Blick zu ihr um.

„Naa, also für heit hab i gnug Abenteuer ghabt", wies Theresa seine Avancen zurück. „Außerdem hab i no a Wäsch dahoam."

Und sie zog ihn mit sich fort Richtung Wohnung.

Pursuit

Sam was rotating his coffee mug in his fingers, pondering. Waltraud had her spreadsheets laid out across the ugly floral tablecloth on the tiny folding table on her balcony. Theresa boldly was leanimg over the flimsy pane of corrugated plastic that basically constituted the railing of the balcony. From this rickety structure, clotheslines were strung over the cheerless concrete courtyard below, all the way across to another balcony on the opposite side. The line was drooping precariously under the weight of the laundry. More than once, Sam had seen items tumble to the dirty ground, and Wolfi or Brigitte had to run down three flights of stairs to recupterate them. The heat had dried today's laundry within an hour, and Theresa was pulling on the plastic string to recover it.

"I know he's dealin weapons," said Sam, who could not get the encounter with Shane Tucker out of his head. "But he had no weapons with him today, jus a piece of paper or sumthin."

"He deals weapons wis us," interjected Walli matter-of-factly, looking up from her meticulous spreadsheets.

"What!? Ya did any more of that?"

Bernd was just stepping through the kitchen door onto the balcony for a smoke, catching the tail end of their conversation.

„Was? Ich dachte, des war nur ausnahmsweise für die Aprilmiete, Mama," he said, visibly taken aback.

„Die Mama ist die größte Waffenhehlerin von ganz Nürnberg," said Max, not without smugness.

„*Hehlen* is des falsche Wort. Und wir machens a ned sooo oft. Wenns halt knapp wird mitm Geld."

„Mama," Bernd reproached, shaking his head in disbelief and disapproval.

„Na, rechen doch selber mal, Bernd: fuchzig Mark die Miete. Dann Gas, die Kohln im Winter, der Strom, des Wasser. Was der Laden abwirft, wasst ja selber. Und die Theresa verdient grad amol…"

"How much ya been sellin to Tucker?" Sam interjected, his voice sharp.

„In letzter Zeit eigentli ned viel."

"I want ya to stop that," commanded Sam with unusual authority.

"Se money, Sam, se money," Waltraud defended her actions, tapping her index finger on her spreadsheet.

"Doan do business with that man, Walli. You can spect some more demand at the store in the cumin months. Ya know I started that book club, and folks gonna buy books in bulk."

The apartment door slammed open so violently that they could hear it from the balcony.

„Ned die Tür so aufhaun!" Waltraud scolded the children, but they were utterly unable to move slowly. They came trampling onto the balcony, which thus reached its critical load. Triumph was pumping through their hot, sweaty bodies.

„Mir ham ihn gfundn!" crowed Brigitte, her hair streaky wet, her little face crimson with excitement and joy.

„Er wohnt in der Bergstaß, fast scho obn am Tiergärtnertor," reported Wolfi breathlessly, then ran back inside to the kitchen sink, opened the squealing tap and let water run directly into his drenched mouth.

"Tell us everythin," demanded Sam. Between his own understanding of the children's agitated accounts and Bernd's interpretation, Sam ascertained that the man in the gray coat had parted ways with Shane once they thought they were safely clear of the prowlers. From the cover of a hedge, Wolfi had even overheard them agree on a new meeting place. The *Katharinenklause*, a dreary ruin where one would not expect to happen on anything more devious than roaming children. Once the stranger had left Shane, Wolfi and Brigitte got on the man's heels, followed him all the way into the city walls and up the castle hill to the very top, where he entered one of the few unharmed historic buildings at the foot of the castle.

„Die treffn si also wieder, in der Katharinenklause. Wir wissn bloß ned, wann. Des hams ned gsagt."

„Ick weiß wann," replied Sam. „Wie heute. Gleiche

Tag, gleiche Uhr, der Mann gesagt."

„Bitte," begged Theresa when she beheld Sam's pondering face. „Geh da bloß ned hi. Des gibt doch bloß Ärger."

"But doan ya see this could be sumthin big?"

"*Too* big," Theresa said forcefully. "Please."

"Hmm," made Sam.

"You are not se police."

"I know, I know."

◆

Sam and Theresa waited until nightfall before they ventured out again. They knew they could walk arm in arm, unwatched, unjudged, where the Pegnitz River cradled the beautiful, swampy Wöhrder Wiese. Patches of shrubbery and clustered trees were scattered all across the large area. Far from any street lamps or lit windows, they strolled along under the waxing moon.

"We were interrupted earlier today," Sam began. „Ick liebe die Sommernacht."

„I aa."

„Und ick liebe dir."

„*Dich*," corrected Theresa, her mouth chuckling,

because she did not quite know how to handle this momentous statement, but her eyes beaming because the feeling was mutual.

"And I love you," she requited. He pulled her into the protection of a nearby cluster of shrubbery. It was evident that children were playing here during the daytime; dirt trails led in and out of the thicket, trodden by busy rascals on whatever adventurous mission their imagination had assigned to them. There was a clearance in the brush, created countless bustling little bodies, just tall enough for an adult to duck in. Sam and Theresa entered a sort of leafy dome. The ground in here was like a smooth floor, stomped by a summer's worth of little bare feet. The crickets were loud, heightening their sense that they were no longer outdoors, but in some enchanted chamber, safe from the world.

They kissed while their bottoms sank to the marshy ground. Sam ventured to tuck on Theresa's cardigan, and she helped him by shaking the sleeves off her shoulders and arms. Emboldened, Sam began to play with the tiny buttons on her blouse, and again, she assisted him in the effort. Soon he caught his first glimpse of her breasts in the moonlight that shimmered silvery and gently through the canopy of leaves. Meanwhile, she was broaching his shirt. He tore it off himself impatiently. Her hands clutched his chest with much more resolve than he expected. He fiddled with the pins in her hair, pulled down her heavy braids and unknotted them with hurried fingers, he wanted her as undressed, as untouched as possible, just the pure Theresa Winkler. He suddenly remembered her as he had first beheld her, in the photograph in her husband's wallet, during that strangely peaceful moment amidst the raging Battle of Normandy. He saw the tattered, love-worn photo so clearly before him that he now believed he had fallen in love with her right there and then, over seven years ago.

Sam was stunned by the sweet simplicity with which they now made love, neither timidly, nor ferociously. They had never before ventured beyond a kiss or a playful caress. Neither had ever known the flesh of another race. And yet their bodies instantly found the same perfect, instinctive familiarity as their minds had shared since their first encounter. Their groins rocked in harmony, and at the end, Sam sank onto her belly like a child, content and warm. He kissed her face … and tasted salt. Sam propped himself up to look at her. Tears glistened in the night, rolled silently along the curve of her neck, onto her chest and then seeped into her hair.

„Mei Ludwig," she mouthed without a sound. When her eyes met Sam's, she jerked. "I'm sorry, I … I hab seither nimmer … die Erinnerung …"

"Doan worry, baby. I understand."

He hugged her tightly as her silent tears heaved into shuddering sobs.

DIEBSTAHL

„Vorsicht", flüsterte Wolfi heiser. In der Ferne schlugen die neuen Glocken von Sankt Sebald mit denen von Sankt Lorenz um die Wette, es war zwölf Uhr am Samstag, genau der Zeitpunkt, an dem Theresa und Sam vor einer Woche den Kindern so ein wunderbares Abenteuer beschert hatten. Wolfi war felsenfest entschlossen, dem geheimnisvollen Mann wieder aufzulauern. Aber bloß nicht von Shane Tucker erwischen lassen, der ja auch jeden Augenblick hier auftauchen musste. Brigitte und Wolfi bewegten sich wie Katzen, über das überwucherte Geröll im ausgebrannten Katharinenkloster, zwischen den hohen Gemäuern mit den Spitzbögenfenstern, die sinnlos und leer in die Luft ragten.

„Da", hauchte Brigitte, die noch schärfere Ohren hatte als ihr Lehrmeister.

Tatsächlich. Schritte auf dem Schutt, viel ungelenker, viel lauter als die der Kinder, die nun geschwind um die Ecke in die Basilika schlüpften. Der Neuankömmling schlurfte mit der Ungeduld eines Wartenden hin und her, geriet dabei mehrmals gefährlich nahe an das Versteck der Kinder. Brigitte hielt so gespannt den Atem an, dass die Haut um ihre Augen blau wurde und Wolfi ihr mit einer unwirschen Geste bedeuten musste, dass ihr Atmen sie schon nicht verraten würde.

"Mr. Brakow", hörten sie nun die unvorsichtige,

gedehnte Stimme von Shane Tucker unmittelbar um die Ecke. Der so angesprochene Mann grüßte flüsternd und unfreundlich zurück, hörbar verärgert, dass der Tölpel Tucker seinen Namen so laut ausgesprochen hatte.

"So, what is it this week?", hörte und verstand Wolfi. Danach aber begann das Gespräch schneller zu traben, und sein von Comic-Heften instruiertes Englisch kam nicht mehr hinterher. Er wagte es also, mit den Augen nachzuforschen. Brigitte klammerte ängstlich die Träger seiner Lederhose, während er vorsichtig den Kopf um die Ecke reckte.

Enttäuscht zog er ihn bald darauf zurück.

„Die ham bloß Zettel."

„Pass auf", warnte Brigitte und hob ihren Zeigefinger zu ihrer Nasenspitze, als die Stimmen wieder etwas lauter, unbefangener wurden. Die Verabschiedung nahte wohl, und mit ihr vielleicht ein neuer Treffpunkt. Und tatsächlich war Wolfi in der Lage zu erhaschen:

"Rochusfriedhof, do you know where that is?"

„Freilich wissen wir des", flüsterte Wolfi. Brigitte hielt sich die Hand vor den kichernden Mund.

"No, sir."

"It's a cemetery. Ask for the *Volksbad*, the public pool. It is right behind it. You can't miss it. I'll be waiting behind the chapel."

"All right. Same time and day?"

"If that works for you."

"Absolutely, sir."

"Good-bye, then."

"Good-bye, sir."

Die Kinder schlichen wieder vorsichtig ins Hauptschiff der Klosterkirche, während sich die schweren Schritte der Erwachsenen in verschiedene Richtungen entfernten.

„Wieder hinterher?"

„Aber sicher!"

Der Fremde namens Brakow ging mit dem zuversichtlichen Schritt eines Ortskundigen davon; die Kinder folgten in sicherer Entfernung. Shane hingegen tapste Richtung Marientorgraben und Straßenbahn davon, er hielt sich eher an die großen Verkehrsarterien, um seinen Weg zurück zur Kaserne zu finden. Brakow überquerte die Pegnitz beim Heilig-Geist-Spital. Sie huschten weiter hinter ihm her, vorbei am beleibten Hans Sachs aus Stein, der etwas vorwurfsvoll auf sie hinunter blickte, quer über den Hauptmarkt, dann die Bergstraße hinauf.

„Der geht wieder ham", stellte Wolfi enttäuscht fest.

„Is ned gsagt", meinte Brigitte.

Doch Herr Brakow stoppte nicht an der Tür, durch die Wolfi ihn das letzte Mal hatte schlüpfen sehen, sondern ging weiter bergan. Kurz darauf war er am Tiergärtnertorplatz, schwenkte nach links ein und steuerte auf die Bänke zu, die vor dem Wirtshaus „Zur Schranke" in der Sonne standen.

„Er geht was essen!"

Tatsächlich ließ der Mann sich an einem der Tische vor dem Wirtshaus nieder. Eine Kellnerin kam unverzüglich angewiesel. Die Kinder schlichen vorsichtig an, wagten sich nicht auf den offenen Platz. Wolfis Blick war sehnsüchtig auf etwas fixiert.

Brakow hatte nämlich seine Aktentasche neben seinem Stuhl abgestellt. Er studierte nun die Speisekarte.

„Eds oder nie", gab Wolfi sich selbst den Startschuss, als Brakow den Blick zur Kellnerin hob. Wie ein Pfeil, lautlos und flink war er mit einem Satz dort. Bevor Brigitte ihren erschrockenen Mund wieder schließen konnte, war Wolfi schon mit seiner Beute wieder bei ihr.

„Eds renn!"

Die Beine der Kinder flogen das Kopfsteinpflaster talwärts. Schon nach ein paar Sekunden hörten sie das schwerere Trampeln eines Erwachsenen über dem flinken Klatschen ihrer eigenen Schritte und dem Hecheln ihrer kleinen Lungen. Sie fegten weiter, einfach den Berg hinab, am Dürer vorbei, der ihnen noch strenger nachschaute als vorher der Hans Sachs, über den Sebalder Platz ... aber Brakow war zäh. Sie legten einen Spurt hin, mit dem sie normalerweise zornige Erwachsene leicht abhängten. Brakow aber war nicht so leicht zu entmutigen, seine Schritte polterten weiterhin im etwa gleichen Abstand hinter den Kindern her. Was Wolfi nicht bedacht hatte, waren die Umstände: Die Erwachsenen, die ihm sonst wütend hinterher rannten, hatten den Schaden meistens schon erlitten, etwa einen Stein ins Bierglas oder ans Hirn bekommen; und das Einfangen des Übeltäters brächte ihnen allenfalls ein wenig Genugtuung. Wenn ihnen aber dann die Lungen zu brennen anfingen und die kaputten Knie sich meldeten, gaben sie die Jagd meist mit ein paar dreckigen Flüchen auf.

Brakow jedoch wollte *seine Tasche* zurück, das gab ihm mehr Antrieb als den üblichen Verfolgern. Endlich erreichten die Kinder die Deckung bietenden Obststände auf dem Hauptmarkt. Als Brakow das rege Treiben auf dem Markt sah, besann er sich auf eine bessere Strategie:

„Diebstahl! Mein Aktenkoffer! Diebe!"

Erwachsene verdrehten die Hälse, erst nach den Rufen des Opfers, dann, begreifend, nach den trappelnden kleinen Gestalten. Wolfi konnte nicht viel schneller, die Tasche wurde langsam schwer. Und Brigitte durfte er auf keinen Fall verlieren. Er hörte sie nur vage hinter sich schnaufen.

Dann packte ein starkes paar Arme ihn direkt um die Mitte, als wäre er eine Katze. Seine Füße verloren den Kontakt zum Boden.

„Den hab i!", röhrte ein tiefer Männerbass. Ein Schutzmann, der sich bis vor ein paar Augenblicken am Hautpmarkt gelangweilt hatte, setzte sich in Bewegung.

Wolfi warf Brigitte eindringliche Blicke zu: Sie solle doch gefälligst im Chaos das Weite suchen! Doch die dachte nicht daran, Wolfi im Stich zu lassen. Sie blieb so angewurzelt neben dem Mann stehen, als hielte er auch sie an der Taille umschlungen.

„So, was hammern da", sagte der Polizist mit einer schmerbäuchigen Genugtuung, die Wolfi augenblicklich zur Weißglut brachte.

„Sie ham mich ja ned amol erwischt, sondern der Mo da", wies er auf den geistesgegenwärtigen Gemüsehändler, der ihn aus vollem Lauf geschnappt hatte.

„Und die junge Dame ghört auch dazu?", fragte der Polizist mit Blick auf Brigitte.

„Naa, die hat nix damit zu tun."

„Doch, i war aa dabei", widersprach Brigitte, als ob sie damit Wolfis Lage verbessern könnte. Der drehte ihr frustriert die Augen raus.

„Und des is des Diebesgut", stellte der Polizist langsam fest, und wand Wolfi die Aktentasche aus dem klammernden Griff.

„Oh, meine Tasche. Tausend Dank", sagte der Bestohlene, der nun auch die Szene erreicht hatte.

„Des is Ihr Taschn?"

„Ja, die wurde mir soeben gestohlen."

„Ja, der Bub hier, und des Mädle, die ham sie entwendet", erläuterte der Schutzmann wichtig. Brakow war zu erleichtert über das Wiedererlangen seiner Tasche, als dass er irgendwelcher Rachegefühle mächtig gewesen wäre:

„Na ja, Schwamm drüber. Die haben Hunger, die Kleinen. Da ist nichts zum Essen drin", belehrte er nun Wolfi und Brigitte über den Inhalt seiner Aktentasche. *Ja, das ist mir klar*, dachte Wolfi, enttäuscht über sein Scheitern. Brakow würdigte die Kinder dabei allenfalls eines flüchtigen Blicks und erstand dann vom Gemüsehändler einen Sack Kartoffeln.

„Da, nimm", sagte er großmütig und überreichte ihn Wolfi. „Und denk immer daran: Mit Stehlen kommst du nicht weit, mein Junge."

Und er grüßte seinen Retter in der Not sowie den Polizisten und machte sich eilig mit seiner Tasche von dannen.

Wolfi machte ein paar zaghafte Schritte rückwärts.

„Auuugenblick", stoppte ihn der Polizist. „Bloß, weil dei Opfer a großzügiger Mensch is, heißt des ned, dass ihr einfach so davonkommt. Ihr kommt mit auf die Wache."

Auf der Wache nahm der Polizist die Personalien der Kinder auf. Wolfi hielt die Kartoffeln auf dem Schoß. Brigitte, zwischenzeitlich vom Ernst der Lage eingeholt, schluckte tapfer ihre Tränen hinunter.

„So, eds. Namen, Eltern und Wohnort."

„Ich heiß Uwe Müller und des is mei Schwester Gisela", erklärte Wolfi ohne mit der Wimper zu zucken. Brigittes Augen weiteten sich, doch sie hielt still.

„Unsere Eltern sind der Wilhelm und die Hildegard Müller. Wir wohnen in der Gerbergasse 12, Parterre." Dann machte er große, flehentliche Kinderaugen: „Bitte sagn Sie unsern Eltern nix."

„Ja sowas musst du dir überlegn, bevorst Sachen klaust", murmelte der Polizist ungerührt, während er die Angaben notierte.

„Bitte, der Papa versohlt uns", jammerte nun auch Brigitte und erntete dafür einen anerkennenden Seitenblick von Wolfi. Die Klage des kleinen Mädchens machte mehr Eindruck auf den Schutzmann. Er streichelte ihr sogar über den strähnigen blonden Schopf.

„Ihr habt Glück, dass wir so viel um die Ohrn ham. Wir kommen in den nächstn Tagen auf eure Eltern zu. Wenn ich du wär", wandte der Polizist sich belehrend an Brigitte, „tät ichs meine Eltern scho heut Abend beichten, was ihr angstellt habt, dann isses ned so a großer Schreck, wenn der Kollege dann vor der Tür steht."

„Des machmer", versicherte Wolfi rasch, denn er machte sich Sorgen, weitere Aussagen von Brigitte in ihrem tiefen Oberbayrisch könnten bei dem Polizisten Zweifel an ihrem Geschwistertum aufkommen lassen.

„Du, Wolfi, wer wohntn in der Gerbergasse 12?",

wollte Brigitte wissen, nachdem sie sichere zweihundert Meter von dem Tor mit dem bayrischen Polizeiwappen entfernt waren.

„Niemand. Des is a öffentliches Scheißhaus. Die Adresse hab i für so an Fall wie heut immer parat."

Brigitte lachte wie ein Glöckchen.

„Aber die Tasche hammer ned. Scheiße."

„Des Gute is, der hat uns kaum angschaut."

„Ja. Der hat überhaupt ned begriffen, warum i die Tasche gnommen hab. Dem kommer scho no auf die Spur. Gehmer heim, der Sam macht bestimmt wieder deiner Mama sei Aufwartung."

Damit lag Wolfi ganz richtig. Sam saß tatsächlich am Küchentisch, auf seinem gewohnten Stuhl und mit seinem gewohnten Humpen Kaffee.

„Heut hätt mers beinah gschafft", verkündete Wolfi.

„Was gschafft?"

„Ich hab dem fremden Mann sei Aktentasche geklaut, vermutlich mit Sachen vom Shane Tucker drin, aber ich bin erwischt worn und er hat se sich wieder gnommen."

Die Erwachsenen fielen aus allen Wolken, redeten alle durcheinander.

"Y'all went to their next meetin?", fragte Sam wissbegierig.

„Mit der Brigitte?", fragte Theresa besorgt.

„Du hast was *gstohln*? Und bist *erwischt* worn?", kreischte Walli.

„Ja, wir beide, in der Katharinenruine. Des heißt, den Koffer hab *i* am Tiergärtnertor gstohln. Und erwischt worn sinmer am Hauptmarkt. Aber mach der kane Sorgn, Mama, ich hab der Polizei a falsche Adresse angebn."

„Der *Polizei*?!" Das kam aus allen Mündern gleichzeitig.

"Okay", nahm Sam die Angelegenheit in die Hand, "ya both are very fine friends to wanna help. Gute Freunde. Aber… is zu gefährlich. Ick will ich nicht, dass ihr das macht mehr. Okay?"

New Member

Wolfi and Max came trudging into the club room, with books stacked all the way to their dirty noses, and crashed them onto the table with a sigh of relief. As they shook out their aching arms, Waltraud surveyed, in book-merchant heaven.

"That it?" Sam wanted to know.

"Yes...." Waltraud swiftly sorted the books into stacks. "Sis here is *Quicksand*, *Les Miserables* here, and I put *Se Count of Monte Christo* over sere."

Sam rubbed Waltraud's shoulders as he passed her. He had certainly lifted some financial trouble off this woman's chest for the moment, and with it, any pressure to traffic weapons to Shane Tucker or any other fool in the barracks. His book club, in just the first couple of months of its existence, had swelled from its original five to almost a dozen regulars, and many more who dropped in on occasion. Waltraud happily scribbled one order form after another.

Whitson Clarke sat at the far end of the table, piercingly peering through those funny glasses of his. They resembled the bottoms of two Coke bottles. The night he first met Whitson, Sam had actually felt compelled to take off his own glasses to see if they looked as strange as Clarke's, but they did not. That was just Whitson, his entire persona was shrouded in a sort of absent-minded, gawky haze. Right now, Whitson had to muster all his mathematical skills to count the money he had collected from the club members – after all, he was a bookworm, not an accountant. Sam, in turn, was counting the books, but lost track when he felt fingers in his back pocket. He quickly swatted the little thieving hand. Brigitte squealed with delight and terror at being caught.

"What ya lookin fo', lil devil?"

„Kaugummi!"

"You *aks* me for some. You doan stick ya dirty lil fingers in ma nice uniform pocket."

Distracted, Whitson dropped the money on the table. He would have to start his count over again. He observed quietly, but with great interest, as Sam picked up the scrawny tomboy like a puppy, sat her onto the table, swept her sweaty blonde hair out of her face, and stuck a piece of gum directly between her chapped lips.

„Und oans fürn Wolfi!" she crowed happily.

„Und fürn Max! Und für die Uschi! Und für die Erika! And God knows who else," Sam crooned, mocking the tinkling pitch of her little voice, and handed her the whole packet. She hopped off the table and made a move to run off, knowing only too well that Waltraud or her mother would immediately prohibit the generous transaction if either of them got wind of it.

„Eds gehst du heim, ja!" Sam called after her. „Machst du keine dumme Sachn!"

„I mach scho nix *fischi*!" she called back, beaming.

„Machst du Hausaufgabe."

„Hab koa Hausaufgabn auf."

„Yeah, righ. Glaub i ned. Bestimmt du hast Mathe."

„A bisserl."

„Also machst du."

„Mach i."

Whitson closely watched Sam, whose glance was melting in utter fondness as the child skipped away.

"You are close to that child," Whitson observed in a gentle tone.

Sam shrugged.

"You talk to her almost like a parent. And she seems to mind you, too."

That's because she practically is my daughter, Sam did not say aloud.

"I'm like the official purveyor of gum to half the neighborhood," he offered by way of explanation.

But Whitson, kind-hearted and sharp-minded, sensed more. The shop was empty except for Waltraud, who was hacking away brutishly at her malfunctioning mechanical calculator.

"Where are you from, Sam?"

"Georgia. Why," drawled Sam, though he knew very well why Whitson wanted to know.

"A-ha."

"And 'a-ha' is spose to mean...."

"You know, that little girl is living proof that racism isn't an inborn trait. If color doesn't matter to little blondie here, why does it matter to a little white child back home?"

"Cuz they been taught."

"Exactly. That means they, too, could grow up differently."

"Hm."

"If the *Germans* can learn? It's a lesson we all must take back home with us."

"Yeah. That is, if I feel any desire to be lynched or burned alive."

"I know it is harder for you."

"You ain got the faintest idea jus how hard it is for *me*," said Sam. He saw Whitson's eyes, so sincere and beady behind his thick glasses. He felt a sudden urge inside, wanted to tell that skinny pale guy everything about his situation. About Theresa. But he didn't.

♦

Tonight, the book club members' minds were glowing ember, fanned eagerly by Carl and Whitson Clarke, and the conversation was just about to flare into hot, sizzling argument, when the door to the meeting room flapped open unexpectedly. Sam jumped, fearing Shane Tucker. But tonight's newcomer had two silver stripes on his shoulder.

"Captain Perry," Sam said surprised, rising from his seat. "Welcome. Thanks for honoring us."

"May I take a listen?" Perry said, sounding quite casual, even though he was fully aware that his presence put the rest of the company ill at ease. He paid quiet attention to the now tongue-tied conversation. When it died down, sooner than usual, Sam as president of the club was expected to propose the topic for the next week. On a normal night, he would have just asked the group what they wanted to read next. But he knew why Perry was here. So he suggested the least compromising book he knew, or rather, the most anti-Communist one:

"Hey, folks, what d'ya say we pick up Orwell next? Animal farm? Should we order a copy for you, too, Captain?"

"Yes, please."

They all got up from their chairs, pushed them back to the tables. Perry and the book club members left. Sam stayed late as always, under the pretense of cleaning up the room. In reality, he was waiting for the person whose job it was to clean the room. A person who intentionally arranged her nightly route around the building in such a way that they could relish a brief, sweet encounter on Monday nights. Tonight, Whitson lingered, as well.

"Good move, buddy. Good job appeasing the mind police."

"You know Shane Tucker probably got him to come check on us."

"No doubt about that."

Again, the tip of Sam's tongue was tingling with the need to tell Whitson something. This time about Shane.

"This fool has this need to get attention. Must be an inferiority complex," Whitson said. "It would make his year if he could, I don't know what he even wants, unearth a nest of Marxists or something. He doesn't even know what he's talking about."

"Well." Sam shrugged. He concurred with Whitson that Shane did not understand the tenets of Communism. And yet he seemed to be quite entangled in it, from what Sam could tell.

"Few do."

"Few do what?"

"Know what Communism actually is all 'bout. Read 'bout its theory and all that."

"You're right about that."

"Have *you?*"

"No," Whitson said reluctantly, hating to admit that there was anything of import that he hadn't read.

"Want to?" Sam now dared offer.

"I don't think our library or Frau Wächter carry that sort of literature," Whitson laughed.

"But the Samuel Harris private collection does."

"Oh, wow," Whitson reacted, instantly intrigued.

"Pop ya head into ma room 'bout five minutes before the end of dinner time, there's usually nobody there."

Whitson neither accepted nor declined this precarious offer, but Sam made plans to be in his room tonight at the time he had proposed. Whitson left the club room. Just in time. The rattle of Theresa's cleaning cart wheels was reverberating at the far end of the hall.

Theresa entered and had a wet kiss pecked onto her nose before she could even maneuver the cart into the room.

„Langsam. Gib Obacht," she said, steadying the bucket that Sam had made quiver. Water swooshed all over the floor. Sam fastened his arms around her lean frame.

"Ya all right?" he asked her when he sensed that her body did not nuzzle into his embrace with the usual ease.

„Des Wetter wahrscheinli. Mir wird die Hitz zviel. Des mog i ned, wenns gar zu hoaß is."

"I auch ned. Well. I'll let ya get to work," he said, letting her go with another kiss. "Doan ya get sick on me."

„Ja, ja, ich will ja mit dir am Freitag auf die Kärwa gehn."

"What is that?"

„A Fest halt. Mit Essen und Bier und Schaukeln und Buden für die Kinder."

"Like a fair?"

„Hm-hm."

"That sounds great. Good night, ma love."

He backed out of the room, happy, humming, oblivious, and unable to take his eyes of his woman. When he sensed a figure in the hallway, he reeled around.

Disgust was sparkling in Shane Tucker's eyes. He shifted back and forth, agitated, undecided, then he lunged forward:

"Listen, Harris, if you snoop around my business any more, then *your* disgusting little secret here...."

"Oh, ya gonna tell on me, are ya. Ya gonna put me in ma place, are ya." Sam took a step towards Tucker. "And then Vaughn would be mighty surprised to hear what ya doin around town off-duty."

"That's one arrogant nigger to assume that his word is gonna count for anything against mine."

"Ya wanna test it?"

Sam felt Tucker' body recoil, ever so slightly, yet Sam felt as if he had gained a mile of ground against Tucker.

"Seems we got a pretty stable gridlock here righ now. Let's keep it that way," he advised Tucker and walked away.

KÄRWA

Wolfi, Max und Brigitte flitzten wie kleine Teufel zwischen den Bierbänken umher. Auf die Krüge war jeweils ein Fünferl Pfand, und manch angeheiterer, gemütlich sitzender Kärwabesucher überließ das Geld gerne den Kindern, wenn es ihm das Aufstehen ersparte.

„Na, des wird ja a gelungene Kärwa für euch, wenn ihr so weiter macht mit die Krüg", sagte Waltraud. Die Kinder glühten vor Vorfreude auf die Zuckerwatte und Schiffschaukelrunden, die sie sich mit dem Krügesammeln verdienten.

Metzger Ahrendt, der ein paar Bänke weiter und im Getöse damit außer Hörweite saß, fand Augenkontakt mit Waltraud und fuchtelte mit seinem triefenden Fischbrötchen, was wohl heißen sollte, dass er sie sprechen wollte.

„Der soll zu uns herkommen, wenn er was will", sagte Bernd, von seiner Maß schlürfend.

Doch Waltraud begriff, dass Ahrendt nur sie allein sprechen wollte. Was wollte er denn? Die letzte Miete hatte sie doch ganz pünktlich zahlen können, dank der erhöhten Büchernachfrage in der Kaserne.

„Grüß Gott", grüßte Ahrendt mit aufgesetzter Gemütlichkeit.

„Hockens Ehner halt amol her zu uns."

„Is was mit der Miete?"

„Naa, naa, des hamms ja offenbar in Griff gricht."

„Ja, es geht besser eds."

„Wen wunderts?", prustete ein angetrunkener Tischgenosse.

„Woher hammsn eds auf amol des Geld, Frau Wächter?"

„Des geht Ehner doch nix oh", blockte Waltraud sofort. „Solang Sie's Geld am ersten ham."

„Ja, na…", wand sich Arendt, bis er schließlich von einem stechenden Blick seiner Gattin animiert wurde, mit dem echten Anlass des Gesprächs rauszurücken: „Es wird halt a weng gredt im Haus."

„Über was denn, bittschön?"

„Es sin halt… recht viel Leit in der Wohnung, und dann a no recht oft a … Bsuch…", mühte sich Ahrendt, die Situation mit Anspielungen zu beschreiben. Endlich hielt es Frau Ahrendt nicht mehr aus; sie nahm das Gespräch in die Hand:

„Dass die Necheer triebhaft sin, des wass ja a jeder. Die anderen Fraun im Haus traun sich scho gar nimmer vor die Tür."

„Bei mir in der Wohnung wohnt aber ka Necher. Bloß mei Familie und die Frau Winkler mit Kind, und des hammer doch mit Ehner geklärt vorher."

„Ja, zwa Frauen allaans mit an Haufn Kinder, des kann ja ned gut geh. Da fehlt a Mo im Haus. Des is ja des Problem in ganz Deitschland, dass die Männer fehln."

„Ja, da könnens froh sein, Frau Ahrendt, dass Ehner Ihr Mo verschont bliebn is, und meiner und der Winklerin ihrer halt leider ned. Aber i hab mei Familie im Griff, und a Essen bring i aufn Tisch, und a Dach hamms überm Kopf."

„Und dann hams no a paar andere Einkommensquellen aa, odä?"

Die Waffengeschäfte zuckten kurz durch Waltrauds Kopf. Doch sie wusste schon, dass dieses Gespräch auf etwas ganz anderes hinsteuerte.

„Die schrecken vor nix zurück, die Amihuren", kommentierte der Angetrunkene, der sich von dem Gespräch exquisit unterhalten fühlte.

„Mir nehma ka Geld von die Ami. Des is doch a Unverschämtheit. Die Winklerin und ich verdiena unser Einkommen redlich mit unserer Arbeit in der Kasern."

„Und die ganzen Konservenbüchsen von die Amis in der Küchn? Die kriecht mer doch sonst gar ned."

„Warn Sie in meiner Wohnung?" Jetzt wurde Waltraud wirklich sauer. Aber was half's, einen Rauswurf konnte sie nicht provozieren. Sie atmete tief in ihren wutschäumenden Bauch. Ahrendt wandte seinen fleischigen Nacken schwerfällig zur Seite, um seiner Frau einen fragenden Blick zuzuwerfen. *Gehst du wohl in die*

Wohnungen?

„Die Necher, die bezahln ja sogar die klanna Kinder, dass sie ihre Schwestern und ihre Mütter mit ehner verkuppeln", setzte nun noch ein dritter Tischgenosse ein, und deutete eine trunkene Hand in Richtung Brigitte und Wolfi, die immer noch emsig Pfandgläser einsammelten.

„Also, Herr Ahrendt, eds sagens halt amol was. Des muss ich mir doch ned anhören."

„Na ja, eds hörens zumindest amol, wie hinter Ihrm Rücken gredt wird. Wenn's des ned wolln, müssens halt dafür sorgen, dass der Verdacht erst gar ned entsteht."

Eine Hand lag plötzlich auf Waltrauds Schulter. Theresa war herübergekommen, als sie im Kirchweihtrubel die erregte Körpersprache an der anderen Bierbank bemerkt hatte.

„Wissens, Frau Wächter, sechs Jahr lang ham wir Widerstand gleistet, und manche gibt's, die könna ned amol anner Tafel Schokolad widerstehn."

„Reden Sie von mia?", wollte Theresa wissen, selbstbewusst, kampfbereit.

„Die Gräber um uns rum, Frau Winkler, die vergessens wohl, wenn Sie sich da mit die Necher vergnügen?"

„*Sie* ham doch goa ka Grab, Frau Ahrendt. Mir zwoa scho. Und i vergnüg mi ned mit *die Necher*. Sondern i bin mit *oam* davo auf der Kärwa, nach ner hardn Arbeitswochn, des wird ja wohl no sei derfen."

„A Schmach fürs ganze Land is des."

„Der Mr. Harris und I? Mir san a Schmach? Da fallmer a poar andre Sachen ei, für die mir Deitsche uns schäma misstn. Früher woarns die Judn und eds sans die Schwoarzen. Irgendjemand muss mer immer hassn, göi?" Theresa keuchte spöttisch. „Und *uns* nennens die Schmach."

Theresa schwang auf dem Absatz herum und mit sich schob sie Waltraud, die sich nun ernsthafte Sorgen um ihren Mietvertrag machte. Sie marschierte zurück an ihren Tisch, hielt ihr Kinn hoch und ihr Rückgrat aufrecht wie einen Stock, ihr sonst so zartes, verschämtes Wesen wie verwandelt. Bis sie allerdings wieder an ihrer Bierbank anlangte, war der steife Stolz, mit dem sie von den Ahrendts weggestorcht war, schon wieder verflogen. Sam bekam von dem Schlagabtausch nichts mit. Er war zu sehr damit beschäftigt, über seiner verbleibenden Viertelmaß zu sitzen und sich über seine Unzulänglichkeit als fränkischer Biertrinker zu grämen:

„Mehr kann ick ned trinken."

„Derf ich?", rief Max und stürzte sich auf den verbleibenden Gerstensaft.

„I will a a weng!", rief Wolfi.

„Aber wirkli ned, do is ja eigentli der *Max* no zu jung dafür", gebot Walli ihm Einhalt.

"Cum on, let's look at the rides", sagte Sam, an Theresas Ärmel zupfend. "You wanna?"

„Na freili."

Ohne das vorhergehende Gespräch hätte Theresa sich vielleicht gar nicht mit ihm aus dem relativen Schutz ihrer überbelegten Bierbank gewagt. Schließlich versammelte sich das ganze Stadtviertel auf der alljährlichen Kirchweih. Aber der Vergleich, den sie in ihrer Wut gerade selbst gezogen hatte, brachte es Theresa erst voll zum Bewusstsein: *Früher woarn's die Juden.* Was für Unmenschen waren das eigentlich, die ihren Sam so verachteten und sie derart beleidigten, ihr alle Ehre und Schamgefühl absprachen? Und da sollte sie klein beigeben, sich verstecken?

Theresa griff nach Sams Arm. Sie ging durch die Menschentrauben, fest bei Sam eingehakt.

"Oh", sagte Sam voller Interesse für die Schießbude.

„Schießn kannst gnuag im Beruf", sagte Theresa und steuerte ihn weiter.

"You know, Sam, traditionally men try to win a rose for their sweetheart", suggerierte Bernd, der dicht hinter den beiden ging.

"I didn know that", freute sich Sam und bugsierte Theresa sofort zurück zur Schießbude. Er kaufte fünf Schuß. Ein paar Halbstarke, die schon zu tief in ihre Maßkrüge geblickt hatten und mit mäßigem Erfolg schoßen, hatten sich vor der Bude breit gemacht.

„So, eds geht ihr amol alle do nüber, ihr belegt ja die ganze Budn. Der Herr da braucht a aweng an Platz", schaffte das Schießbudenmädchen beherzt Ordnung am Stand, damit Sam anlegen konnte.

„Zehn Schuss kost übrigens bloß a Zehnerl mehr", schlug sie vor und verwies auf ein Pappschild mit ihrer ausgeklügelten, zu höherer Schusszahl verlockenden Preisstruktur.

„Naa, brauch ick ned mehr", lehnte Sam selbstsicher ab und legte an. Das Schießbudenmädchen grinste und trat beiseite.

„Kauf lieber glei zwanzig", kommentierte der schon etwas schief dreinblickende Halbstarke, der neben Sam fast schon auf dem Schießtisch lag und angestrengt auf sein Ziel schielte.

Sams Hand blieb ruhig. Mit dem ersten Schuss segelte gleich eines der Zielscheibchen aus seiner Halterung.

„Jawoll!", freute sich die Verkäuferin, „Sie brauchen wirkli ned mehr als fünf Schuss. Welche Farbe?", fragte sie, die Hand bereits zu den künstlichen Rosen an der Seitenwand ausgestreckt.

„Rot." Er überreichte Theresa ihren Preis mit ritterlicher Geste und legte wieder an. Als das zweite Plättchen fiel, rief er nach Brigitte. Die Kleine empfing ihre erste Kirchweihrose mit funkelnden Augen.

„Dankeschön", hauchte Theresa und wollte es ihm mit einem Kuss vergelten.

"Wait, I ain done yet", sagte er, schob sie sachte zur Seite, gewann noch eine dritte Rose und steckte sie ein.

„Für wen ist die denn? Muss i eifersüchtig sein?", fragte Theresa neckend und unverdrossen, obwohl sie die Antwort tatsächlich nicht wusste. Nun bekam Sam seinen Kuss.

„Schokoladensau", tönte es hinter ihnen. Die Halbstarken lungerten noch immer etwas wacklig auf betrunkenen Beinen an der Schießbude.

„Wie bitte? Ick hab ned gut gehört", knurrte Sam.

„Schwerhörig bist wohl a no. Schokoladenhure hab i gsagt."

Sams ganzer Körper zuckte wütend in seine Richtung. Bernd, fast halb so schmächtig wie die Kerle an der Bude, schnellte unmittelbar hintendrein, ungeachtet der Tatsache, dass er in einem Gerangel keine Minute auf den Füßen bleiben würde. Theresa packte Sam.

„Bitte. Bitte. Du tust uns koan Gefallen."

"Didn ya hear them bastards?"

„Wenn du di mit dene anlegst, bin i stocksauer auf di, hörst mi? Die sin doch bsoffen. Du aa, Bernd. Reiß di zam."

Ihr Griff war fest. Sam gab nach und ließ sich von ihr wegziehen, nicht ohne den Frevlern noch einen bitterbösen Blick nachzuwerfen. Bernd hoppelte noch eine Sekunde sinnlos von einem Bein aufs andere, dann besann auch er sich und wich langsam rücklings weg, sein Gesicht purpur vor Wut und Hilflosigkeit.

Die Halbwüchsigen lachten schmutzig.

REVELATIONS

After the next weekly book club meeting, Sam lingered in the room in vain. Theresa failed to show. He spent a restless Tuesday. On every occasion, he would find an excuse to scour the barracks. But the rattling of Theresa's broomsticks and swishing of her buckets was nowhere to be heard. Finally, on Wednesday, he spotted her cart through the half-opened door to the Officer's Mess, which was strictly off limits for the other ranks. He entered, anyway. Theresa was startled up from her work, reeled around, and strangely, did not relax at the sight of him.

"It's just me."

„Hier drin in der Offiziersmesse darfst aber eigentli ned sein," she said aridly.

"Hey. How 'bout 'hello'? I missed ya on Monday night."

She continued to vigorously scrub the large dining table.

"Girl. What is it?"

He seized her shoulder and turned her towards him. He felt her whole body edgy and flustered. She went rigid in his embrace. Her eyes fretfully avoided him. As he searched her face for an explanation of her odd behavior, Sam noticed a strangely frayed strand of hair that stuck out from her blue head rag. And that rag was pulled unusually tight around her head today.

"What's that?" He pulled on it. She cupped her hands over her head, too late to stop him.

Her hair was gone. Some shaggy strands hung limp around her ears; the rest was uneven, stubby, as if it had been rasped off her head. She turned her face away in embarrassment.

"What happened?" Sam hollered more than he asked, in bubbling panic.

She tried to wriggle away from him.

"And that? What is that?" he asked as he discovered scratches and welts on her shoulders and neck.

„Nix. A paar Deppen warns."

"That ain *nix*," Sam raised his voice further.

„In a poar Wochen is des scho wieder in Ordnung," Theresa said drily as she pulled her headscarf back into place. „Trägt ma doch heitzutag eh kürzer, die Frisuren."

"What the hell are ya talkin 'bout? Doan shrug this off! I'm concerned 'bout ya safety!"

„Die ham ihrn Spaß ghabt und jetz werdns scho a Ruh gebn."

Sam grabbed her chin, for she was still squirming away from his glance.

"What did they do to you?" he asked, in a much

lower voice that was grating with horror.

„Des hast doch grad gsehn."

"I mean, what *else* did they do to you."

He sank on a chair. His breathing was heavy with fear of her reply.

"Jus tell me, okay. Did they rape you?"

Theresa looked at him, only guessing what the word meant.

„Naa."

"Tell me the truth."

„Naa, hams ned."

Sam buried his face in his hands. Theresa knelt on the floor in front of him, and repeated:

„Wirkli ned."

"All right." He raised his glance to her. "Who are they? Where can I find 'em?"

Theresa shook her head quietly.

"Cum on. Ya know who they are."

She kept shaking her head.

"Was it the bastards from the Kärwa? You tell me *now*!"

„Was bringt des denn, außer dassd in Teifels Küchn kommst? Was willtsn machen, die verdreschen? Und dann? Dann heißts doch bloß: Schaut her, wie dieser Gemeingefährliche diese armen Buam zugricht hat."

Sam understood that she was not going to tell him who attacked her. He decided not to press her any further. He would find out one way or another. The adrenaline subsided and with it, all strength oozed out of him. His shoulders slackened.

"This is ma fault. What the hell am I doin." He rolled his eyes at the ceiling, cupped his hands over his face. He shook his head as he continued to ramble self-accusations. "Who the hell do I think I am. Gettin you in that kinofa situation."

„Rednmer nimmer davon, bitte. I hab… i mein, *mir* ham ganz andere Sorgn."

"Other than gettin attacked, an shorn, an hurt by a gang of fuckin bastards?"

„Mir war doch in letzter Zeit öfter ned guat", she reminded him, hoping he would understand what she was hinting at. When she saw that he did not catch on, she said, very quickly:

„I glaub, i krieg a Kind."

"Ya mean… ya mean ya're *pregnant*?!" he asked, frantically gesturing towards her belly.

„Ja."

In a span of five minutes, Sam's emotional state had surged from the simmering, slightly anxious impatience of a waiting lover into a violent panic, then plunged into the dull void of guilt ...

Now his mind went flying in all directions.

He stared at her, and she at him.

"That's good news. Ya hear me? It's *good* news."

He held his hand out to her.

"Sit with me."

She finally regained her normal body language, slunk into his lap, soft and limber as he knew her, and he easily clutched her entire slender frame in his arms. They were having a child. In this small woman's womb, there was a child. *His.* The thought barreled over him unlike anything else that had ever crossed his brain. There he was, at thirty-two. He who always complained of having nothing ... was sitting there, holding two infinitely precious treasures right there in his arms, one inside the other. Theresa had finally begun to weep, after these long, chilling minutes of paper-dry coolness that were so unlike her.

"I got a vision for us, baby," Sam said after some silence. "I'm gonna take y'all home with me. You, and sweet Brigitte, and that sweet baby. I'm gonna save every dime here and we gonna rent some farmland. Ya gonna teach me how to grow hops. We'll do what ya love. What you and Ludwig used to love. Ya show me how, and we gonna do it together." He even smirked at the thought: "We gonna grow some decent hops so those *Amis* can make some decent beer."

„Hopfen in Amerika, des hab i ja noch nie ghört," Theresa snuffled doubtfully, but with a tiny smile in the misery on her face.

"We gonna do it. That country is so big, there must be places where the climate is kinda like here where it can grow well. I'll find out. And where there's no hate, where folks will jus leave us be. I'll find us a place like that."

She smiled through her tears:

„Soll des hier so was wie a Heiratsantrag sein, Mr. Harris?"

"Am I aksin you to marry me? I... I am. Ja! I am! "

Die Seidenrose

Sie schritten auf Ludwigs Grab zu. Auf der dunklen Marmorplakette leuchtete schon von weitem sichtbar etwas Grelles, Unnatürliches in der Sonne. Brigitte hüpfte mit dem Gesteck und der Kerze voran.

„Mama, schau mal."

„Na, des habt's doch ihr her, oder?", vermutete Mutter Winkler.

Theresa trat näher. Ihre Schwiegermutter kniete sich ohne Umschweife in den Dreck, um emsig die Blumenbeete vor den Urnenreihen zu bearbeiten. In der Blumenhalterung an Ludwigs Grab steckte eine knallrote Seidenrose. Eine Schießbudenrose.

„Is des deine, Brigitte?"

„Naa, Mama, freili ned. Mei Rose steckt doch an meim Schulranzen."

Theresa kniete sich hin.

„Der war hier", sagte sie leise zu sich selbst. Ihre Finger spielten mit der weichen Seide, noch nass vom letzten Regenguß.

„Na, wer hat'n die künstliche Rosn dann hi, wenn ned ihr?", wunderte sich Frau Winkler.

„Na, wer wohl?", fragte Brigitte. „Der Sam Harris."

„Der Ami? Na, so was."

Frau Winkler maß der Sache nicht die gebührende Bedeutung zu. Sie war zufrieden mit dem Zustand der Bepflanzung, raffte sich auf, klopfte den Schmutz von den Knien.

„Also, ich hätt's dann scho. Ich geh scho amol vor und setz die Klöß auf. Bleibt's ihr no a bissl da?"

Theresa nickte.

„Brauchst du no die Geräte, Spatzl?", fragte Frau Winkler und wies auf Schaufel, Pflanzgabel und das Gießkännchen.

„Na, Mutti, dankschön. Mir bleibn einfach no a paar Minuten hier", sagte Theresa sanft.

„Na freili, lassts eich nur Zeit", erwiderte Frau Winkler und strich im Gehen ihrer Enkelin übers Haar. Als ihre Schwiegermutter außer Hörweite war, ließ sich Theresa auf die feuchte Erde sinken.

„Brigitte?"

Das Kind sah den Ernst in den Augen ihrer Mutter und kniete sich neben sie.

„Des war aber liab vom Sam, dass er an Papa dacht hat, oder?", begann Brigitte, als ihre Mutter sprechen wollte und die Worte nicht gleich fand.

„Ja, des war liab. Und i glaub, i weiß a, warum er da war."

„Um die Rose hizusteckn."

„Ja. Und reden wollt er mitm Papa. I glaub, er wollt ihn was fragn."

„Aber den Papa kann mer doch nix mehr fragn."

„Freili ned. Aber manchmal hilfts die Lebendn, wenn ma einfach am Grab steht. Dann tut mer so, als könnt mer no mitanand reden. Und des hilft oft, wenn mer ned woaß, was ma tua soll."

„Und was wolltn der Sam beredn?"

„I glaub, er wollt wissn, obs dem Papa recht wär, wenn i wieder heiratn tät."

Brigitte blickte sie still, aufmerksam an. Theresa fuhr nicht gleich fort. Also tat es Brigitte:

„Du moanst, wenn du und der Sam heiratn täten?"

Theresa nickte. Brigittes wasserblaue Augen begannen zu leuchten.

„Und der Sam wär dann mei Papa?"

Ihre Mutter nickte wieder.

„Des wär dem Papa bestimmt recht! Dass i den Sam als Ersatzpapa hätt, wenn er doch ned da sei koa."

Theresas Augen schwammen nun.

„Und di, *di* wollt i a fragn, ob's dir recht wär."

„Ob *mir* des recht wär?", lachte Brigitte. Theresa packte sie und drückte sie an sich.

„Ich kriag endli an Papa", hörte sie Brigittes Stimmchen dumpf durch den dicken Stoff ihrer Wolljacke juchzen.

„Und es gibt nu was", sagte Theresa, wischte sich mit dem Ärmel das Gesicht ab und sah Brigitte fest ins Gesicht. „A kloans Gschwisterla kriegst nämlich aa, mei Schatz."

Brigitte quieckte vor Glück und vergrub ihr Gesicht wieder in Theresas Halskuhle. So blieben sie ein paar Minuten sitzen, bis Brigittes Gesicht so heiß und rot war, dass sie sich aus der Umarmung befreien musste. Durch ungehemmte heiße Tränen starrte Theresa auf das kleine, messinggerahmte Glasoval an der Urnenplatte. Dahinter, verblichen und gewellt, aber wohlwollend wie immer, blickte Ludwigs ernstes Knabengesicht sie an. Sam war ein Jahrzehnt älter, als Ludwig je geworden war.

Theresas Tränen versiegten, sie blinzelte angestrengt, atmete tief durch. Mutter Winkler sollte in ihrem Gesicht nur Wind und Wetter sehen. Sie richtete ihr Kopftuch. Die Bescherung darunter der Mutter Winkler zu erklären, war schon schwierig genug gewesen.

„Und der Oma, der verraten mers no ned, in Ordnung?"

„Warum ned?"

„Weil... i glaub, die Oma is no ned so weit."

„Okay", sagte Brigitte verständig.

„Okay", ahmte Theresa sie lächelnd nach. „Klingst ja scho wie a kloana Ami."

ENGAGEMENT NIGHT

"Since when you been so concerned 'bout your looks, Sam?"

Greg was intrigued by the intensity of Sam's grooming tonight, the vigorously brushed suit, the meticulous shave, the shining shoes.

"Goin out tonigh."

"I gathered that much."

As on any Friday night, the quarters were bustling with eager anticipation. Half a dozen men were elbowing in front of a single dull mirror, tie-knots were being jiggled, jacket sleeves being shrugged into place, hair was being combed. Tonight, Sam took part in the general hustle. He padded his chest with both hands as he made a final inspection of his appearance.

"Where ya goin?"

"Dunno yet, what ya recommend?"

"The Tally-Ho, fo' sure."

Sam frowned. "And that ain one of them places were ya get in trouble?"

"This one's fine. They got the best music."

Herman came swinging into the room, humming, tapping his feet on the floor and drumming his fingers on any available surface. He was giddy and restless, ready for some smooth jiving, hot kisses and cold booze – his usual Friday night routine. Tonight, Sam also felt some of the jittery excitement that normally made him want to throw objects down at the romping revelers beneath his bunk bed.

"Ya cumin?" Sam asked Carl. He did not want to be stuck with Herman and Greg again.

"Sure," confirmed Carl.

"Ya cumin with us tonigh?" Herman could hardly believe it.

"Yes, sir, I'm takin ma girl out."

"Sam – is – taking – his – *girl* – out!" Greg whinnied in disbelief and amusement. "I didn know ya knew what a girl was!"

"I'm also takin ma girl out," said Herman. "That's great, that way our ladies got someone to talk to."

Sam was afraid that Herman's involvement with a German girl was slightly different from his. But he said nothing.

"Cum on, let's go before all the tables fill up."

♦

"Where we headed?" Herman wondered after all four

of them had squeezed into a taxi, and Sam gave the driver an address Herman had never heard before.

"I tole ya, I'm takin ma girl out. Gotta picker up, doan I?"

"From her *place*?"

Theresa was already waiting on the street. She had wrapped a yellow headscarf over her ruined hair, which made her look much more melodramatic than she was.

"Good evening, gentlemen," she greeted the company in the cab as she clambered in, very carefully, because her skirt was tighter than what she was used to. All other men in the vehicle nodded silently, Herman and Greg in surprise, Carl in appreciation, the taxi driver in tight-lipped disapproval.

"But... y'are the lady who cleans the offices!" Herman exclaimed, recognizing her now. "I had no idea that you an Mr. Harris... Ya know, Miss, cuz I'm in the same situation."

"How so?" snorted Greg.

"I'm also in luv with a *Frollein*. Very fine lady, jus like you."

"Oh, gimme a break, Herman," Greg huffed.

"It's true. German ladies are all so pretty. Ya know, Miss, I'd do anything for ma *Frollein*."

"Cept tell her ya got a wife back home?" Greg said,

cutting off Herman's syrupy ramblings.

"Oh, ma God," Sam moaned, shaking his head in frustration. But Theresa chuckled.

"Okay, folks, before y'all go on 'bout anythin else that's either inappropriate or stupid", Sam warned Herman, Greg and Carl. "Tonight's a special occasion for us. Tonigh, we're celebratin our engagement," he announced.

"Wow. So all drinks are on you, I reckon," huffed Greg. Sam sighed and pushed himself deep into the leather of the taxi seat.

„Tut mir so leid, Schatz. Ick soll ned kommen mit diese Kerle da," he whispered to her, needlessly, because neither of the others understood German.

„Macht nix, is doch lustig."

The taxi entered the city walls, then turned behind the Frauentormauer and pulled up by the curb. Sam helped Theresa fold her legs out of the cab. Then he dispensed a banknote that was much larger than the fare they owed, the taxi rolled away contentedly, and his fiance stood on the sidewalk, looking mellow and misplaced as if she had been cut out from a pastel painting and stuck onto this garish scenery of dancing neon lights. Sam tucked her skinny forearm tightly under his elbow and guided her through the stream of people. Despite her flat-heeled shoes, her step was teetering awkwardly among the confidently swaying hips of the other merrymakers.

A sudden roar made Theresa bounce and press up against the wall of the building they were passing. Sam whirled around to see a fin-tail car, arrogantly heavy and large in the narrow old-town street. It had veered off the street and trundled onto the sidewalk right behind them, barely slowing down. Now it bucked back down from the sidewalk onto the street and roared away under the curses of the party it had nearly squashed. A group of onlookers across the street was laughing. Greg and Sam restrained Herman's visceral urge to run over there and engage in trouble.

„Ja, woar der wohl scho bsoffen?" asked Theresa, her back still flat against the wall.

"Na. That was deliberate," Sam grunted.

Theresa looked across the street at the snide grins. It pained Sam to watch her innocent face as it dawned on her that they had just been run off the sidewalk because they dared walk on it arm in arm.

He slid his right arm back under her left, with heightened determination, and walked her to the Tally-Ho.

Herman yanked on the dark wooden door. Heavy and solid, it was a sullen reminder of the respectability and bourgeoisie that had once reigned in this building. It was almost censoriously difficult to open, as if it opposed itself to its frivolous patrons. Theresa's nose wrinkled as a tide of sweaty body heat, nicotine and pizza cheese washed over them. The Tally Ho was firmly in black American hands, female patronage excepted. The music was familiar, the company lively.

„I bin die Lydia," a woman who had suddenly materialized in Herman's arms introduced herself to Theresa.

„Grüß Di," Theresa replied affably. Sam was not as pleased as Theresa. He surveyed Lydia in sore awareness of the contrast between Herman's Veronika and his fiance. With her brashly painted lips, her tiny skirt that revealed expensive American nylon stockings, and her savagely bleached hair, she embodied a ruthless determination with which she most likely went after all her life's pursuits. And tonight, that happened to be Herman. Her English was inferior to Theresa's, and yet she managed to talk ten times as much, at lightning speed, randomly, happily oblivious as to whether her words were actually understood and processed or not. Despite her obvious pleasure of being the GIs' center of attention, she did not consider Theresa a rival, but rather a welcome opportunity to vent even more of her many fleeting thoughts in her native tongue.

„Mensch, der Herman hat mir grad erzählt, ihr wollt im Ernst heiratn? Des is ja der Wahnsinn!" Lydia had to scream over the storm of music that was raging around their heads. It made it difficult for Sam to follow, but had the advantage that no one else could, either.

„Du, Lydia, i kenn di zwoar ned, aber i find, du solltests wissn: Der Herman hat scho a Frau dahoam," Theresa enlightened Lydia, holding Lydia's hand in advance sympathy. But Lydia had not exactly been dealt a blow:

„Ach, des macht doch nix."

Theresa threw Sam a grin. Sam did not find it amusing at all. But he did like Theresa's blunt frankness. That was his girl.

„Tansen wir auch," Sam suggested, trying to escape the table with its awkward conversations. Theresa let Sam maneuver her around, gaping at the swirling skirts, bare thighs and probing hands all around them on the dancefloor. Sam's glance also skipped from couple to couple. He noted that this was not an all black place, after all. There were some white GIs steering German girls across the floor, as well. Regardless of the race of the male, however, all females seemed to have one thing in common: Expensive gifts jingled from the ladies' ears, wrists and necks, their dancing legs were draped in fine nylon or silk, their incessantly talking lips were glossy red. The kinds of gifts Theresa categorically refused, and for good reason. Sam and Theresa scuffled around at the very edge of the floor with little rhythm. Sam liked being close to the entrance, because every new customer who opened the heavy door brought a small whiff of oxygen into the stifling room. There it was again, a second-long pleasant draft of fresh air. Sam looked to see who had arrived this time. A group of five men, clearly GIs.

„Find i ja gut, dass die Ami si hier a bissl vermischn," commented Theresa on the fact that the newcomers were white.

"Woah. But I could do without *this* particular fellow," said Sam, recognizing one of the newcomers. "Why the hell would *he* even wanna be here?"

Shane Tucker walked among his group with an unenthusiastic gait. Sam did not want to examine him any closer lest they made eye contact. He foxtrotted Theresa away towards the other side of the floor.

"I'm sorry," he said close to her ear.

„Wieso denn?"

"This ain a nice place. You doan belong here."

„Eds musst ned glei so schwarz sehn, da sind a ganz Nette dabei. Ganz Anständige."

„*Schwarz* sehen?" Sam asked, arching his eyebrows.

„Des sagt ma halt a so," laughed Theresa and they both came to a complete stop, chuckling at each other.

„Eds komm, i hab dacht, du fihrst mi heit zum Tanzen aus!"

She tugged on him, wanting to continue their clumsy dance. Sam complied, and when they resumed dancing, he mustered enough spirit to give her a little jive, to which she responded happily and gawkily. Sweet happiness lit up Theresa's face, her eyes were twinkling, her mouth twitching as she laughed about her own wrong steps, and she took many wrong steps. For split seconds at a time, Brigitte's sunshiny expression would flash up on Theresa's face, even though Sam usually thought the kid favored Ludwig. For the first time, he felt impatience to know what their baby would look like. Sam shivered with the thought that when the time came to leave Germany, he would take three women with him, one grown, one small, one unborn – for the child growing there between their swaying hips had to be a girl, he was sure of it.

Samuel Harris was coming home a rich man.

So absorbed was Sam in the bliss of this thought that he did not even feel the bottle hit his temple. It was the sounds that yanked him back into reality, the shattering of glass as the bottle landed on the dance-floor, the frantic hollering all around him. Then a red glaze blurred his vision. Through it, he saw Theresa stare at his forehead in horror. Women were squealing, but Theresa just stood there, pale, her mouth closed tightly. She squatted down and scooped up something that Sam just now realized he was missing. She gave him his glasses back.

Then a breathless silence fell over the turmoil, abruptly like a heavy curtain. Sam turned to see what had so suddenly arrested the rowdy crowd. Herman had taken hold of the room. Sam put his glasses back on, blinked the bloody shroud from his eye to see how Herman managed to hold sway over a whole bar full of intoxicated, agitated patrons.

Herman had drawn a gun on Shane Tucker, whose face was twisted by hate, disgust and the shock of looking down the barrel of a .30 caliber. Sam understood that Tucker had thrown the bottle at him.

"Herman!"

Sam was by Herman's side with a single bound, seized his shooting arm from behind and pushed it down. The startled shot that Herman fired as he felt his arm being grabbed went into the shiny parquet. Wood splinters flew. Gunsmoke wafted through the room. Guests lost their minds. A full brawl erupted before the females even realized that they had better get out of the way. Fists flung right next to dainty purses and whirling petticoats, the heads of tumbling men landed on the floor among dangerously high heels that were traipsing around in panic.

"MP!"

At this, the women rapidly got their act together. They trampled over the combatants. When Sam saw them swarm to the backdoor with the swift efficiency of startled cockroaches, he remembered something, in horror. Something that someone had told him a while back, long before he cared: Military Police routinely conducted raids of German women in local bars, which they termed 'VD checks'. Regardless of whether or not the MP were actually here for a prostitution raid, or just responding to the commotion, the policemen rode right into the heart of the brawl with truncheons, going after the colored offenders with natural precision. By that time, the bar was clear of females … with one exception.

„Geh!" Sam hollered at his petrified bride. Unlike the

other women in the bar, Theresa had never witnessed anything like this before. She had no notion of what was about to happen to her. Her stunned attention was focused solely on Sam and the sticks drumming down on him.

„Geh! Denk an die Baby!"

Reluctantly she turned, made a vague move towards the door that led to the kitchen and back exit, the escape route through which all the other girls had just scrambled out. One MP spotted her, interrupted his order-restoring activities, and seized her just as she reached for the knob of the grease-stained glass door.

Verhör

Zunächst nahm Theresa nur den Geruch wahr. Ein Wall aus altem Fett, billigem Fleisch und matschigen Kartoffeln drängte aus der Küche, traf auf die dicke, vor Schweiß und Nikotin stehende Luft der Gaststube, und Theresas empfindlicher Magen drehte sich fast um.

Gott, ich bin wirklich schwanger.

Die selten geputzten, vergilbten Küchenfliesen waren mit Soßenspritzern und Fett besprenkelt. Zwischen den metallenen Herden standen noch andere Frauen. Ihre schrill geschminkten Lippen und knallbunten Blusen zeichneten sich grell und irritierend gegen die faden Farben der Küche ab. Der eine Polizist, der gerade nicht damit beschäftigt war, schwarze Männer in der Gaststube in Grund und Boden zu knüppeln, verhaftete die versammelte Frauenschar mühelos, denn keine wagte sich zu rühren oder auch nur einen Ton von sich zu geben. Handschellen rasteten ein, enger als nötig. Auch während der rütteligen Fahrt zum MP-Hauptquartier in einem amerikanischen Kübelwagen sprachen die Verhafteten kein Wort. Theresa musste ohnehin ihre ganze Kraft darauf verwenden, sich nicht zu übergeben.

Die Aufnahme der Personendaten ging still und zügig von sich. Jede der Frauen hatte im Umgang mit eben den Amis, deretwegen sie nun in dieser misslichen Lage waren, genug Englisch gelernt, um Fragen nach Namen,

Wohnort, Beruf oder Familienstand beantworten zu können. Schwieriger wurde es, als die MPs versuchten, den vermuteten Tatbestand festzustellen.

"Have you had intercourse with any of the men present at the Tally-Ho tonight?", fragte der Polizist. Theresa verstand die Frage nicht, ließ sich aber von dem nüchternen Ton, in dem sie vorgetragen wurde, nicht beschwichtigen. Sie schlotterte, vor Übelkeit, Scham und Angst.

"I don't understand."

Der Polizist hechelte ein kurzes Lachen.

„Obsd mit jemand von die Ami dort gvögelt hast, will er wissn", erläuterte eine Leidensgenossin. Sie saß hinter Theresa auf einem der Stühle, die entlang der Wand aufgereiht waren und wartete auf ihre Abfertigung. Theresa wandte sich langsam zu der Frau mit den knallroten, verschmierten Lippen und abgebrühten Augen unter aufwendig toupiertem und dennoch zerzaustem Haar. Sie hatte die Beine übereinander geschlagen; ein hochhackiger roter Schuh wippte lässig von ihren Zehenspitzen. Die so sichtbar gewordene raue Ferse hatte eine Laufmasche in den Nylonstrumpf gerieben.

"No!", antwortete also Theresa dem Polizisten.

"What are you doing in a place like this, then?"

Das verstand sie.

"I was wis my... my...." Sie wusste das Wort gar nicht, stellte sie fest. Widerwillig drehte sie sich noch einmal zu der überschminkten, überparfümierten und trotzdem schlampigen Person um, die offenbar des Englischen mächtiger war als sie.

„Wie sag inn Verlobter?", bat sie um Hilfe.

"Fiance", antwortete ... nicht die Vogelscheuche, sondern ein flüsterndes, trauriges Stimmchen neben ihr. Tatsächlich, da saß noch eine Person auf dem nächsten Stuhl. Im Vergleich zu der ersten Frau war sie so unscheinbar, dass Theresa sie gar nicht wahrgenommen hatte.

„Danke."

Sie wandte sich zurück.

"I was wis my fiance", beendete sie ihren Satz, doch der Polizist hatte bereits zu lachen begonnen, als er den Übersetzungsvorschlag der schüchternen Frau vernommen hatte.

"All right, all right." Er verdrehte lakonisch die Augen und machte mit abfälliger Geste eine Notiz.

"I was wis my fiance. His name is...."

"I'm done here, the Lieutenant will see you in a minute", unterbrach der Polizist sie, schälte sich aus seinem Sitz und schwang Theresas Akte in einer routinierten Bewegung mit sich.

„Verrat bloß niemand, wie deiner heißt, wennst ihn

wirkli gern hast", hisste die Aufgetakelte nun Theresa zu. Die Blasse nickte zustimmend:

„Ja, des gibt sonst bloß no mehr Ärger."

"Are we at an ice cream social or a police station?", disziplinierte der Polizist die Frauen. Er hielt immer noch die Akte und klopfte mit den Knöcheln derselben Hand an das Blindglas einer Bürotür. Eine gedämpfte Stimme antwortete, und mit dem Zeigefinger seiner freien Hand bedeutete der Polizist Theresa, zu kommen.

Die Aura des Leutnants war sanftmütiger, selbstbewusster als die des blechernen jungen Kommisars, der die Vorarbeit geleistet hatte. Fast väterlich legte er seine Hand auf Theresas Schulter, geleitete sie zu ihrem Stuhl vor seinem schweren Eichentisch.

"Miss Winkler...."

"Not miss, it's *Mrs.* Winkler", korrigierte Theresa und erschrak über ihre eigene Bestimmtheit.

"Hm", machte der Leutnant, in der Akte blätternd. "Hutson?"

Der jüngere Polizist steckte seinen Kopf wieder zur Tür herein.

"Why did you put 'unwed'? She says she's married."

"She said 'no husband'. But you know how it is, sir, these women don't know much English."

"I said 'no husband' because he's dead", mischte

Theresa sich ein und berichtigte dabei gleich einmal die Unterstellung, sie verstünde nichts.

"Oh, I see", sagte der Leutnant ruhig und korrigierte den Akteneintrag von 'unwed' zu 'widowed'. Der jüngere Mann verschwand wieder.

"Okay, Mrs. Winkler", begann er von vorne. Er sprach sanft, mit beinahe wohlwollendem Blick, wie mit einem Kind.

"Listen, I will tell you something. Personally. You must know that a colored man is no good for you. You may not understand this at this point, but they are not like us. They may seem wealthy to you here, but in fact are poor. A lot of them carry disease. There….."

"Can I now have my….", unterbrach Theresa ihn und merkte mitten im Satz, dass sie das Wort für ‚Strafe' nicht wusste. Der Leutnant ließ sich aber nicht beirren.

"People will call you a nigger-lover, and worse. As a matter of fact, I'm sure they are already calling you that. And you will have a really hard time ever getting a white man after this."

"My white man is dead and when I marry my fiance, I never need one again."

Fall-out

„Wissns, des beste is, ma kommt erschd gar ned in so a Situation," the German police officer said with a shrug, distractetly fishing for his rubber stamp on the desk so he could clear Theresa's dismissal slip. Sam was observing her deflated body language from behind; she had not even noticed who was sitting there in the reception hall. She also did not reply to the policeman's comment. Sam understood. Talking to these people was like a boring, predictable game of chess. You already knew what reply any of your statements would provoke, what you would then have to say back, what they would say in return. So what was the point of saying anything in the first place? And Sam could see, just by looking at her back, that Theresa was tired. Very tired.

„Sie sin doch ned *so* anne," the policeman added genially. Theresa wordlessly accepted the dismissal papers. The policeman lifted his glance, beheld Sam, and visibly regretted his – what he considered – kind words. Because there he was! The very man who had gotten her into this trouble! Only now did Theresa's eyes follow the policeman's indignant gaze and she saw Sam in the waiting area.

„Mein Gott, i hab dacht, di hams in die *Stockade*."

"I'm so sorry, baby." He embraced her ruefully. "I keep thinkin we can make this work, and it keeps gettin worse."

She inspected his face, yet found no damage other than the cut on his temple.

"If ya lookin for bruises, they know not to hit the head. They go for the back and the legs."

Saltwater flooded Theresa's eyes, with the force of an opened floodgate. Those tears had been battling with her pride all night.

„I muss zur Brigitte," she sniffed, moving towards the exit.

„Die is bei Waltraud, natürlich," Sam reassured her. Together, they stepped out onto the cobbled road.

„Hast wohl scho nach ihr gschaut?"

„Freilich."

„Und was hoast ihr gsagt, wo ihr Rabnmutter is?" Theresa asked, rattled by a sudden sob.

"Okay — stop!" Sam reigned her in. He had to hold both of her skinny shoulders to make her face him. "We ain gonna give in to that. We're a young couple that wanted nuthin else but celebrate their engagement. It ain our fault how it turned out. We did nuthin wrong. Doan let them do that to us. They're all wrong. We're right."

Theresa just stood there in the slightly drizzling rain.

When they were back home, around the kitchen table, with Brigitte cuddled up like a ball in her mother's lap,

Sam made one concession:

"Now, I *am* sorry we went to that place. We shoulda jus gone to, I dunno, *Café am Hauptmarkt* or sumthin, and sat 'mong the ole grannies with Kaffee and Kuchen. Nuthin would of happened then."

Theresa nodded.

"But, hell, we're two young people. We oughta be able to go out for a dance without gettin beaten up and arrested. It ain right."

„Was isn mitm Herman?"

"Detention. Fcourse."

„Und was passiert mit eam eds?"

„Keine Ahnung."

„Und was is mit dir? Wird des alles no a Nachspiel hoam?"

„Keine Ahnung."

„Mama, was is a Nachspiel?" asked Brigitte. Wolfi, who was also in the kitchen, idling over a blank page of math homework, responded gloomily:

„Dass der Sam aa no eigsperrt wird. Oder heimgschickt nach Amerika."

"Since when you been an expert on military discipline?" Sam snapped at Wolfi. "No one said anythin 'bout that." But the damage was done. Brigitte's small face twisted in horror.

„Heimgschickt?"

„Naa, hunny, des passiert ned."

„Aber du sollst doch mei neuer Papa wern!" she wept in instant despair as it can only seize a child. She sprang up from Theresa's lap and clasped Sam as if an MP was standing right there in the kitchen, and she could save Sam from repatriation by clinging to his neck like a little millstone. Sam wrapped his arms around her tiny waist. Wolfi intervened:

„Komm, Brigitte, komm mit mir. I hab a Idee," he lured her with an encouraging, conniving glance.

„Ja, geht spielen," Sam seconded Wolfi's proposal. He wanted to see the girl distracted from their worries.

„Setz ihr bloß koane neuen Flausn in Kopf," warned Theresa, more keenly aware of Wolfi's mischievous nature. Only after the children's clattering steps had reached the bottom landing of the staircase, Theresa asked:

„Meinst, des könnt passiern?"

„Was."

„Dassd weg versetzt wirst?"

For lack of an answer, he kissed her.

ÜBERGABE

Der Samstagmorgen war mild. Spatzen hüpften über das Kopfsteinpflaster und pickten in den Ritzen herum. Brigitte warf ihnen winzige Brösel von ihrer Breze zu. Bald waren die Kinder von aufgeregtem Flattern und Piepsen umringt.

„Na, wunderbar."

Wolfi zerrte Brigitte weg, weiter hoch auf den Tiergärtnertorplatz.

„Mir is langweilig."

„Glaubst du, der Sherlock Holmes fands langweilig, seine Verdächtigen zu beschatten? Kein Fleiß, kein Preis."

„Mir san aber ned der Sherlock Holmes. Und der Brakow is letzten Samstag ned raus kimma, und vorletzn a ned. Vielleicht wohnt er gar nimmer da."

„Es is aber unser einziger Anhaltspunkt", beharrte Hobbykommisar Wächter.

„Gehmer doch was spüiln," jammerte Brigitte. „Der Sam hat eh gsagt, mir solln des Rumschnüffln sei lassn."

„Der Sam is ned unser Vadder."

Das verletzte Brigitte. Sie schob eine beleidigte Unterlippe vor.

„Schau, Brigitte", sagte Wolfi versöhnlicher. „Wenn mir zwei rauskriegn, was der Tucker da treibt, was glaubstn, was dann in der Kaserne los is?"

„Die Hölle is dann los."

„Der Tucker ist doch derjenige, der dem Sam den ganzn Ärger macht. Wenn mir rauskriegn, was der Tucker da macht, dann kommt er ins Gfängnis und ihr habt euer Ruh."

Brigitte glubschte ihn an.

„Verstehst?"

Plötzlich stülpte Brigitte ihre schwitzig-schmutzige Hand über Wolfis Mund. Mit großen wasserblauen Augen starrte sie auf das Gebäude gegenüber: Die schwere hölzerne Eingangstür des Fachwerkhauses quälte sich auf. Diese mit der Schulter aufstemmend, erschien Brakow. Wortlos, atemlos beobachteten die Kinder, wie Brakow aus dem Hauseingang ging und mit gehetzt wehendem Mantel die Bergstraße hinunter verschwand. Eben noch kaum an Detektivarbeit interessiert, drängte Brigittes ganzes kleines dürres Wesen jetzt unbändig vorwärts, dem Herrn im Mantel nach, so dass Wolfi sie an der Schulter halten musste wie einen ungestümen jungen Jagdhund.

„Abstand halten."

Wolfi tat wohl mit seiner Vorsicht. Denn während sie Brakow behände folgten, drehte der sich tatsächlich ständig nervös um. Jedes Mal fegten die Kinder wie

Kaninchen in Nischen, Ecken und Hauseingänge. Brakow hielt sich links. Bald kam er am Rathenauplatz an.

„Oh, bitte kei Straßenbahn nehmen!", hoffte Wolfi. Damit wären sie hoffnungslos abgehängt, denn ein Zehnerl für die Fahrkarte hatten sie nicht. Doch Brakow überquerte den Marientorgraben, marschierte weiter am Prinzregentenufer entlang.

„O mei, bald isser bei uns dahoam", hechelte Brigitte.

Endlich verlangsamte Brakow seinen Schritt. Er war am Wiesengrund angelangt. Der schwere Regenguß der vergangenen Nacht hatte das Grün noch sumpfiger gemacht als sonst. Brakow lüpfte den langen Mantel und begann zu stapfen. Wolfi und Brigitte klebten hinter der letzten Häuserecke vor der freien Wiese und wussten nicht so recht, wie sie ihm nun so ganz ohne Deckung folgen sollten. Brigitte löste sich schließlich aus dem Schutz der Häuserreihe, flog wie ein Pfeil über die Straße und warf sich auf der Wiese auf den Bauch. Wolfi, blieb nichts übrig, als zu folgen. Bäuchlings auf den Latzen ihrer Lederhosen robbten sie zwischen den hohen Halmen hinter Brakow drein. Weil der in seinen guten Hosen und Schuhen recht zaghaft stakste, kamen sie sogar ganz gut hinterher. Wolfi hörte ihn jedes Mal fluchen, wenn sein Schuh mit einem schmatzenden Geräusch tief in den Schlamm sank. Endlich langte er da an, wohin er wollte, eine Anhöhe mit festerem, trockenem Boden und ein paar Bäumen und Sträuchern. Tatsächlich erspähten die Kinder eine ungeduldig wartende Männergestalt hinter einer Weide.

„Ja, ja, i seh ihn selber", bremste Wolfi Brigittes aufgeregt wedelnden Zeigefinger. Brakow kam unter dem Baum zum Stehen, die Kinder verlangsamten ihr Kriechen. In Hörweite blieben sie auf dem Bauch liegen.

"Excuse my delay."

Ja, das war Brakows rostige Stimme.

"No problem, sir." Und das war die träge, gedehnte Zunge von Tucker. Aber die saloppe, betont lässige Arroganz, die er normalerweise durch die Barracks trug, fehlte ihm. Er war steif vor Beflissenheit – und Bange.

"So... do we know anything?"

"Yes. It will be on September 8th. Your next border tour assignment has not changed, I assume?"

"No, sir. Camp Pitman, as scheduled."

"September 8th, at 22:00 hours, at the Rozvadov border crossing."

"Okay."

Obwohl sie gute zehn Meter von den beiden Männern entfernt waren, hörten die Kinder den schweren Atem, mit dem Tucker seine Antworten aushauchte. Wolfi spannte sich an, wollte kein einziges Wort verpassen. Brigitte, die weniger verstand, hielt sich dennoch mäuschenstill.

"You will make yourself known to them with the

following word."

"Okay."

"Ready? You must not forget it."

"Okay."

"You tell them носитель."

"Okay."

"Repeat it for me."

"Nay-see..."

Brokaw wiederholte geduldig und langsam das Wort, ein dutzend Mal, während beide Kinder es lautlos mitsprachen. Wolfi wurde nach dem vierten oder fünften Mal langweilig, doch Tucker schwerfällige Zunge brauchte einige Versuche mehr, bis Brakow es für zumutbar hielt.

"You will not forget it."

"No, sir", versicherte Tucker, allerdings mit wenig Zuversicht.

"If this code word does not produce an immediate reaction from your Czech counterparts, abort the operation immediately. Do not attempt to explain anything."

"I won't, sir."

Es gab einen Moment der Stille. Wolfi reckte seinen Hals in die Höhe, wollte zwischen den Grashalmen hindurch sehen, was Brakow da tat. Eine Akte.

Vorsichtig, fast feierlich hielt er sie mit beiden Händen, während Tucker eifrig und mit zittrigen Fingern die Tasche öffnete, die er offenbar eigens für den Transport der Papiere mitgebracht hatte. Er empfing die Akte von Brakow, schob sie in die Tasche, und zur Tarnung stopfte er rund um die Aktendeckel – Wolfi erahnte es mehr, als er es sah – ein paar der billigen Schundheftchen, die Tucker so gerne im Kiosk erstand. Brakow sah ihm ruhig dabei zu, bis ihm alles gut gesichert erschien.

"If anything happens – if you are reassigned on short notice, or you have to abort the handover at Rozvadov for whatever reason – you will keep the file safe and return it to me at our next meeting."

"Yes, sir."

"Guard this file with your life."

"Yes, sir." In Tucker Stimme zitterte ein leichtes Schaudern, das hörten die Kinder bis in ihr schlammiges Versteck.

"Any other questions?"

"No, sir."

"Whatever happens, I will see you right outside the Neutor on September 30th at eighteen hundred hours", gab Brakow ihren nächsten Treffpunkt bekannt. Die Kinder horchten aufmerksam. "In the very corner on the outside of the city wall."

"Got it, outside of the wall."

"Okay."

Grußlos verschwand Tucker. Im Gegensatz zu Brakow machte er sich um seine Hosenbeine keine Sorgen, drückte seine wertvolle Last an die Brust und patschte hastig zurück in den knöcheltiefen Schlamm. Brakow stand still. Sie würden den Treffpunkt natürlich nicht gemeinsam verlassen. Als Tucker weit genug in die Gegenrichtung gegangen war, raffte Brakow wieder seine Hosenbeine und trat, noch widerwilliger als zuvor, in den Matsch zurück. Er stapfte geradewegs auf Wolfi und Brigitte zu. Wolfi drückte seine Hand fest auf Brigittes bebenden Rücken. Ruhig bleiben. Sie spähten durch die hohen, saftignassen Halme. Wenn sie ganz still hielten, würde Brakow vielleicht einfach an ihnen vorbei gehen.

Doch die Schritte kamen immer näher. Bald hörten sie die einzelnen Halme unter seinen Schuhen nachgeben und in den sumpfigen Boden knatschen. Da zuckte Brigittes knochiger Rücken unter Wolfis Hand weg; wie eine Katze wischte sie dicht am Boden entlang und rappelte sich erst voll auf, als sie schon fast in vollem Sprint war. Wieder blieb Wolfi nichts anderes übrig, als es ihr nachzutun. Brakow entfuhr ein kehliger Schrei, er blieb vor Schreck starr stehen, starrte sprachlos den kleinen, dünnen und völlig besudelten Gestalten nach, die er so unversehens aufgescheucht hatte. In der Ferne blieb nun auch Tuckers Silhouette stehen, wandte sich alarmiert um. Brakow winkte hektisch ab: Tucker solle sich gefälligst lieber um die Akte sorgen! Tucker hastete also mit seinem kostbaren Gut weiter. Brakows Schuhe befreiten sich mit einem schmatzenden Geräusch aus dem Matsch und er nahm ungelenk die Verfolgung auf. Wolfi schloss schnell wie ein Windhund zu Brigitte auf. Er kannte den Wiesengrund wie seine Westentasche, wusste genau, wo der weiche Boden, unvermittelt in knöcheltiefes Wasser überging. Wolfi rannte mit dem Mädchen an der Hand geradewegs von der schlammigen Wiese in den seichten Sumpf hinein. Brakow stolperte die ersten Schritte ins Wasser, ruderte wild mit den Armen um sein Gleichgewicht. Nachdem er sich gefangen hatte, stellte er den Kindern weiter nach. Wolfi und Brigitte schlugen einen scharfen Haken nach links, rannten knapp zehn Meter, dann gleich wieder nach rechts. Brakow sah in dem scheinbar chaotischen Zickzack der Kinder eine Chance, ihren Vorsprung einzuholen und sprintete geradeaus. Klatschend und tösend stürzte er in das bauchtiefe Wasserloch, das die wiesenkundigen Kinder flink umlaufen hatten.

Ihr Vorsprung war nun zu groß. Brakow gab auf. Er würde nun aus dem schmutzigen Wasser kraxeln, nach Hause gehen, die Schweinerei in einem kleinen Waschzuber säubern. Zum Glück waren es nur Kinder gewesen. Dass diese elenden kleinen Streuner aber auch ausgerechnet an seinem Teffpunkt spielen mussten.

The Note

„Na, des tätns doch so ned schreibn," said Waltraud. „Außerdem wärs eh gscheiter, ihr geht glei zum Captain."

Sam huffed sarcastically, thinking of Captain Perry's so-called *investigation* of the altercation at the Tally Ho. Dozens of black eyewitnesses to the fact that Tucker had started the aggression had done nothing to change the outcome: Shane Tucker went unpunished, Herman, the fool, was in the stockade. The other black GIs who had had the ill fortune of being present that night tended to their bruised backs and legs in private – and in silence.

Therefore Sam was quite certain that his word, the testimony of two small German children, or that of a German cleaning lady who had just been arrested in a prostitution raid, would hardly persuade his Captain.

„Naa," Sam declined, shaking his head as he continued to scribble.

„Aber ihr habt den Tucker doch eds scho mehrmals bei krumme Sachn erwischt, langt des ned?"

"What am I gonna tell them, Walli? 'Bout his weapons deals? And get *you* fired over it? Or 'bout the shit he's doing with Brakow – ma word against his? Or theirs?" He pointed to the children. They looked indeed very small and did not exactly make convincing witnesses as they were, sitting on the floor, playing with dirty beer bottle tops, which they both collected and traded with great passion.

"I need *sumthin.*" As if to emphasis his point, he grasped something invisible out of the air. He needed something tangible. Something that even Captain Perry could not dismiss.

„Ja, so is besser," said Bernd, nodding over Sam's shoulder.

Operation delayed due to unforeseen circumstances.

Report to convened location one week later at same hour.

Same procedure.

"Sign his name?"

„Des tät der Brakow doch nie machn."

"But if it's anonymous, maybe Tucker ain gonna take it seriously 'nough to act on it."

„Also gut, unterschreib's."

Bernd and Sam stared at the finished note as if they

had just given birth to something.

"Now, when an how do I slip it to him?"

„Des mach i scho." Theresa snatched the paper out of his fingers. „I legs zu seiner Post, wenn i den Mailroom sauber mach. Wenn ihr alle auf der Großn Straß seids."

They all glanced somewhat blankly across the table, each lost in their own contemplation of the folly they were about to undertake, except for Waltraud, who senselessly picked up and rearranged objects around the room, finding comfort and distraction in her hyperactivity.

"How can you be sure that *you* will have duty at that checkpoint that night?"

"There are ways. I know the sergeant who's in charge of the duty roster. He's a pretty chummy chap. Tucker gonna wanna change his schedule once he gets *this*. If I time it right, I'm gonna come in right when they gotta change the schedule for Tucker, and I'll volunteer to take his shift."

There was a silence, filled with skepticism.

"Well," Sam broke it, "At least the thrill of doin sumthing incredibly stupid's gonna make it less painful to leave y'all for four weeks of border duty."

„Und für mi machts des bloß umso schwerer," grumbled Theresa.

A Russ

Theresa stand vor der üblichen Ferkelei, die die Offiziere nach ihrem wöchentlichen Poker-Treff in der Offiziersmesse hinterließen. Doch heute schwang sie sich nicht voller Elan in den Raum, sammelte nicht flink die verschmutzten Servietten ein, schrubbte nicht beherzt den Boden. Heute nicht. Sam war erst eine Woche im Border-Camp und es schien ihr schon eine Ewigkeit. Lustlos zog sie die Stühle beiseite, wischte so ein bisschen um die Stuhlbeine herum, schaute mehr aus dem Fenster als auf den Boden, ihren Blick in einem leuchtend roten Herbstbaum verloren.

Da sah sie draußen einen Mann umherlaufen. Erst packte sie ihren Mopp fester, damit der vermeintliche Offizier sie nicht beim Trödeln erwischte. Doch dann drehte sie ihren Kopf unwillkürlich noch einmal zum Fenster. Irgendwas hatte da doch nicht gestimmt. Da stand er noch. Statt der schlanken, schnurgeraden Hosenbeine, denen Theresa insgeheim gerne nachschaute, wölbte sich die Beinkleidung dieses Mannes über polierten schwarzen Lederstiefeln zu einer wuchtigen Reiterhose. *Des is ja wie bei die Nazis!*, erschrak Theresa, bis ihr Verstand ihr sagte, dass das ja kaum möglich war. Ihr Blick wanderte nun weiter an dem seltsamen Mann hinauf. Die Jacke war knapp, moosgrün wie die Hose, ein brauner schlichter Gürtel, die Schnalle golden, ebenso wie die drei Knöpfe der Jacke. Auf der

Schirmmütze prangte – ein roter Stern!

„Mei, des is ja a Russ!", entfuhr es Theresa, ihr Mopp polterte zu Boden. Siedende Sorge um Sam stieg ihr ins Gehirn. Heute Nacht sollte sein geheimnisvolles Treffen an der böhmischen Grenze stattfinden. Was ging hier vor? Und wie konnte ein russischer Offizier einfach ungehindert auf dem Gelände der Merrell Barracks herumlaufen? Theresa stürmte aus dem Offizierskasino, über das Kopfsteinpflaster ins Hauptgebäude, klapperte über den spiegelblanken Marmorboden bis zu Vaughn's Büro, an Frau Kellermann vorbei, die vor Schreck nur ein entrüstetes „Na hoppla!" herausbrachte. Theresa hämmerte gegen das blinde Glas in Vaughns Tür.

Der öffnete persönlich.

„Da draußen steht a Russ!", rief Theresa. Dann besann sie sich: "I mean, a Russian! Shere is a Russian!"

"Where?", fragte Vaughn, seltsam unaufgeregt.

"Walking around! Outside!"

Vaughns strenger Mund spannte sich zu einem breiten Lächeln.

"My goodness", sagte er halb zufrieden, halb verärgert. "Two thousand men in the barracks. He's been out there for almost forty-five minutes, and who reports him? The cleaning lady."

„Hä?", machte Theresa, noch außer Atem.

"He's a plant. Not like this one", lachte er, als

Theresas verwirrter Blick zu seinen Kakteen am Fensterbrett wanderte. "I *planted* this man. He's not real."

"Not real?"

"No. He's here to test the soldiers' reaction to an intruder."

Jetzt schmunzelte auch Theresa, erleichtert, dass der Vorfall nichts mit Sam zu tun hatte.

"Goodness. It takes a German cleaning lady to detect a Russian intruder right on our grounds."

Er schüttelte den Kopf.

Rozvadov

The night air was too wet and slicing for September, Sam opined, though he could not be sure if it really was the outside temperature, or if his own blood was running cold in his veins. Sam had been checking his watch constantly since he left Camp Pitman. As he left, he had seen Shane Tucker out on the camp road scrubbing a Jeep. Sam was on duty with his book-club-mate Whitson Clarke, who was reading in the pale light of the little passenger-side lamp. Whitson did not even question why, or maybe was not even aware that Sam was idling there near the border crossing instead of steadily patrolling the border strip, as they were supposed to. Whitson in his book-nerdy obliviousness was the perfect sidekick for tonight's undertakings. It was a quarter to ten. Sam did not know the two GIs who were anxiously awaiting the end of their shift over at the border booth. *Good*, he thought.

"Whitson?"

Clarke looked up from his book with the slightly confused gaze of someone who had just been ripped from a different dimension back into dreary reality.

"Ya know the guys over there?"

Whitson leaned towards the windshield, straining his eyes.

"No."

"Good. Cuz sumthin unusual gonna happen tonight."

"What?" said Whitson, his finger firmly pressed on the line where he had stopped reading, expecting to return to it within the next few seconds.

"Close that book."

He did, leaving his finger between the pages.

"Ya know this was spose to be Shane Tucker's shift?"

"Yes, I was wondering why *you* showed up."

"Sumthin curious gonna happen tonight. Sumthin that was spose to happen to *Tuck*."

"I'm not following you."

"Ya'll see. Jus wanted to warn you 'head a time."

Sam knitted his forehead, staring into the black wet night. One more glance at the phosphor markings on his watch in the darkness. Ten to ten. He started the engine and drove the short distance up to the booth and barbed-wired gate.

"Finally!" they were greeted by the other soldiers, who were happy to call it a night. The changing of the guard was swift and professional, soon Sam and Whitson were alone. The rain was whipping the glass panes of the booth. Sam kept the door open so he could continue to peer out into the blackness, much to Whitson's frustration.

"A little chilly to be keeping that door ajar, isn't it?"

"Can't see a thing through those wet windows."

Whitson put his book down and looked at Sam seriously through his thick lenses.

"You really *are* expecting something, aren't you?"

His question was answered by the muffled sound of a starting motor. A car on the opposite side of the Iron Curtain had done exactly the same as Sam, had been hanging around near the crossing until it was time to take action. Except that the soldiers in the other car did not conceal their actions from the border guards on duty on the Czech side. They were saluted militarily. The car rolled up to the gate deliberately and slowly. Its headlights illuminated the streaking rain, then they went out. Sam left the booth. Whitson hesitated a moment, then curiosity, as well as a sense that he better stay with the more informed party, persuaded him to follow Sam, yet not without first grabbing a raincoat from the hook inside the door. He caught up to Sam who was calmly walking up to the gate.

"носитель," said Sam.

"You are not our contact," replied the gloomy figure on the other side of the border gate. The voice was rusty, the consonants chiseled. The vowels quivered just a tiny bit, which boosted Sam's confidence: His counterpart was also nervous. The hair on the back of his neck was bristling with thrill. This was real. Between himself and the kids, Sam already had plenty of proof that Shane Tucker was involved in something mighty devious. But standing here, right on the Iron Curtain in the soggy shadows, face to face with Communist spies – it was wrenching his bowels with fear and satisfaction at the same time.

"Ya contact couldn't come. But that's not a problem. Ya can talk to me," Sam said, slowly, trying to sound commanding and level-headed.

"And where is he?"

"That's not important. I'm his replacement, ya talk to me."

Whitson's distressed breathing was so heavy that Sam could hear it through the prattling rain. Yet, Whitson said nothing.

"The file, please," demanded Sam's interlocutor.

"It's been destroyed. The file was burned in a fire at Mr. Brakow's apartment," Sam had prepared to say, curious to see what reaction that would provoke. He had no idea what kind of repercussions such a bold lie would have. But since he didn't know what he was doing, anyway, he might as well stir up this crazy hornet's nest as much as possible, and then watch the fall-out.

"Burned?"

"Yes. I assume Mr. Brakow will procure a replacement soon," Sam said in a tone that could be taken both as a question or a statement.

"How soon?"

So, Sam's words had been interpreted as a statement, proving that the fellow on the other side didn't know much about the mechanisms of this odd deal, either.

"It'll probably be a few weeks," Sam replied randomly. The other man started to turn away.

"Might I have your name?" Sam asked in a last-ditch attempt to get something tangible out of this crazy maneuver. The man began to walk away.

"Or a number?"

The man got into the car, which veered away.

"Holy shit, Harris," Whitson behind him said in uncharacteristic vulgarity.

"That's right," confirmed Sam.

"Explain what the fuck just happened, please."

Sam looked into poor Whitson's stupefied face. What had Sam hoped to get out of this? Part of him had hoped they would give him something, a document, whatever. But they hadn't, and neither had they told him anything of import.

And yet, Sam concluded, tonight had been worth the folly. For a male white American adult *had seen it all*. Had seen it all and knew that Shane Tucker was supposed to have been there in Sam's stead. In Whitson Clarke, Sam finally had a witness that his superiors would not just dismiss.

"Cum on, I'll explain it all in the booth."

EHRUNG

„Ach, Herrgott nu amol."

Waltrauds frustrierten Fingern entwischte zum zigten Male die fransige blonde Strähne, die sie auf einen Lockenwickler zu zwängen versuchte.

„I bring deine Haar ja ned amal um den Wickler rum, des hält so ned. Willst ned lieber a Kopftuch aufsetzen?"

„Naa, will i ned."

Erst gestern hatte Theresa eine unerhörte Summe darin investiert, dass ein Friseur an ihrem gerupften Schopf einen Rettungsversuch unternahm. Nun konnte freilich selbst ein Meister seines Fachs nicht viel mit der Bescherung anfangen. Trotzdem wollte Theresa sich heute nicht verstecken.

„Heit Namittag trag i meine Zotteln wie an Orden. Sollns ruhig alle sehn, was mir passiert is. Und dass mir nix ausmacht. Die solln nur alle weiter versuchn, dem Sam und mirs Lebn schwer zu machen, i lass mi nimmer einschüchtern," sagte Theresa entschlossen und forderte Waltraud auf, sich weiter dem Aufwickeln ihrer unfrisierbaren Haare zu widmen. Achselzuckend fuhr Waltraud fort.

Um drei Uhr, hatte Vaughn ihr gesagt, sollte sie direkt zu seinem Büro kommen. Fünf vor drei stand sie bei Frau Kellermann auf der Matte.

„Grüß Gott, Frau Winkler."

„Sagns doch Theresa zu mir", forderte Theresa die Sekretärin auf. Durch deren strenge Fassade wollte sie schon lange mal brechen. So dienstlich war die Frau Kellermann immer, so unnahbar, obwohl es doch in der ganzen Kaserne nur eine handvoll deutscher Frauen gab, die Theresas Meinung nach eigentlich zusammen halten wie sollten Pech und Schwefel.

„Luise", gab Frau Kellermann noch ein bisschen widerwillig nach, kehrte dann aber sofort zur Sache zurück: „So, der Lieutenant Colonel hat gsagt, Sie... i mein, du sollst dich bei uns bei die Verwaltungsangestelltn mit hinstelln, bis er dich aufruft."

Sie stand auf, strich ihren steifen Rock glatt und stöckelte voran. Theresa blieb der Atem weg, als sie auf den Kasernenhof traten. Die gesamten Mannschaften standen in Reih und Glied auf dem Hof, mit Ausnahme der Männer, die zurzeit im Border Camp Dienst hatten. Da war auch Sam noch.

Vaughn kam aus dem Hauptgebäude, schritt zügig in die Mitte des Platzes, bediente sich eines Mikrophons, das schon bereit stand. Theresa verstand am Anfang nicht viel und wunderte sich darüber. Den Sam verstand sie doch in der Zwischenzeit so gut. Musste wohl hauptsächlich gestelztes politisches Palaver sein. Was sie Vaughns Tonfall allerdings schon anhörte, war, dass es sich um eine Standpauke handelte. Da knarzten Vorwürfe und Belehrungen in seiner Stimme, die blechern über die Lautsprecher schepperte. Die Soldaten hätten gerne betreten auf ihre Stiefelspitzen geschaut, durften aber nicht, denn sie standen ja die ganze Zeit über in Habachtstellung. Vaughns Ausführungen wurden dann weniger theoretisch, weniger politisch, klangen ärgerlicher, direkter, und Theresa verstand mehr.

"Now, apparently, as you go about your business here in the barracks, you are too concerned with your next meal, or your next dance, or your next movie, to feel that threat. Constant vigilance is a must. Not just when you are out there along the border. Not just when you are in the tank or the helicopter. *Always*. Always. A threat could be walking right in front of you, and you would not even notice."

Hierauf reagierte die Menge, gemurmelte Entrüstung flatterte über die Köpfe.

"No", gebot Vaughn dem Raunen Einhalt, "This is no rhetoric. It already happened. One of our men was able to walk the barracks disguised as a Russian officer, in full uniform, for exactly forty-five minutes before he was detected and reported."

Das Gelispel der Menge wurde unruhig.

"There is one – *one*! – member of our staff who does not walk around with blinders, and this member will receive the Exceptional Service Award today. This member of our staff is not even part of the U.S. Armed Forces. Frau Winkler, if you please."

Theresa wollte nach vorne treten und ihre Füße gehorchten ihr erst einmal nicht. Vaughn musste ihr erst zweimal auffordernd zunicken, bis sich ihre Beine endlich in Bewegung setzten. Die endlose Reihe von Gesichtern erdrückte sie, allesamt, ob sie nun amüsiert dreinschauten oder betreten, wohlwollend oder ablehnend. Jeder Soldat hatte seine eigene Reaktion darauf, dass Vaughn sie so bloßstellte. Bis vor ein paar Minuten hatte Theresa die ganze Angelegenheit als eine Ehrung verstanden, hatte sich darauf gefreut. Jetzt fühlte sie sich plötzlich missbraucht. Ihre Auszeichnung diente dazu, die Soldaten zu beschämen, ihnen zu zeigen, was für Flaschen sie doch alle waren, wenn sogar die doofe deutsche Putzfrau wachsamer war als sie! Theresa schlurfte langsam, fast widerwillig in die Mitte des Platzes, direkt in die Sichtlinie tausender Augen, wo Vaughn schon mit der Medaille bereit stand, die er ihr anzuheften gedachte.

"You go, girl!", hörte sie plötzlich.

Das war eindeutig Gregs vorlaute Stimme. Gelächter brach aus, warm und gutmütig. Theresa kannte in der Zwischenzeit den tiefen, sonoren Klang gut genug, um herauszuhören, welche Soldaten es waren, die da so aus voller Brust lachten. Theresa wurde klar, dass alle über sie und Sam Bescheid wussten. Die kleine dünne Frau, die so verloren in die Mitte des großen Platzes tapste, war *ihre* Theresa. Und die hatte es den aufgeblasenen Offizieren ganz schön gezeigt.

Theresa war bei Vaughn angekommen, der ihr offen

und freundlich ins Gesicht sah.

"Now, I know you all love our Frau Winkler, and we're proud of her vigilance and service to our Regiment, but you're supposed to be ashamed of yourselves, men!", sagte er ins Mikrophon. Er hatte seinen Punkt gemacht. Dass die ganze Sache nun in Belustigung umschlug, schien ihn gar nicht so sehr zu stören. Ganz anders war dagegen das Gesicht, das Theresa nun über Vaughns Schulter hinweg wahrnahm, während dieser ihr ihre Medaille an die Bluse heftete. Captain Perrys Blick war scharf wie ein Dolch.

◆

Bei *Stars and Stripes* stand mal wieder Inventur an, und daher kniete Theresa im Buchladen und half mit. Sie kontrollierte die langen Bestandslisten, die Bernd und Max am Vormittag aufgestellt hatten. Die Tür ging auf.

"Closed for inventory!", rief Waltraud, woraufhin normalerweise ein verirrter Kunde mit einem gemurmelten 'Sorry' die Tür wieder zuzog. Nicht diesmal. Die Tür klappte ganz auf, ließ die Herbstluft rein.

"We are closed", sandte Waltraud den ungebetenen Kunden mit frostiger Stimme fort. Doch der ihr unbekannte Soldat stand unbeirrt in ihrem Laden.

"I'm looking for Frau Winkler, I figured you'd know where to find her."

Theresa stand aus ihrer Ecke auf.

"I'm right here."

"Captain Perry needs to see you. Follow me."

Theresa tauschte mit Waltraud einen langen Blick aus, folgte dann dem Soldaten aus dem Laden. Der Weg aus dem Seitengebäude über den Hof, entlang den Korridor im Hauptgebäude erschien ihr ewig, und gab ihr viel zu viel Zeit, über den Grund ihrer Vorladung zu grübeln. Bis sie endlich in Perrys Vorzimmer stand, war sie zittrig und verschwitzt. Sie schaute den engen Bürogang hinunter zu Vaughns Tür. Aber das Milchglas war trüb, der Raum dahinter dunkel. Vaughn war nicht da.

"Frau Winkler!"

Perry schüttelte ihr nicht die Hand, wies nur auf einen Stuhl vor seinem Schreibtisch.

"That was quite a spectacle the other day. You caused quite a stir", sagte er ohne Freundlichkeit.

"I didn't... I just saw the Russian and I thought...."

Wo war ihr Stolz, ihre Entschlossenheit? Theresa wollte sich ohrfeigen, denn fühlte sich wieder wie immer: klein und nervös, irgendwie ertappt.

"I wanted to talk to you because it has come to my attention that you will... require some assistance in the near future."

"Assistance?"

"Help."

"Help, with what?"

"I want to point out some options for you in your *circumstances*. Time flies, and before you know it, there you'll be with a... you know." Er deutete vage auf ihren Bauch, dem man noch nichts ansah.

"You are not the only case in Germany. It's actually... I don't want to say *rampant*, but definitely a problem. Just last year, the Brown Baby Plan was instituted to address it."

"Brown Baby plan?", fragte Theresa verständnislos und unheilvoll.

"There are plenty of decent black families back stateside who would adopt the child and give it a home."

"What?", hauchte Theresa, während ihr Gehirn mühsam verarbeitete, worauf Perry hinauswollte. "You want to take my child?"

"Well, I would hope that you would *want* that child to grow up where it belongs, amongst its own kind. You should be grateful. It's very generous of these families to take in these unfortunate creatures."

"You want to take my child?", wiederholte Theresa.

"There is no question that a black woman has a better capacity to nurture and understand a black child."

"Better than se mosser? Better san I?"

Theresa saß schwach auf dem Stuhl.

"Do you not understand that it would be better for the poor thing?"

„No, no, no", schüttelte sie nun den Kopf. Sie hatte nun keinen Zweifel mehr, was Perry meinte, hatte ihn nicht falsch verstanden.

"First: It is *my* child. And second: I know how it is over sere in America. Everysing separated, white here, black sere. And a mixed baby, where does *it* go? My fiance tells me all that."

"You have no fiance, Mrs. Winkler," sagte Perry abschätzig.

Theresa verstummte. Wozu noch mit diesem Mann sprechen? Sie atmete tief durch und sagte sich selbst, dass ihre Panik unnütz war. Perry hatte keine Macht, ihr ihr Kind zu nehmen. Sie war Deutsche, und sie würde ein deutsches Kind zur Welt bringen. Perry konnte ihr nichts anhaben, wenn sie sich nicht von ihm ins Bockshorn jagen ließ.

„Mei Kind mir nehmen. Und i hab dacht, ihr Amis seid hier, um uns *Nazis* a bissl Menschlichkeit beizubringen", sagte sie nun bitter. Perry verstand sie nicht.

"Can I go?"

"Take this form and study it carefully. You can leave it with Frau Kellermann once you have filled it out."

Theresa stand auf, schnappte den Adoptionsbogen aus Perrys Fingern, machte auf dem Absatz kehrt. Sie fegte grußlos an Luise Kellermann vorbei, ging auch nicht mehr zurück zu Waltraud, um mit der Inventur zu helfen. Sie ging heim.

Return

"Was sagstn da dazua?"

"That's what I say to this," said Sam, who was back from four long weeks of border camp. He reached for his back pocket, produced his gas lighter and held its flame to the offending paper. The blue flame began to eat into the adoption form, crumbling it. Glowing little black-rimmed flakes sailed onto Waltraud's kitchen table where they disintegrated into ash. Sam and Theresa watched the paper burn, and the visitor who sat across from them was keenly observing them. When the fire had eaten up all but one last corner of the sheet, Sam dropped it onto his empty dinner plate into the puddle of brine that was left of Theresa's Kartoffelsalat. Theresa looked at ease, snuggled up against Sam.

"What was that?" asked Hannes.

"Adoption papers to send away our baby," said Sam.

"Who gave you that?"

"My captain gave it to her."

Hannes sighed.

"Once we're married, jerks like him woan be able to...."

"Do you have a permit to get married?"

"I been here only fifteen months, and they doan let ya apply until eighteen. Then it's gonna take a few more months after we apply."

"That's a long process. The baby might be born by then."

"Well, they want ya to be back home in the States by the time ya get the permit, in the hope that ya passion is gonna cool and ya gonna give up on the idea. Outa sight, outa mind, ya know. But I ain going anywhere until we're married. I'm gonna try to extend ma tour here til we get the permit." Sam's voice trailed away at the end. Hannes' face was wrinkled in skepticism.

"Bloody hell, Sam they might post you away," Hannes concluded in his typical pharmacological pragmatism.

"Nah," Sam said, trying to silence Hannes and rolling his eyes meaningfully towards the corner where Brigitte was nestled in a little blanket on the floor, industriously working a page in the pretty coloring book Hannes had brought. Indeed, her red crayon was hovering an inch above the paper, she was gawking at the grown-ups, trying to follow their conversation.

"Let's not get *her* all worked up," Sam said, in a low voice. Hannes nodded, he had understood.

"So do you think you want to stay in the Army? You think you *can* stay in the Army?"

"We'd rather settle down somewhere as private

citizens, ya know."

„Und deine Witwenrente?" Hannes asked Theresa. Theresa exhaled in a way that betrayed that she had not even considered her widow's pension until now. Hannes was dissecting their dreams with the cool precision of a surgeon. It did not feel good, but both knew that they ought to have faced all these hard questions without a visit from Hannes.

„Die verlierst du nämlich bei Wiederheirat. She's going to lose her widow's pension."

"Look, Hannes, we ain sayin we're in any way prepared fo this. All we know is that baby's cumin. Everythin else is gonna have to fall into place. Gonna have to."

"You need a plan, my friends," Hannes said, keeping them hostage with a very sober, dry look. They both nodded in silence. Of course they needed a plan, one that answered questions about money, work, housing....

Brigitte was still looking at everyone. Her mellow eyes were dark blue with worry about the adults' grave talk.

„Wie findest du dein Malbuch, Süße?"

„Hab scho zwoa Seitn ausgmalt."

NEUTOR

Wolfi war sehr zufrieden mit seinem Zögling. Brigitte kletterte fast so flink wie er, in seiner alten Lederhose, die so viele Helden- und Schandtaten gesehen hatte und die Brigitte nun in allen Ehren weiter auftrug. Der Baum war so hoch wie die Stadtmauer, und seine starken Äste wucherten so breit, dass manche den trutzigen Sandstein der Neutorbastei streiften. Brigitte zeigte keinerlei Höhenangst. Wolfi hatte für ihren heutigen Lauschangriff einen luftig-hohen Logenplatz gewählt, damit sie nicht noch einmal in so eine Bredouille kämen wie beim letzten Mal im matschigen Gras. Außerdem genossen sie hier oben auch eine bessere Akustik. Brigittes Einwand, dass sie eigentlich in einer Sackgasse säßen, wenn sie denn entdeckt würden, winkte Wolfi ab. Sie mussten lediglich still sein.

Pünktlich erschien Brakow, stellte sich genau dahin, wo er es mit Tucker abgesprochen hatte, 'in the very corner', lehnte seinen Rücken gegen die sandsteinerne Neutormauer und wartete. Schon von Weitem sahen die Kinder Tucker seine Unruhe an. Sein breitbeiniger, watschelnder Gang war gehetzt. Eine Ledertasche hing an einem Gurt über seiner Schulter, doch presste er sie zusätzlich auch noch an seine Brust. Ihr Inhalt war kostbar. Natürlich, denn er hatte ihn ja am Grenzübergang nicht loswerden können. Sehnsüchtig blickten die Kinder auf die Tasche. Was würden sie dafür geben, sie in ihre eigenen Kinderhände zu bekommen. Absurde Ideen kamen Wolfi, konnte man irgendwie vom Baum aus danach angeln? Das Gespräch begann und Wolfi schlug sich die albernen Gedanken aus dem Kopf. Angestrengt horchten die Kinder in die Abenddämmerung hinein.

"Good evening."

Brakow erwiderte den Gruß gar nicht, denn er hörte gleich das Unheil in Tucker Stimme.

"What news?", fragte er ohne Freundlichkeit.

"No one showed."

"I doubt that." Brakows Stimme war scharf wie eine Klinge.

"No, really." Tucker hingegen klang immer mehr wie ein Schuljunge in einer Zwickmühle. "I swear I was there, no one showed. I came exactly at the time you wrote."

"I *wrote* you?"

"The note... you wrote me...."

"I wrote you no note. You are telling me no one showed at the border crossing on September 8th?"

"It wasn't September 8th, remember? You moved it back a week."

Die Kinder horchten, doch für ein paar ewige Sekunden fiel kein Wort. Wolfi versuchte, sich die

Gesichter vorzustellen als beiden klar wurde, dass etwas massiv schief gegangen war.

"The file", verlangte schließlich Brakow, dessen Vertrauen in Tucker schlagartig auf null gesunken war. Wolfi reckte seinen Hals, um zwischen dem im letzten Tageslicht glühenden Laub hindurch zu beobachten, wie Tucker die Tasche übergab. Brakow riss sie an sich, mit einer Besorgnis, die Bände sprach. Dieser Narr von einem Amerikaner hatte es tatsächlich geschafft, die Übergabe an der Grenze zu verbocken. Sollte er mit diesem unfähigen Mann fortfahren oder alles ganz neu aufziehen? Und was hatte es mit dieser bizarren Geschichte von einer Nachricht und einer Terminverschiebung auf sich? In exquisiter Schadenfreude stellte Wolfi sich vor, wie Brakow diese Fragen durchs Hirn schwirrten. Zu Wolfis großer Enttäuschung senkte Brakow nun die Stimme, und dazu noch fuhr eine leichte Herbstbrise in den Baum, die welken Blätter begannen zu rauschen und rascheln. Wolfi hangelte sich weiter an dem Ast voran, um besser hören zu können.

Da knackte es furchterregend. Brigitte atmete scharf ein und zuckte mit ihrem kleinen Körper in Wolfis Richtung, packte ihn bei den Hosenriemen, zerrte an ihm. Der Ast war angebrochen. Wolfi kraxelte in Panik zurück. Einen Sturz aus über zehn Metern Höhe hatte er gerade noch so vermieden. Doch die Aufmerksamkeit der Männer am Boden galt nun ihm. Wortlos, atemlos erklommen Wolfi und Brigitte den nächsten Ast, dann den nächsten – da war die Basteimauer. Wolfi wagte sich vor auf den langen, geschmeidigen Ast, der die Mauer sanft streichelte. Er bog sich unter Wolfis Gewicht, doch brach nicht. Wolfi starrte auf die Mauer. Der Sandstein war rau und porös. Wolfi kannte ihn wie sich selbst. Wie oft waren sie beide schon den steilen Ölberg zur Burgfreiung hinaufgejagt wie kleine Gemsen.

Wolfi machte einen Satz, grub seine Finger in den weichen Stein, fand genug Reibung, schwang seine Beine über die Bastei. Dann sah er Brigitte im dämmernden Licht. An dem fahlen Schrecken, der ihr ins Gesicht geschrieben stand, erkannte er, wie irrwitzig sein Manöver gewesen war. Zwölf Meter unter ihm drehte sich der Neutorgraben, denn nun auf einmal schwindelte ihm. Der Ast, von dem er abgesprungen war, wippte noch. Aber er war drüben. Brigitte noch nicht. Unter ihnen stampften erregt die Schritte der ertappten Männer, die in das dichte Geäst hochspähten, sehen wollten, wer zum Teufel denn da oben war. Das Herbstlaub war schon verfärbt, aber noch dicht. Noch hatten die Männer sie noch nicht erkannt, glaubte Wolfi zumindest. Er warf Brigitte einen eindringlichen Blick zu. Auch sie musste nun irgendwie in die Neutorbastei herüberkommen, denn an einen Abstieg vom Baum war nicht zu denken. Brigitte begann, den Ast entlang zu kriechen, der sich unter ihrem Gewicht senkte. Dadurch kam er der Wand zwar näher, doch der Abstand zur oberen Mauerkante, über die es zu klettern galt, wurde größer. Wolfi wagte ihr nichts zuzurufen. Die Männer unten sollten keine Kinderstimmen hören. Er lehnte sich über die Brüstung, so weit er konnte, und streckte ihr seine Arme entgegen. *Komm schon, jetzt,* bedeutete er ihr mit dem Blick. Das Mädchen stieß sich mit ihren dürren Beinen vom Ast ab, beide Arme nach oben gestreckt, sprang ins Nichts. Wolfi ließ sie nicht im Stich. Er packte ihre Hände. Ihr Gewicht überraschte ihn. Seine Füße verloren kurz Kontakt zum Boden, dann fing er sich wieder. Brigitte stieß und trappelte gegen Sandstein, bis auch sie oben war. Wolfi packte ihre Taille und zerrte sie über die Mauer. Beide sackten im Schutz der Brüstung entkräftet auf den Boden der Bastei, sahen sich in die Augen, atmeten tief.

„Oh Gott", flüsterte Brigitte.

„Wir müssen weiter", hechelte Wolfi.

„Ja", schnaufte das Mädchen.

Noch einen Moment saßen sie, dann rappelten sie sich auf. Wie schnell konnten Tucker und Brakow hier hoch kommen? Wolfi berechnete fieberhaft, wie die Männer laufen mussten, um sie zu fangen. Erst mal mussten sie raus aus dem Stadtgraben, durch das Neutor, um den Turm herum, dann... Na, bis dahin wären er und Brigitte längst weg.

Sie rannten die Neutormauer entlang, über die Straße, über den Kettensteg, durch den kleinen Fußgängertunnel und dann über die Brüstung hinunter in den Uferschlamm der Pegnitz. Es war nun fast dunkel, doch die Kinder brauchten nicht zu sehen. Erst im Kontumazgarten kraxelten sie die Böschung wieder hoch und verschnauften. Brigittes Atem röhrte ein wenig.

„Hammerse abghängt?"

„Keine Ahnung. Ich hoff."

Sie gingen nebeneinander im Dunkel. Die Pegnitz schimmerte. Sie hörten nur ihre geschundenen Lungen hecheln und ihre erschöpften Schritte auf dem Gras. Dann ein Trappeln, ein Stampfen, ein Streifen von Büschen — am anderen Flussufer, gegenüber von ihnen.

„Scheiße, die sin da drüben auf der Hallerwiese!", hauchte Wolfi.

„Ned renna, sonst hörns uns bloß. Die komma so schnell ned auf unser Seitn", versuchte Brigitte Wolfi zurückzuhalten, doch dessen Beine waren schon wieder in einen kopflosen Spurt gefallen. Aufgebrachte Männerstimmen am anderen Ufer – sie hatten die Regung natürlich bemerkt. Schritte polterten wild, blind und ziellos durch das Dunkel.

Dann fiel ein Schuss.

Keine Schritte mehr, weder auf der Hallerwiese, noch im Kontumazgarten. Brigitte wagte sich nicht zu rühren. Sie konnte Wolfi im Finstern nicht sehen. Die Männerstimmen am anderen Ufer begannen nun wieder zu sprechen, zwar unverständlich, aber nicht mehr panisch, sondern abwägend, beratschlagend.

Wo war Wolfi? Brigitte bebte am ganzen Körper. Versteckte er sich hinter einem Baum oder Busch? Oder lag er blutend im Gras, angeschosssen, erschossen? Brigittes Unterkiefer begann zu schlottern. Ihre Zähne klapperten, sie wusste nicht, was sie tun sollte. Suchen? Rennen? Rufen? Tränen der Hilflosigkeit stiegen ihr in die Augen. Da packte sie etwas von hinten.

„Wolfi?!"

„Psssst."

„I hab dacht, die ham di erwischt."

„Pssst", wisperte er. Er biss sich die Unterlippe wund. Seinen rechten Arm presste er an seine Brust. Im Dunkeln schimmerte es feucht und dickflüssig.

„Wolfi, du blutest!"

„Des weiß i selber, wir müssn aber weiter, die kommen bestimmt eds übern Kettensteg", presste Wolfi zwischen vor Schmerz und Angst verbissenen Zähnen hindurch.

„Die Kinderklinik!", schoss es Brigitte ins fieberhafte Hirn. Die Cnopfsche Kinderklinik war auf der Hallerwiese, genau wo sich Brakow und Tucker befanden, nur ein paar Hundert Meter von ihnen. Um dorthin zu gelangen, mussten sie noch einmal die Pegnitz überqueren.

„Die sind in Richtung Neutorgraben zurück. Wir gehn einfach übern nächsten Steg."

„Und in die Cnopfsche nei werdns uns ja wohl ned nachrenna", beschied Brigitte. Sie gingen hastig flussabwärts weiter und überquerten den Großweidenmühlsteg.

Cnopfsche

In his frenzy, Sam forgot to pay the taxi driver. The man snarled at him and he produced a bill febrile fingers. It was way too much for the fifteen-minute ride from the barracks to the clinic, but before the taxi driver could alert him to the mistake, Sam had rushed through the double door into the white-tiled room. He blinked under the glaring electric lights. In the waiting area, women were holding children in various stages of fevers and distress.

At the very back sat Waltraud and Theresa with Brigitte, whose expression was as frayed as her hair and clothes. Then Sam spotted Wolfi, who was sitting between the women, looking remarkably young and tiny.

„Wie geht es, Wolfi?"

„Es geht scho," the boy answered.

"When will he be seen?" Sam stretched his back, throwing a judging glance around the room to assess the severity of the other cases in the waiting area.

„Er kommt bald dran," Waltraud tried to calm him.

"What happened, Wolfi? Who did that?"

„Na ja, entweder der Brakow oder der Tucker, kann i ja ned wissn."

"Oh, my God!!" Sam uttered in a sort of suppressed

holler. He thrust his head back in emotion, paced a senseless circle around the waiting room, then cupped his hands over his overwhelmed face. The other mothers and little patients goggled at him.

"Oh, my *God*."

"Sam."

He looked at Waltraud and Theresa, could not believe their calm acceptance, their meek patience. How could they sit there and appear to be neither angry with Tucker and Brakow, or this incompetent hospital staff... or at least with *him*?

Finally a nurse appeared behind in the glass door that led to the treatment rooms, and which all waiting patients were eying anxiously, ready to jump up when called.

„Wolfgang Wächter?"

„Ja, hier," Waltraud said, rising quickly, as if another Wolfgang Wächter might snatch their turn. She steered Wolfi through the door. Brigitte, Theresa and Sam stayed behind. Theresa got up from her chair and walked over to Sam, wrapped her arms around his waist and craned her face towards his. At first, Sam could not really answer her embrace.

"This all ma fault."

„Dass dir der Tucker in der Kneipn a Flaschn ans Hirn schmeisst? Dass der Herman daraufhin a Knarre rausholt? Die krummen Dinger von der Drecksau Tucker? Dass die uns des Kind wegnehma wolln? Dass der Wolfi und die Brigitte, die elendn Fratzn, ned auf ihre Mütter hörn? Is alles *dei* Schuld?"

"From here on out the kids are gonna stay put."

„Wie willstna des durchsetzn? Mir arbeitn ja n ganzn Tag."

"They're grounded. Have them stay with Waltraud in the bookstore after school."

Brigitte's eyes had followed the conversation, of which she only really understood the German half. But she was a keen reader of body language, and when Sam and Theresa sat down, she retreated to a corner of the waiting hall to pout in advance about her impending grounding.

They sat silently, Theresa stared into the air, Sam kept his eyes cast down. After a while, Waltraud and Wolfi emerged. They rushed to meet them.

„Und?"

„Streifschuss," Wolfi reported smugly. This was one of the classic war wounds that Wehrmacht veterans would often mention, and he was quite proud of his.

„Zum Glück," Waltraud added soberly, „hat's kan Knochn erwischt."

"So there was no bullet?" Sam whispered to Waltraud.

„Zum Glück ned," she shrugged, „sonstn hättens uns die Gschicht, dass er mit der alten Luger vom Vater gspielt hat, ja ned glaubt."

„Aber es war ja zum Glück a Streifschuss," summarized Wolfi. Then his smugness gave way to some disappointment: „Aber glohnt hats sichs überhaupt ned. Nix Neues, gar nix."

"Doan matter. Theresa and I jus decided that you brats woan be dogging Tucker or Brakow or anyone else no more. Do ya hear?"

„Hm," said Wolfi in a tone that promised nothing.

"Wolfi, he *shot* at you."

„Er hat ned gwusst, dass mir Kinder sin. Die ham uns nie richtig gsehn."

"Ya go straigh to the bookstore after school and stay with ya mother til she gets off work. Every day."

The prospect of being indefinitely grounded in the bookstore made Wolfi turn paler than being shot at by a Russian spy or American traitor.

„Bitte!"

„Na, stimmt scho, des is a gute Idee," seconded Waltraud.

They took the tram home. When the children were in bed, Waltraud, Theresa and Sam conferenced around Waltraud's kitchen table.

„So, i glaub, eds langts aber mit der Spioniererei. Geh morgen zum Vaughn und sag ihm alles," Waltraud demanded.

"I still ain got nuthin to go on. No proof."

„Der Whitson war doch dabei an der Grenz. Würd der aussagn?"

Sam slowly raised his glance from his cup of malt coffee.

„I weiß ned. I need to talk to him."

All three nodded.

♦

Sam knocked on the door to Whitson's six-bed room. Several mumbling voices invited him to enter. He opened, and around the rectangular wooden table in the middle of the room sat four men playing Poker. Sam could not even tell whether Whitson was among them, because before he was able to scan all the faces present, the sight of Tucker sent his blood whirling. This plain, self-satisfied face seemed grotesquely ugly to Sam at this moment. His brain shut down like a rolling gate, and wrath propelled him into the room, he was but a blind, mindless sack of muscle and bones. There was no anticipation in Tucker's face when Sam punched it. He was making no apparent connection between the events on Hallerwiese and the raging man descending on him like an avenging angel.

It all went so fast that the other three players were still holding their cards in neat little fans when their Queens, Jokers and Aces were suddenly sprayed with blood.

"Whoa," Sam heard the others as they dropped their cards. He vaguely heard them telling him to stop, and wondered why it took them so long to physically intervene. Were they just so stunned? Or did they secretly enjoy that Tucker was getting his ass beaten? Were they afraid of Sam, who at this moment was nothing less than a furious wrecking ball? Finally, they took it upon themselves to grab Sam from behind, hold down his punching arms, force him to his knees. Sam was panting, assessing the damage he had done to Tucker and finding it insufficient. Blood was dripping from the corners of his mouth. Looked like Sam had gotten a good swing at his cheek, perhaps cracked his cheekbone, judging by how the skin right underneath Tucker's eye that was rapidly filling with air and blood. Instead of the glistening hate that Sam expected, Tucker's expression was one of teary confusion.

"What the fuck, man?" he heard the others say.

Sam never found out if Whitson actually was in his room or not. Officers came rushing, MP showed up. The next time Sam was able to grasp a clear thought, he was looking at bars.

♦

"This is the disciplinary hearing in accordance with Article 15 of the Uniform Code of Military Justice for PFC Samuel James Harris, born on June 2nd, 1920, in Jesup, Georgia."

The oval conference table seemed larger than last time Sam had been here, maybe because of the lack of clutter on it. Instead of a busy disarray of papers, the desk was clean but for one file in the exact center. Sam could read his name and number on the tab. He sat down on his chair, which was lower and less sturdy than Captain Perry's seat, as well as very far away from him. Sam had the very ill fortune that Lieutenant Colonel Vaughn, who should have presided over this meeting, was in the States attending his mother's funeral. Perry was acting commander of the Regiment. He took his task very seriously:

"Infractions to be reviewed are...." Perry raised a displeased eyebrow at the length of the list of Sam's offenses. Frau Kellermann was in the room to type the minutes. She took great care not to make eye contact with Sam.

"Disturbance of the peace in a civilian locality, indecency, propagation of subversive ideas.... that was the list *before* you apparently felt you had to add disorderly conduct as well as assault and battery."

Sam sat silently as he tried to connect the list of accusations with things he had done.

"Let's begin with the riot at the Tally-Ho."

"Riot," Sam let out in a huff, then checked himself: "Sir, ma involvement in the brawl consisted of me receiving a beer bottle to ma head while dancin." He pointed to the cut on his temple that was still visible. "But I didn start it, I didn even fight back when I was attacked...."

"You know, Harris, I'm really hardly interested in the exact details of how you people get into your fights. I am concerned with the troops' reputation. I cannot have any of this. Period."

"I understand, sir," Sam said, deciding to hold still for the moment.

"This is number one. Number two," Perry went on, "is an issue of moral turpitude. It has been reported that you have been engaging in illicit, immoral acts with local prostitutes."

"Now, that is a lie!"

"Sit down, Harris."

Sam did not know he had risen.

"Who's sayin that?"

"Sit down, Mr. Harris. If I find you unable to participate in this hearing in an orderly fashion...."

Sam made an effort to pull his anger back like a

cowboy a wild horse. He had to consider his prospects and choose the wisest course of action rather than the most proximate.

"I'm sorry, Captain," he was able to say. "This accusation upsets me cause I'd actually hoped to apply for a marriage permit. Nuthin could be further from ma mind than intercourse with a prostitute."

"Well, Harris," Perry smiled, his face ugly with sarcasm, "That is probably the oldest phrase in the book: 'I'm going to marry her.' The problem is rampant, and there is not a line we haven't heard. But the saddest thing is, not only do you use such lies to justify your depravity before your officers, you are also encouraging those poor wretches."

Sam sat breathless.

"I ain ever had intercourse with no prostitute."

"Yes, you have, Harris, you even got her pregnant. Don't deny it, it is all over town."

"It's ma *fiance* who's pregnant. I ain had contact with no prostitutes."

"Please, stop this farce. Do you know how much harm you're doing to this poor woman, financially, socially?"

Flaming red anger crept up Sam's spine as he finally understood that Perry was referring to Theresa as the prostitute.

"Ma fiance ain no whore!!"

"I understand the person in question was arrested in the turmoil at the Tally Ho."

"By the MP, yes, and as soon as they handed her over to German police *they* let her go, cuz they saw through all this nonsense right away."

"Sexual favors in exchange for material compensation, Mr. Harris, do our definitions not concur? It doesn't have to be a monetary transaction. According to my reports, Frau Winkler has received clothing for herself and her daughter, groceries and cosmetics. You bought no fewer than twenty buckets of coal in December, delivered to Nunnenbeckstraße 46 where Frau Winkler resides … and that is only what we have documented."

"This is ma *fiance*, Captain," said Sam, incredulous, terror kneading his stomach like a cold hand. And how did Perry know all this, anyway?

"I's makin sure ma fiance and her daughter had coal to get through the winter. She's pregnan with ma child!"

"We know that. She never returned the form I gave her, in a well-meaning attempt to help her sort this out and provide this poor creature with a chance at a decent life."

"We ain givin up our child for adoption! What is this nonsense? I'm tellin you, this is ma fiance!"

"Harris," sighed Perry, getting impatient. "Don't pretend that you don't know what the deal is. A German widow. With a colored man. If you really think that these girls are in it for anything else than the dollars and the lipstick...."

If I punch him, I'm going to jail, Sam thought.

"The bottom line is, we're going to have to suspend her from her job here. This is the kind of trouble that you are getting these poor women in, Harris."

Jail. Jail. Jail. With this thought, he managed to restrain himself. Perry took Sam's heavy silent breathing as a cue to continue down the list of grievances.

"Let's continue with the gravest of the issues. This book club that I was naïve enough approve has turned out to be a nest of subversive minds, where seditious ideas are being hatched, right under our noses, every Monday night."

"I didn know Mark Twain or hundred-year-old stories 'bout factory girls and orphans was subversive."

"Yes, I'm aware that you are hiding behind a front of so-called classics," interjected Perry. "You are also in possession of an excessive amount of books, which have been confiscated for investigative purposes."

"Ya mean ya took ma books? Since when do ya have the right to take a man's books? And what is too many books?"

"I did not say too many."

"Ya said excessive."

"The point is, your book club has been suspended."

Perry closed the file.

"Do ya even know what we're readin?" Sam provoked him.

"Yes, I do. From a member of your club," Perry said. "Who, as a matter of fact, is a witness in this hearing."

With this, Perry gave a nod to Frau Kellermann, who went and ushered Shane Tucker enter the room. Although his face bore the traces of his last encounter with Sam, he looked quite content.

"Tucker was never a member of our club! He sat in once or twice, hopin to hear sumthin he could use 'gainst us. I demand you ask someone that actually shows up every week and reads our stuff."

"We have vetted potential witnesses and Sergeant Tucker was the one whose reliability was the least questionable."

"What are you talkin 'bout?"

"Well, who are the regular members of your club? Herman Foster? Who drew a gun on a comrade at the Tally Ho, unleashing a massive riot that had to be broken up by MP?"

"Whitson Clarke!"

"Declined to testify."

"How can a soldier decline to testify at a hearin?"

"Sergeant Tucker, can you elaborate on your experience with PFC Harris's book club?"

Shane had been sitting on a chair to Perry's right, relishing Sam's frazzled anxiety. He eagerly replied to the Captain's question:

"Well, they were using those big old novels as a pretext to then have these really unpatriotic, disloyal discussions. Got all riled up. And they did read other things, too."

"Like what?"

"Like negro stuff. Rebellious stuff."

"Rebellious," Sam echoed, in ever greater disbelief that this was really happening.

"And Communist books and such."

"Oh, cum on!" Sam cried out, unable to contain himself.

"Well, Mr Harris," said Perry and pulled something from an envelope in front of him. "This was found in Whitson Clarke's possession. Which is probably why he declined to comment at this hearing."

And Perry produced a book that looked immediately familiar to Sam. It was the book Bernd had procured him months ago, the English version of *The Communist*

Manifesto. Sam groaned inwardly. Why had he given it to poor Whitson?

"Look, this is... This kin of jus fell into Whitson's lap, really – he never sought it out...."

"So this book came to him from *you*," Perry ascertained, scribbling in his file with eagerness. Sam did not deny it.

"Well, I's under the misconception that I live in a society where I can read whatevr I damn well please," Sam said, giving up. There was no way to reason his way out. Sentence had already been passed. With nothing left to lose, Sam decided to go on the offensive.

"I'm not the traitor here. That guy is," he now pointed directly at Shane Tucker's swollen nose. Tucker huffed incredulously, in perplexed amusement.

"Tucker is in contact with a Russian agent. He's met with him multiple times over the summer. He was spose to transfer secret documents at the Rozvadov border crossin on September 8th, but he failed to do it. He gave the file back to his contact, a man named Brakow, on September 30th. He shot and wounded a child that happened to witness the handover. That's why I lost my composure on Thursday night when I saw him," Sam reeled off this desperate last-ditch effort to get through Perry's thick skull. He spoke louder with each word, because every bit he said made Perry shake his head in more dimissive indifference.

Shane's arched eyebrow betrayed a certain surprise at the amount and precision of the information Sam possessed, but other than that ... he was unruffled.

"Sorry, Captain," he drawled, "but I'm startin to think Harris got some kind of mental problem. This man attacked me twice, out of the blue, and now he's rambling about God knows what crazy cloak n dagger stuff I'm sposedly involved in ... he sounds, like, deluded or somethin."

"He attacked you *twice*? I only know of the incident yesterday."

"Yes, but the first time Colonel Vaughn didn deem it necessary to pursue any action", drawled Shane, skillfully exploiting the ill will between Vaughn and Perry and steering Perry's attention away from Sam's 'delusional rant'. Perry never processed his words. *That nigger just lost his fucking mind*, was all that penetrated to his Captain.

"Well, I think I have gathered enough information so I can come to a conclusion."

Sam stared at his henchman. That man *believed*, from the bottom of his bigoted conscience, that he was right and Sam was wrong on every count. Shane Tucker was wearing his battered face like a trophy, visible proof of Sam's moral inferiority, his lack of self-control, his indecency. There was nothing Sam could say to be heard, nothing he could do to be understood. It was surreal. He might as well be a protagonist in one of his many, no 'excessive' novels: He was trapped in Kafka's *Trial*, watched by Big Brother, running from Javert, being judged by De Villefort.

It was all over.

Nach dem Sturm

Das Klopfen an Waltrauds Wohnungstür war so schüchtern, dass es nicht der Vermieter sein konnte. Und wer sonst würde denn um diese Uhrzeit etwas von Wächters wollen? Waltraud schlurfte in Pantoffeln über die Dielen, zog ihren alten Morgenmantel straff um ihre Mitte, spähte erst mal durch den Türspion.

„Na, so was."

„Wer isn?", fragte Bernd von der Küche.

„Anner von die GIs. Anner, der viel kauft. Waß eds nimmer, wie er heißt."

Theresa, die kraftlos und scheinbar dösend im Baststuhl neben der Balkontür lag, erhob sich nun wie ein Geist. Sie griff an Waltraud vorbei nach dem Türknauf und öffnete. Im Dunkeln stand, gekrümmt vor Zerknirschung, seine Dienstmütze verlegen mit beiden Händen knetend, Whitson Clarke.

Theresa schloss die Tür wieder, Whitson steckte seine Hand dazwischen, verbiss sich den Schmerz, als Theresa trotzdem weiter zudrückte.

„Frau Winkler..."

Sie hörte auf zu drücken, nicht versöhnlich, sondern ermüdet.

"I had to come."

"Come in", übernahm Waltraud. „Komm, hogg di hi, hör ihn dir an, schaden kanns ned", wies sie Theresa zurück in die Küche und auf den Baststuhl.

In der Küche blieb Whitson stehen, immer noch mit schuldbewussten Fingern seine Mütze bearbeitend.

"Frau Winkler, I had to come and... check on you, I guess? And try to explain myself."

"No need," sagte Bernd nun. "You're a fucking coward, and a hypocrite, because deep inside you don't care about a colored man as much as you would about another white man. No matter how many righteous books you read."

Whiston stand versteinert. Die Kappe hörte auf, sich in seinen Fingern zu drehen.

"Coward, that I must accept. But I did not let down Sam because of his race. I'm such a coward that I would probably have failed any friend, be he black, white or green."

"Or red", suggerierte Bernd.

"Well, that is the problem. See, the United States is in a state of mass hysteria. There are two government committees doing nothing but hunting down what they perceive as Communists, real or imagined. And that book ... got me in a good deal of trouble myself...."

"I doubt that anything that is happening in the U.S. now could even come close to what happened here between 1933 and 1945," warf Bernd ein.

"Well, and I'm sure I would not have been a hero had I lived here between 1933 and 1945. I have not come here to defend myself. I wanted to apologize."

Bernd stand nun auf.

"You should have testified in defense of the book club. You should have kept that stupid book safe. You should have testified at this Mickey Mouse hearing about what you saw at the border. You should have thought about the fact that there is a pregnant woman here and that a family was about to be torn apart if you did nothing. And yet, you did nothing."

"Is Sam… where… I mean, have you heard any….", stotterte Whitson.

"I have no news from him since he left", sagte Theresa trocken wie Staub.

"You haven't… I mean, even… I mean, talked on the…."

"We have no phone here, he has no phone there. Mail is slow", übernahm Bernd für Theresa, weil er ihr ansah, dass sie kaum Kraft, geschweige denn Interesse hatte, sich weiter mit Whitson und dem Schmerz auseinanderzusetzen.

"Anything I can do to help… I'll gladly do."

"Good night, Mr. Clarke", schloss Theresa das Gespräch. Whitson tropfte davon wie ein Schluck

Wasser.

„Also, so grob hättet ihr eds a ned mit ihm umspringa müssn", kommentierte Waltraud, nachdem er gegangen war. „Der hat wahrscheinlich gnuch Ärger kricht wegen dem Scheiß Buch, und du Bernd, hättest es dem Sam nie aufdrängen dürfen."

Bernd starrte betreten auf die Tischplatte, hatte ausnahmsweise einmal keine schlagfertige Antwort parat.

Back home

"So, what y'all up to tonigh?" asked a co-worker named George on the lunch bench. The old tune. It sounded so familiar to Sam as if Herman himself was sitting there.

"Nuthin," Sam munched.

"It's pay day!" George crowed with delight.

"Didn ya notice that Sam here doan spend no money? He guards his check like a treasure," Louis laughed and padded Sam's leather briefcase, where he kept his paycheck. Sam's hand inadvertently jerked to his bag in a protective gesture. The other two men laughed.

"What's a mill-worker doin with a briefcase, anyway?" George asked mockingly.

This check was another tiny installment towards coming back to life. Paycheck by paycheck, Sam got a little closer, painfully slowly. In the course of any given day, he would do the math in his head about half a dozen times while feeding the hungry saw. He calculated how much of each paycheck he would have to spend on food and living expenses. At the current rate, it was going to take him a year and a half to get back to Germany.

The eternity that had passed so far ... had been only three weeks.

"He doan eat, either. Look at that," Louis added, pointing at the frugal lunch in at Sam's tin box: a sandwich with one single slice of cheese, an apple, some crackers.

"Trouble is, no matter how hard I try, I gotta eat almos half of ma pay. I tried eatin less, but it's hard to get thru the shift if ya doan have any strength in ya."

"What ya savin up fo, anyway?"

"I gotta get ma family over here. Got a baby on the way."

"You *married*? I didn know that," George said, taking eager advantage of Sam's relative verbosity. The Harris family had been around forever. Everyone knew the Harris family. And yet people knew hardly anything about the odd one, Sam. Had been kind of quiet as a boy, and practically tongueless during his intermittent returns home since the war.

"Engaged."

"Got a picture of her?" George demanded to see.

Sam reached into his briefcase, carefully extracted his wallet, making sure the check did not fall out in the process. He opened it and produced a picture of Theresa with Brigitte on her lap. It was in the exact same state as Ludwig's photograph of her had been in 1944: battered, thumbed around the edges, kissed a thousand times.

The jaws of George and Louis dropped.

"Put that away, man," Louis hissed between clenched teeth. Sam followed his advice.

"Ya out of ya mind? That righ there could get ya beaten up."

"Or worse", added Louis ominously.

"It's a calculated risk," said Sam, swinging his legs over the bench in order to get up. He felt the other two men stare as he walked away. He made his way down the hallway, lunch was almost over. He stopped by the fountain.

No water came out.

"Ya kiddin me."

Sam rattled the button. He hadn't really paid attention to it the first couple of weeks here, but now that it was malfunctioning, he inspected the contraption and found it was still the same old botch job as two years prior, an old rusty pipe leading from the real fountain to a little separate basin.

"That damned thing still keeps breakin down, huh?" he asked someone who had come up behind him.

"Oh damn it, is it out again? It happens all the time. Fuckin thing's been breakin down fo' years. The whole thing gotta be replaced, but they jus keep fixin the valve."

"I know," Sam said. He straightened up and walked the two steps over to the actual fountain, bowed his head under the large, block-lettered sign that read "Whites only" and drank. He took his time, too. He did not need to look up to sense that the entire bustling end-of-lunch corridor had ground to a halt behind him.

"That nigger's drinking from the whites-only fountain!" someone hollered, quite gratuitously as everyone within earshot was already staring at the scandal. Sam turned slowly and looked into the hostile, washy eyes of the offended party.

"The other one's broken."

Sam looked around at his black fellow workers to see how far they would go with him. Not very far, as he saw immediately. They were all trying hard to put a layer of indifference over their anxiety, the same look as George and Louis when they had seen Theresa's picture. *It ain worth it, man*, their eyes were pleading with him. He couldn't blame them. It had taken him and his mates at the book club months to work up any kind of courage in the *desegregated* military, and the present party was in Georgia, and utterly taken by surprise.

"We work in a fuckin mill, we all gotta drink water for the sawdust," Sam said to everyone.

"Y'all better get back to work," a foreman tried to defuse the situation. A wall of shoulders formed around the fountain and Sam.

"He can't jus get away with that!" There was a dangerous gnarl in the voice that said it. It belonged to a young guy. Sam discretely sized him up, even though he knew that he better not get into any brawl. The guy looked scrawny enough, though.

"Course I'll get back to work", said Sam to the foreman, "and next time I'm thirsty, I'll be righ back here."

"Look," Louis took it upon himself to intervene. "This ole fountain keeps breakin and he's right, with all the dust we all do need water. If we could get it fix....," he suggested to the foreman.

"Doan fix the damn thing, get rid of it," said Sam. "It shouldn be there in the first place."

"Will someone shut up that bigheaded nigger?" the young skinny guy demanded. He shuffled forward towards Sam. He lunged forward and smashed into Sam, clutching the strap of his briefcase, which flew off his shoulder. His lunch tin, his wallet, his paycheck and a book clattered across the floor. Sam backed away further, he was not going to fight. *He was not going to fight.* But he *was* going to pick up his things, especially his paycheck and his wallet. His opponent still blocked his way.

"Let me get ma stuff!" Sam's voice was angry, he could not help himself any more. The spectators craned their necks, hoping or dreading to witness further derailment.

"Well, are y'all gonna help me or do I have to deal with him all by myself?" Sam's aggressor provoked the bystanders. Soon a handful of them were shuffling Sam as he was scrambling around, picking up his effects as swiftly as he could. The skinny man with the runny eyes bumped him again, and Sam did little more than stand his ground. The guy let himself tumble backwards. The crowd gasped. Another one swung at Sam in unexpected viciousness.

Sam could feel his willpower slip, his anger foam over. Runny-eye scrambled up from the ground, and when he came charging back at him a second time, Sam swung his fist. Oxygen flooded him, liberated by this first satisfying punch. Sam no longer had to quell or suppress anything. He had begun to fight; he could just let it take its course now. His adversaries' blows were fueled by undiluted hatred as well as a good deal of outrage at the fact that he was figthing back, and yet the energy behind their punches paled in comparison to the rage that had unleashed the animal in Sam. Part of the crowd circled the combatants in eager curiosity, others sneaked away. Confounded voices clamored something about the police.

FELSENKELLER

Max schliefen langsam die Beine ein. Er und Wolfi wechselten sich brüderlich ab, erfanden tausend Kniffe, um die Kleine auf andere Gedanken zu bringen. Doch seit Sam weg war, konnte man mit dem sonst so leicht zu unterhaltenden Mädchen einfach nicht mehr viel anfangen. Ihre kleine Stirn war finster und wolkig, sie wollte nichts spielen. Dafür aber zog es sie magisch in die Bergstraße. Vor Brakows Wohnaus, wo sie nun mehr Ausdauer bewies als Wolfi in seinen besten Detektivstunden. Den Jungen blieb nichts anders übrig, als sie zu begleiten. Nun saß sie schon wieder seit zwei Stunden auf der steinernen Schwelle eines Hauseingangs und starrte auf die Tür, hinter der Brakow wohnte. Max versuchte es, wie so oft, mit sanften Appellen an ihre Vernunft.

„So, und wenn er eds tatsächlich rauskommt?"

„Dann hinterher."

„Und dann?"

„Dann sehmer scho. Der Wolfi und i habn bis eds immer was gsehn, wenn mer den Brakow beobachtet ham."

„Und... des bringt dir den Sam wohl zurück?"

„Naa. Aber vielleicht wird zumindest der Tucker bstraft."

Dem hatte Max nichts entgegenzusetzen. Trotzdem wäre er gerne woanders hin gegangen. Noch zehn Minuten, dann würde er Brigitte einfach nach Hause schleppen.

Am Ende war es Max, nicht Brigitte, der einen verstohlen, gehetzt wirkenden Mann aus dem Gebäude schlüpfen sah.

„Isser des?", fragte er, Brigitte in die Seite rempelnd.

„Oh, ja!", bestätigte die so freudig, dass er ihr seine Hand über den Mund stülpen musste. Brakows Route war günstig, die beiden konnten ihm bequem in gebührendem Abstand folgen, während er beim Dürerhaus in die Albrecht-Dürer-Straße einbog. Er trat recht plötzlich in einen Laden ein, in einem der wenigen Häuser, die den Krieg überstanden hatten. Max stand einen Moment lang gedankenverloren. Denn er erinnerte sich hieran. An genau dieses Haus. Als es noch von anderen Fachwerkhäusern umgeben war statt von Baustellen. Als er klein war.

„Des is der Feinkost-Scherer."

„Geh du nei, mi kennt der Brakow", drängte Brigitte. Einen Augenblick später stand Max in der Ladenstube. Da stand er tatsächlich, der alte Scherer, als ob die Altstadt nicht vor acht Jahren um seinen Laden herum in Flammen aufgegangen wäre – hinter genau dem gleichen Tresen hielt er genau die gleichen Waren feil: die Schnäpse, den Essig, das ekelhafte Kraut, ein paar Sorten Räucherwurst. Dies alles vermengte sich in der moderigen Luft des uralten Bauwerks zu einem schauderhaften Gestank. Als ‚Scherer-Delikatessen' hatte er das seltsame Sammelsurium schon damals angepriesen, als die Wächters mitunter dort eingekauft hatten. Und schon damals war Max davon überzeugt gewesen, dass das Sortiment der sogenannten Delikatessen nicht etwa aufgrund der erlesenen Qualität der Ware, sondern rein nach Zweckmäßigkeit ausgewählt war. Scherer hielt feil, was sich im Laufe der Jahre so für ihn an günstigen Geschäftsverbindungen ergab: Da kannte er einen Schnapsbrenner, dort einen Schlachter.

Max hielt sich unauffällig zwischen den wuchtigen Schnapsgefäßen auf und beobachtete durch das bauchig gewölbte Glas etwas verzerrt die Szene, die sich nun zwischen Scherer und Brakow abspielte. Der alte Lebensmittelhändler drehte sich nach kurzem Gespräch hinter seinem Tresen zur Wand und hangelte nach einem Schlüssel, der zwischen der Hausordnungstafel, einem Schuhlöffel und einigen weiteren Schlüsseln an einem Holzbrett hing. Dieser Schlüssel aber war ungewöhnlich. Er war fast doppelt so groß wie die anderen, aus Messing, hatte eine ovale, verschnörkelte Räute und einen umso einfacheren Bart. Max ertappte sich dabei, dass er seinen Kopf hinter den Schnapsgefäßen hervorgereckt hatte, um den kuriosen Schlüssel sorgfältigst zu studieren. Hastig zog er sich wieder zurück.

Scherer übergab den Schlüssel an Brakow, und sie beide verschwanden zusammen in die Schwärze einer Tür hinter dem Tresen. Max hatte sie erst gar nicht wahrgenommen. Max ging ein Licht auf. Scherers Laden war einer der Ausweichorte gewesen, wo seine Mutter und Brüder hätten hingehen sollen, falls ihr eigener Luftschutzkeller je überfüllt oder unzugänglich gewesen wäre. Max hatte bei solchen Sachen immer genau aufgepasst, mit siebenjährigem Todesernst, denn die Vorstellung, am Luftschutzkeller abgewiesen zu werden und mitten im Bombenhagel zu stehen, hatte ihn damals schwer beschäftigt. Wann immer der Fliegeralarm losheulte, hatte er mindestens drei verschiedene mögliche Schutzräume im Kopf gehabt. Und deshalb wusste Max: Durch diese Tür ging es hinunter in die Felsenkeller. Daher bestimmt auch der seltsame Schlüssel; es war ein uraltes Monstrum, mit dem bestimmt jahrhundertealte Bierkeller aufgesperrt wurden.

Scherer erschien allein wieder im Laden.

„Grüß Gott, Herr Scherer!"

Es dauerte einen Augenblick, bis ein vages Erkennen im Blick des Feinkosthändlers aufging.

„Der Wächter-Bu, erinnerns sich? Der mittlere, der Max?"

„Mei, bisdu groß worn", sagte Scherer, ohne dass Max dabei erkennen konnte, ob er sich wirklich erinnerte oder es nur so dahinsagte.

„Ich wollt fragn... I such nach a bissl Gelegenheitsarbeit. Hättns was für mich?"

Scherer sah ihn überrumpelt, aber nicht interesselos

an. Wohl unbewusst fasste er sich mit der Hand an den eigenen Rücken.

„Ja, die Schlepperei... Ma is ja a nimmer der Jüngste und i habs scho ganz schee im Kreiz..."

„Fässer nunter und nauf tragn und so? Mach i gern, Herr Scherer!"

Scherer sah ihn an. Die Vorstellung, dass ihm ein junger geschmeidiger Spund die schweren Fässer und Steigen tragen könnte, was sehr verlockend.

„Zahln kann i aber ned viel."

„Des machd nix, es geht ja bloß drum, dass i mir a weng was dazu verdien. Dass i ab und zu amal ins Kino kann und so. Oder im schlimmsten Fall könners mi a in Naturalien bezahln, mei Mutter kann immer Glas Kraut brauchn oder a Wurscht."

Scherer kam das ganze ein bisschen zu gut vor, um wahr zu sein. Doch er besiegelte das Angebot von Max per Handschlag.

„Dann kumm glei amol morgn nach der Schul vorbei."

„Danke, Herr Scherer!"

Max wetzte aus dem Laden und zerrte die ungeduldig wartende Brigitte mit sich. Sie fanden eine Ecke, von der aus sie Brakow herauskommen sehen konnten. Max berichtete Brigitte von seinem Geistesblitz.

◆

Wolfi las das gleiche Superman-Heft zum dritten Mal. Er lehnte gegen das Bücherregal. Er hatte die Beine lang von sich gestreckt und zog sie nicht einmal für Kunden ein, die an ihm vorbei wollten. Waltraud schimpfte ihn noch nicht einmal. Sam war zwar Wolfi nicht als Stiefvater in Aussicht gestanden wie der Brigitte, dennoch fehlte er ihm als Vaterfigur und Freund. Dass Tucker immer noch wie ein Pfau durch die Kaserne stolzierte, dass seine Mutter diesem Mann jede Woche mit eisiger Miene neue Schundheftchen verkaufen musste, sah Wolfi als persönliche Niederlage. Sein Streunen war seit ein paar Wochen so gut wie eingestellt. Vor lauter Rumsitzen und Trübsal blasen schrieb er sogar bessere Noten in der Schule. Und Waltraud konnte sich noch nicht einmal so recht darüber freuen.

Brigitte fegte in den Laden und landete krachend neben Wolfi auf dem Boden.

„I woaß, wo die Akte is", keuchte sie.

„Ach komm."

„Doch, echt."

„Wo?"

„Im Burgberg. Gleich nebn dem Kaiser Barbarossa."

„Ja, der liest sie nämlich grad", ertönte nun die

Stimme seines mittleren Bruders, leger, vor Triumph krächzend. „Und morgen holnmer se uns."

◆

„Grüß Gott, Herr Scherer", sagte Max, voller Elan in den Laden wehend. Scherer blickte perplex auf die beiden schmutzigen Kinder, die er im Schlepptau hatte.

„Ach ja...", tat Max so, als fiele ihm seine Begleitung jetzt erst auf. „Sie erinnern si ja bstimmt an den Wolfi, mein klan Bruder." Scherer nickte vielsagend und wenig begeistert. „Und di Klanne da wohnt bei uns, und bei meiner Mama in der Arbeit dürfens heit ned sei, na hab i dacht, obs ned hier im Laden einfach hoggn könntn."

Scherer schaute widerwillig drein, hob den Blick zum Schaufenster und sah, dass sein erster Gedanke – *solln die klann Vregger doch draußn spilln* – eines massiven Regengusses wegen wohl zu hartherzig wäre.

„Na, heit kenners da bleim, aber dass mir des ned zur Regl wird."

„Na, na, des is bloß heit, weil mei Mama in ihrer Arbeit Inspektion hat."

„Also gut, dann geh amol mit nunter in Keller, ich zeich der, wo die Krautfässer sin, die heut no hoch missn."

Max begann zu schleppen. Nach einer Viertelstunde

packte auch Wolfi mit an. Scherer ließ sie gewähren, nachdem er ausdrücklich betont hatte, den Kleinen würde er aber nicht gesondert bezahlen. Die Buben bestätigten das mit eifrigem Kopfnicken. Brigitte setzte ihren keimenden weiblichen Charme ein, plauderte süßlich mit dem alten Herrn, und packte dem nächsten Kunden die Räucherwürste unaufgefordert und so beherzt in Packpapier ein, dass Herr Scherer sich nach einer Stunde sogar traute, in seine Wohnung hinaufzugehen:

„I bin in zehn Minutn wieder do, du passt mir schee auf, gell?"

„Mach i!", versprach Brigitte. Sowie Herr Scherer die krummen wurmzerfressenen Treppen hinaufgeknarzt war und die Dielen des ersten Stocks unter seinen greisen Schritten ächzten, schoss Brigitte wie ein Pfeil zur dunklen Kellertreppe.

„Eds wär a guater Moment!"

Die Jungen waren binnen Sekunden bei ihr. Alle drei starrten gebannt auf das Schlüsselbrett, das sie schon seit ihrer Ankunft im Laden beäugten, besonders den antiken Messingschlüssel.

Wolfi schnappte ihn, wie ein Hund ein Stück Fleisch aus einer fütternden Hand schnappt. Zusammen hetzten sie die steinerne Treppe hinab. Max, der die steilen Steinstufen inzwischen schon gewöhnt war, flog voran. Wolfis ungeduldiger Fuß glitt auf dem schmierigen, von Jahrhunderten schwerer Tritte geschmirgelten Stein aus; er landete auf dem Steiß, verbiss sich den Aufschrei.

Brigitte zerrte ihn an seinem Hemdkragen hoch. Danach klammerte er sich an die kalte rostige Metallstange, die das Geländer sein sollte. Mit jedem Schritt wurde die Dunkelheit undurchdringlicher. Obwohl draußen die Februarluft wie kleine Nadeln in ihre Backen gestichelt hatte, war es hier unten längst nicht so kalt. Sie tapsten im Dunkeln voran, folgten dem Stapfen von Max, zwinkerten ungeduldig die Augen, während diese sich an die neuen Lichtverhältnisse gewöhnten. Endlich zeichneten sich Formen ab. Die Wände waren nass. Wie ein gleißendes Licht schoss die Erinnerung in Wolfis Gehirn: Er war schon einmal hier unten gewesen, in den Katakomben. Er erinnerte sich an den Durst, den er gehabt hatte, den unerträglich dringenden, panischen Durst eines Kindes, das nicht weiß, wann es zum nächsten Mal ein Glas Wasser bekommen wird. Ja, genau. Er hatte mit seiner Zunge die nass perlende Felsenwand geleckt. Bernd hatte ihn vor den Giften gewarnt, die das Wasser auf dem Weg durch den Burgsandstein vielleicht mitgenommen hatte. Tatsächlich schillerte es ungesund grün. Ein dicker Tropfen löste sich von der Decke und platschte ihm auf den Kopf. Ihm schauderte. *Giftig.*

„Früher wars doch hier unten ned gar so nass?"

„Der Scherer hats mer vorhin erklärt", flüsterte Max, während sie sich den Gang weiter voran arbeiteten. „Die Keller hier warn früher alle belüftet, und im Krieg hams die Luftschächte zugmacht, weger die Druckwellen. Und eds wird's hier unten nimmer belüftet und alles fängt an zu verrotten. Irgendwann kracht des hier alles zam."

„Hoffentli ned heit", klang ein kleines Stimmchen von hinten. Ach ja, Brigitte war ja auch noch da.

Sie passierten grauschwarze vergitterte Kellergewölbe. Die Gitterstäbe waren großmaschig, kein Hindernis für Ratten oder sonstiges Ungeziefer. Da hindurch sah man deutlich die Lagerwaren: Scherers Glasballons mit den Schnäpsen glitzerten im Dunkel, Kisten stapelten sich, Fässer lagen gefährlich rund aufeinander, als warteten sie nur auf einen kleinen Stoß, der sie alle ins Rollen brächte. Dann gab es da auch noch massive Türen in den Wänden. Manche waren uralte Holzportale, manche moderne Stahltüren, die ungeschickt in die mittelalterlichen runden Türbögen eingekeilt worden waren.

„So", sagte Max, während er seinen Schritt verlangsamte. „Die Türen hier gehörn alle dem Scherer, und ich war noch ned drin. Probiern mer einfach mal den Schlüssel."

„Probier zuerst die altn Türen, der Schlüssel schaut so alt aus."

„Ja, ja."

Max' Finger waren zittrig. Er stocherte linkisch und grob mit dem Schlüssel in dem ersten Schloss herum.

„Lass mi amol!"

„Nein!"

„Die hier isses", erkannte Brigitte gleich, als Max den

Schlüssel in die dritte Tür steckte. Der Mechanismus setzte sich erstaunlich geschmeidig in Gang. Es klackte zweimal und der Riegel gab nach. Die Kinder starrten gebannt ins Graue, konnten noch nichts erkennen.

„Los, rein!", gab Wolfi das Kommando. Sie schlüpften ins unbekannte Nichts, schlossen die Tür hinter sich.

„Sperr von innen ab!"

Max, der sich unter normalen Umständen niemals seinem kleinen Bruder unterordnen würde, leistete Folge, ohne zu zögern. Das Schloss klackte wieder. Die Kinder fühlten einen Moment der Erleichterung, befreit von dem gruseligen Gefühl, jeden Augenblick einen bohrenden Blick im Rücken haben zu können. Die überreizten Nerven entspannten sich, die Muskeln in Schultern und Nacken schmolzen.

Sie sahen sich um. Der Raum war felsig und kahl, und nicht stockfinster, sondern grau. Warum? Die Kinder blickten nach oben. Ein Schacht führte steil nach oben und mündete in einem Gitter. Darüber stand der graue fränkische Februarhimmel. Wolfi bemerkte nun auch, dass dieser Raum viel trockener war und stabiler wirkte als die Gänge, durch die sie gekommen waren. Das lag an eben diesem Schacht – dieser Raum war noch so belüftet, wie seine mittelalterlichen Erbauer es so klug vorgesehen hatten. Sein Blick wandte sich wieder dem Raum zu. Ein Tisch mit metallenen Beinen stand verloren und unpassend in der Mitte. Brigitte war bereits hingegangen, stützte eine Hand auf die Tischplatte. Der

Tisch wackelte auf dem unebenen Steinboden. Sie reckte ihren Hals vorsichtig, wagte nicht anzufassen, was da auf dem Tisch lag. Aber in Augenschein nehmen wollte sie es, so gut es im grauen Halblicht möglich war.

„Des isse", flüsterte sie ehrfürchtig.

„Des is was?", fragte Max, mit der Unbedarftheit eines gerade neu auf einen Fall angesetzten Kommissars. Ihm war die Angelegenheit noch nicht so in Fleisch und Blut übergegangen ist wie den alten Hasen.

„Die Akte!", sagte Altkommisar Wolfi ergriffen, und war mit einem Satz neben Brigitte.

Da lag sie, und strahlte papierne Banalität aus, wie es nur ein maschinengetipptes Dokument vermag. Und dennoch kam sie den Kindern nicht weniger eindrucksvoll vor als der Heilige Gral. Hiernach hatten sie nun schon seit Monaten gejagt. Wolfi hatte sie vielleicht sogar schon einmal in Händen gehalten, für die paar Minuten, als er in Besitz von Brakows Aktentasche war. Hätten sie sie früher gefunden, vielleicht wäre dann alles anders gekommen... Aber hatten sie ja nicht. Jetzt standen sie davor. Sie wagten sie noch immer nicht zu berühren, und mit den paar englischen Zeilen auf dem Deckblatt konnten sie nicht viel anfangen. Es waren keine Ausdrücke, die sie aus ihrem täglichen Umgang mit GIs und Comicheften kannten, sondern lange, kompliziert aussehende Wortungetümer. Aber so musste es ja auch sein, wenn es etwas Wichtiges war. Ehrfürchtig starrten sie.

„Und jetzt?"

„Na, wir müssense mitnehmen."

„Wir brauchen aber einen Plan, falls der Scherer scho wieder zurück im Laden is."

In die kurze Stille, in der sie alle drei über eine Strategie nachgrübelten, brach ein Geräusch. An der alten Tür wurde von außen gerüttelt. Die Kinder erstarrten. Draußen erschollen Stimmen, zu dumpf, als dass man Worte verstehen konnte, doch nah genug, dass die Kinder erkannten: das eine war der fränkische, von harten Konsonanten freie Bariton des Feinkosthändlers, nervös, sich frenetisch entschuldigend. Das andere... Brakows gemeißelter, kantiger Akzent, ebenfalls nervös, entrüstet. Nun rappelte es im Türschloss. Wolfi und Brigitte sanken unter den Tisch, als könnten sie sich in dem leeren Raum irgendwie verstecken. Max blieb aufrecht, bedeutete ihnen mit einem bedächtigen Kopfschütteln: *Wir haben den einzigen passenden Schlüssel, die können da draußen rumprobieren, bis sie schwarz werden.*

Tatsächlich kapitulierten die Männer nach ein paar erfolglosen Versuchen. Ihre Schritte entfernten sich.

„Haun wir ab?", wisperte Wolfi.

„Jetzt ned, sonst rennen wir denen direkt in die Arme", sagte Max.

„Meinst, die können die Tür eintretn?"

Max schüttelte den Kopf. Diese massive Eichentür wachte seit mindestens fünfhundert Jahren über diesen Raum. So schnell bekam die keiner klein.

„Oder mit am Generalschlüssel?"

„Für so a antikes Schloss?"

Sie standen ein paar Minuten in der Stille, dachten nach.

„I glaub ned, dass die so schnell hier reinkommen. Und die wissen ja a ned, dass mir hier drin sin. Die glaubn bestimmt, mir habn den Schlüssl gestohln und sin abghaut. Und wennmer eds blind hochrenna, schnappt uns der Scherer. Ich glaub fast, wir müssn abwarten, bis Nacht is, bevor mer uns rausschleichn."

Brigitte schauderte leicht, aber nickte zustimmend.

Also saßen sie auf dem harten Boden. Dann drehten sie Runden durch den fahlen Kellerraum. Dann legten sie sich hin, kuschelten sich gegenseitig die Köpfe auf den Schoß, denn es war verdammt trüb und trotz des Schreckens ... ganz schön langweilig hier unten.

„Wie spät?", wagte Wolfi kaum zu fragen. Max zog seine heißgeliebte Taschenuhr aus der Hosentasche und las das Zifferblatt im Licht des Lüftungsschachts.

„Wir sin erst seit einer Stunde hier."

„Ach du liebe Zeit. Meinst ned, mir könna eds raus?"

Brigitte schüttelte entschieden den Kopf. Max' Einschätzung der Lage erschien ihr vernünftig, und um nichts in der Welt wollte sie sich jetzt erwischen lassen, so kurz vor dem, was ihr als das Ziel erschien: endlich Rache an Tucker üben können, ein wenig Gerechtigkeit, ein wenig Genugtuung auf ihrer und Mamas geschundenen Seele.

„Was isn des?", fragte Wolfi plötzlich, fast lautlos. Sein Blick war hoch zum Lüftungsschacht gerichtet. Er packte Max' Arm und riss seinen Bruder beiseite, der nämlich genau darunter stand. Sie lauschten. Tatsächlich nagte etwas über ihren Köpfen. Es sägte. Die drei steckten ihre Köpfe dicht zusammen, hauchten ihre Worte fast lautlos mit ihrem fieberhaften Atem aus.

„Da macht sich wer an die Gitterstäb zu schaffen."

„Wolln die wohl durchn Lüftungsschacht rein?"

„Da passt doch ka Mensch durch. Ned amal du tätst da durchpassen", meinte Max, auf Brigittes klapperdünnen Körper deutend.

„Was zum Kuckuck machn die dann da oben?"

"All right", hörten die Kinder, als ein verrostetes Stück Gitterstab durch den Schacht auf den Kellerboden klirrte. Sie sahen sich mit riesigen Augen an. Das war *Tucker*. Brakow hatte Tucker zur Hilfe geholt.

Da fiel noch etwas auf den Boden, doch es klirrte nicht wie der metallene Gitterstab. Es plumpste eher, schlug auf dem Weg nach unten mehrmals gegen die Schachtwand, rollte die letzten Meter die steile Schräge entlang. Es war länglich und bauchig ... eine Flasche? Zu einer näheren Analyse kamen sie nicht mehr, denn als das Ding auf dem Boden aufkam, zerschellte es. Eine Flamme stach aus den Scherben und ging in einem gleißenden Lichtball auf.

„Scheiße! Des is a Brandsatz!", krächzte Max. Er stieß Brigitte, die in der Mitte des Raumes zögerte, zur Tür. Wolfi war bereits dort und streckte panisch die Hand nach seinem Bruder aus: *Wo war der Schlüssel?* Fieberhaft rüttelten sie den Schlüssel ins Schloss, waren zu fahrig; der Bart wollte nicht greifen. Wolfi und Max rissen sich gegenseitig den Schlüssel aus der Hand, versuchten es abwechselnd. Mit einem dumpfen Knacken explodierte die Flamme hinter ihnen. Sie spürten die Hitze auf ihren Rücken, der Rauch stieg ihnen in die Augen und Kehlen. Endlich sprang die Tür auf. Sie brachen aus dem Raum. Während sie rannten, sah Wolfi Brigittes Pullover glimmen. Im vollen Lauf klopfte er die Glut auf ihr aus. Auch Wolfis Jacke war versengt. Wie Ratten schwärmten sie die glitschige Treppe hinauf, preschten in den Laden, vorbei an Herrn Scherer, der entgeistert hinter seinem Ladentisch stand und mit offenem Mund das panische Pack Kinder anstarrte, das durch seinen Laden hetzte.

„In Ihrm Keller brennts lichterloh!", brüllte Max über seine Schulter zurück, bevor sie durch die Tür verschwanden. Die Ladenklingel bimmelte verwirrt.

♦

Erst als sie in der heimischen Küche standen und in die entsetzten Gesichter ihrer Mütter blickten, wurde den

Kindern klar, wie sie aussahen. Ihre gereizten Luftröhren rasselten, sie keuchten, dazwischen husteten sie. In ihren Gesichtern stand noch der Schrecken, die Backen waren knallrot von der Gluthitze, der Todesangst und dem wilden Spurt durch die kalte Winterluft. Ihre Haare waren verrußt und verschwitzt. Wolfi sah Schrammen und Schwielen auf den Händen und Gesichtern von Brigitte und Max und wusste, dass auch er welche hatte, auch wenn er sie noch gar nicht spürte. Brigittes Strümpfe waren am Knie kaputt, die weiße Wolle blutig.

„Die ham ned gwusst, dass da jemand drin is", hechelte Wolfi. Dann merkte er an den entgeisterten Blicken von Theresa und seiner Mutter, dass er zur Erklärung wohl weiter ausholen musste. „Mir ham die Akte gfunden, im Keller vom Feinkostscherer, und der Brakow und der Tucker ham durchn Lüftungsschacht an Brandsatz runtergschmissen", erläuterte er also atemlos.

„Die wolltn die Akte verbrennen", ergänzte Max. „Beweismittel vernichten, weils ja ned wussten, wer den Schlüssel zum Raum hat."

Theresa und Waltraud standen starr vor Grauen, als ihnen dämmerte, was ihren Kindern gerade widerfahren war.

„Beweismittel vernichten. Des is ihnen gelungen", sagte Wolfi, und seine hektische Aufregung wich plötzlich tiefer Bestürzung.

Die Akte war weg.

„Naa, is ned."

Alle schauten auf Brigitte, die still im Hintergrund gestanden war.

„Is ihnen ned gelungen", sagte sie nüchtern. Mit einem schiefen Grinsen zog sie die Akte unter ihrem Pullover hervor.

♦

Bernd stürmte in die Wohnung, legte noch nicht mal seinen Mantel ab. Die Frauen und Kinder saßen um den Küchentisch, letztere inzwischen gebadet, reichlich mit Brandsalbe eingeschmiert und ihre verräucherten Kehlen mit Pfefferminztee spülend. In ihrer Mitte trohnte die Akte. Bernd stürzte sich erst gierig darauf, bremste sich dann aber. Er blätterte ehrfürchtig und behutsam. Die anderen folgten ihm erwartungsvoll, er war der Einzige in der Familie, der mit dem Kauderwelsch vielleicht etwas anzufangen wüsste.

„Ach, du liebe Scheiße."

Bernd blätterte durch die Seiten mit langen Formeln und verwirrenden Zeichnungen. Fast alle Graphiken zeigten längliche Ovale, durchzogen von Rechtecken und Linien, ein wenig wie ein ahnungsloser Versuch eines Kindes, ein elektrisches Schaltbild abzuzeichnen.

Bernd ließ die Seite los. Er schüttelte erregt den Kopf.

„Des Ding muss aus unserm Haus raus."

„Was isses denn?"

„Pläne."

„Freilich sins Pläne, aber für was?"

„Des is a..." Er schüttelte wieder verstört den Kopf. „Des is a Waffe. Des is was Größeres. Theresa." Er ergriff ihre Hand.

„Komm mit."

Bernd zog die benommene Theresa von ihrem Stuhl hoch. Er schnappte ihren Mantel vom Türhaken und wollte ihn ihr zuknöpfen als wäre sie ein Kind, bemerkte dabei, dass der mittlere Knopf sich nicht mehr um ihren schwangeren Bauch schließen ließ. Er nahm sie mit hinunter auf die Straße, setzte sie auf sein Moped und los fuhren sie. Theresa fragte gar nicht, wohin es ging. Sie wusste es schon. An der Schranke zu den Merrell Barracks ließ der wachhabende Soldat die ihm wohlbekannten Gesichter passieren, obwohl Theresas Geländeausweis eigentlich längst abgelaufen war.

Die beiden gingen wie selbstverständlich durch die Flure. Ein paar verstreute Soldaten auf dem Flur grüßten, manche geistesabwesend, manche überrascht, doch Theresa und Bernd gaben keine Gelegenheit zu Fragen. Im Sekretariat schreckte Luise Kellermann von ihrer Schreibarbeit auf.

„Suchen Sie uns die Stubennummer für Whitson

Clarke raus, bitte", forderte Bernd ohne Umschweife. Die Sekretärin sah Bernd an, dann Theresa.

„Bitte, Luise."

In ihrem Blick sah Theresa, dass Luise das Ausmaß der Ungerechtigkeit verstand, die Theresa widerfahren war, und dass es nun an ihr war, ihrem Gewissen zu folgen anstatt des Reglements. Langsam stand Luise auf, ging hinüber zum Aktenschrank und holte den Ordner mit der Stubenbelegung.

„I geh mit euch hin", sagte sie. Sie führte die beiden zum Flügel mit den Unterkünften. Bald standen sie vor der richtigen Tür. Bernd hämmerte autoritär, die Tür ging entsprechend prompt auf.

"Clarke!", rief Bernd an dem öffnenden Soldaten vorbei ins Zimmer. Whitsons bleiches Gesicht erschien, in einer seltsamen Mischung aus Überraschung und Ahnung.

"Remember when you said you would do anything to help her?"

Whitson nickte, gefasst, bereit diesmal das Richtige zu tun, auch wenn ihm recht schleierhaft war, zu was sie ihn denn jetzt noch gebrauchen konnten.

"We need you to testify about the night you were at Rozvadov with Sam."

Whistons Blick war tief und ernst.

"I will."

Delayed

Once again, Sam found his eyes and attention trapped in a blind stare. The letters were swimming and bopping around on the bone-white paper. A headache was thumping the base of his skull, sending pain all the way across his scalp. The others in the cell were so loud. Everything they did was so damn loud. Did they never need a moment of quiet for themselves? The light was too dim, too. And he had to return this tomorrow, the first good read he had gotten his hands on since he arrived here. Sam swiveled his head despite the pain, trying to shake off the bleariness.

"What ya readin, professor?"

"Cum on, as if you gave a shit what I'm readin. Jus leave me lone."

"Sorry, professor." His cellmate laughed. Irritation was bristling Sam, his finger sought the line he had lost.

The lights went out.

"Damn it."

"Sweet dreams, evrybody," huffed Lloyd. They all sought their bunks in the darkness. One could hear the nuzzling and rustling as the inmates twined and wiggled their threadbare blankets. Sam was still holding the open book in his hands in the pitch-dark cell. Shit. He would have to return it to the prison library without really having read much of it.

He tried to sleep, but the screeching saw of the prison workshop was still ringing in his ear. During the day, it sliced right through his awareness, nine hours at a time. After that, there would be a flavorless supper, invariably followed or accompanied by a brawl or some other unnerving commotion. There were four to a cell that was built for two. Toileting was a challenge, so was elbowing one's way to a spot under one of the few rusty, trickling showerheads, which they got to use once a week. By the time he made it through the evening routine, his headache was usually so vicious that he could hardly finish his nightly letter to Theresa, let alone read.

Once a fortnight, his mother would come for a thirty-minute visit that lasted an eon. She would sit there, wordlessly, ashamed beyond words. Yet she came. Sam tried to appreciate that dutiful motherly gesture. But the truth was that he would rather use this precious half-hour for himself than sit and stare into her worn, sorrowful face with the silent reproach.

"Any mail, mother?" he would ask each time, and she would shake her head no.

"Ya sure there's been no mail for me, mother?"

Her eyes were blank as she confirmed once more:

"No mail."

Sam would then abandon the subject. She did not sound like her old self, who would have said something like *What kina letter ya spectin?* or *Who's got any business writing to ya, anyways?* She said nothing of the sort. Was is possible that she was lying? Or was he betrayed and forgotten? Either way, it was another reason to wish she would not come.

Sam's subconscious mind came to the conclusion that by now, he had to be little more than a sore memory of a mortifying mistake to Theresa. A mistake of dreadful consequence that she was still carrying around inside her. She would soon be relieved of it, for the baby was due in a few short months. Had she already arranged everything, were the adoption papers signed? Would Sam's child be shipped across the Atlantic under the *Brown Baby plan* as soon as she was big enough for the journey? Would she grow up with a *respectable* family, never knowing, but maybe wondering why she was a few shades lighter than everybody else in the household?

His mother was still sitting across from him. Sam looked at the big clock on the wall.

"Almos time to go."

Heim

Mit dem geübten Blick einer Mutter erkannte Frau Winkler Theresas Bauch unter dem Wintermantel.

„So ehrst du mir des Andenken an mein Sohn?" sagte sie, hart wie Eis.

„Dei Sohn is aber nimmer", gab Theresa im selben Ton zurück.

Theresa machte Anstalten, an ihrer Schwiegermutter vorbei ins kleine Haus zu wischen, Brigitte forsch an der Hand lenkend.

„Wird's a Negerkind?" fragte Mutter Winkler. Sie war ja nicht ganz doof.

Theresa blieb nun im Türrahmen stehen, drehte sich zu ihrer Schwiegermutter.

„Ja."

Mutter Winkler sah den traurigen Schimmer in Theresas Augen. Sah ihre Enkelin Brigitte, die sich schützend vor den schwangeren Bauch ihrer Mutter stellte und mit ihrem klaren, klugen Blick der Großmutter geradewegs ins Herz schaute. Das Eis in Mutter Winkler schwamm in einer lauen Pfütze davon. Wen hatte sie denn sonst auf der Welt, außer diesen beiden kleinen Frauen, die so aufrecht da standen in ihrem Elend. In ihrem Türrahmen, weil sie sonst nirgendwo hingehörten. Sie waren doch das Einzige, was ihr von Ludwig blieb.

„Was is mit der Wächterin?"

„Der Hausherr hat's rausgschmissn. Wega der Mietn."

„Und wo wohnt die eds?"

„In ner kloana Wohnung. Recht kloa. Zu kloa fir uns."

„Na, des kriegn mer aa no groß, des Kind", gab Ludwigs Mutter schließlich der Realität nach. „Kumm rei und setz di erst amol. Derfst di ned so strapaziern in deine Umständ."

„I dank dir, Mutter."

Small Redemption

"Ma fiance got a unfair disciplinary transfer and I want sat it is reversed."

Vaughn looked at her. That spine, as erect as one could possibly sit with an almost full-term belly. That fierce resolution in those sky-blue eyes. That fascinating English she spoke, picked up exclusively from black American males, colored in a heavy Bavarian accent, and carefully armed with some technical terms like *disciplinary transfer*, which she had undoubtedly looked up in a dictionary in preparation for this meeting. Vaughn remembered how much he liked this woman.

"When did you last speak to Mr. Harris, Frau Winkler?"

"Before he left."

"Have you had no correspondence since?"

She did not answer. Vaughn sighed. Thus went the conventional cautionary tale: Naïve German girl falls for black man, gets knocked up, black man goes home, never to be seen or heard of again. A case in point? Was Harris really like that? Vaughn could not imagine, and yet, here sat the woman, without news from the expectant father for months.

"I'm sorry, Frau Winkler. Mr. Harris is no longer in the armed forces, and if he still were, in order to seek any form of redress, *he* would have to make the appeal himself."

„Er müsst selber an Antrag stelln," interpreted Frau Kellermann. Theresa nodded. Vaughn could sense her deep sorrow, and once again, was pained that he couldn't do anything for her.

"What happened to Tucker?" she now wanted to know.

Vaughn was not supposed to share such information with civilians. But did not give a damn right now. The least he could do was give the poor woman at least a sense of poetic justice. He went over to his cabinet and hauled out the huge file that had accumulated on Shane Tucker. He fished out the last page in it and read it to Frau Winkler verbatim:

"Sergreant Shane Andrew Tucker was found guilty of espionage, conspiracy to commit espionage, larceny, sale of government property, and violations of military regulations. He was sentenced to twelve years confinement, reduced in rank to E-1, forfeited all pay and allowances, and received a dishonorable discharge."

"Twelve years?" was all that Theresa could gather from all the legal gibberish, but it sufficed. "And Brakow?"

"They are looking for a ghost, it seems. And if he *were* found, I doubt we would ever know. This whole thing was much bigger than us, you know."

"It was some kina horrible bomb, right?"

Vaughn did not comment. The CIA had snatched the whole case from him as soon as they got wind of it, with a swiftness and fierceness that told Vaughn Frau Winkler's conjectures had to be pretty spot on.

"Sank *God* the Russians didn't get se papers. I sink my fiance should get something like a...." She was fishing for a word and found it, for she had received one from Vaughn once, for *her* own vigilance: "Like a *award*."

"Unfortunately, that's not how the world works, Frau Winkler. I really...." He stood up and took her hands. "I really wish you all the best. I have a little son, you know.... If yours is a boy, please have Frau Wächter stop by my office. We have plenty of clothes and toys for him."

"Sank you, Lieutenant Colonel."

Vaughn watched her waddle away, she was very pregnant indeed. He was a Lieutenant Colonel of the most powerful army in the world, and all he could do for a brave, mistreated little woman was hand down some layette.

Vormund?

Hannes Kröger saß am Tisch mit der ihm eigenen Lässigkeit, seine Frau Mathilde aufrecht daneben. Theresa saß rechts von ihnen, hatte sowohl Brigitte als auch Klara dabei. Brigitte saß mit aller Würde, die eine Zehnjährige aufbringen kann, und hielt die prallen Ärmchen und erstaunlich starken Beinchen ihrer Schwester im Zaum, so gut es ging — achtzehn Monate geballter Neugier, die alles erkundenswert, alles faszinierend fand, vom Heizkörper an der Wand über die Aktenordner auf dem Tisch bis hin zum Kaktus auf dem Fensterbrett.

„Und was ist nun konkret Ihr Interesse daran, als Vormund benannt zu werden? Sie haben doch keinerlei Verwandschaftsverhältnis zu Mutter oder Kind."

„Der Kindsvater hat im Krieg mir und dem verstorbenen Mann der Mutter das Leben gerettet. Ich habe seit meiner Rückkehr aus der Kriegsgefangenschaft ein Auge auf die Witwe meines Kameraden gehabt."

„Na, da hatten Sie aber ein schlechtes Auge auf sie", erlaubte sich der Mann vom Vormundschaftsamt zu scherzen.

„Ist es nicht eher im Sinne des Staates, dass ein Freund der Familie die Vomundschaft innehat, als irgendein vom Gericht benannter Fremder?", argumentierte Hannes ruhig, und Theresa wünschte, sie hätte

Hannes auch in anderen Lebenssituationen da haben können, mit seiner souveränen, gefassten, allen Unsinn mit Logik bezwingenden Art.

„Fremder, na ja. Es handelt sich um einen Bestellten des Jugendamts, und wenn Frau Winkler sich nicht so querstellen würde, wäre er ja bald kein Fremder mehr."

„Lassen Sie die Frau Winkler in Ruhe. Sie ist verwitwet, ihr zweiter Mann wurde aus Böswilligkeit und Rassenhass strafversetzt, und jetzt will ein Freund der Familie helfen, und dem würden Sie sich auch noch verweigern? Zeigen Sie doch ein bisschen Herz. Und gesunden Menschenverstand. Meiner Ansicht ist es albern genug, dass eine ausgewachsene Frau und Mutter Ihren sinnlosen Bestimmungen nach überhaupt einen Vormund für das Kind braucht."

Theresa schaute Hannes an, voll glühender Verehrung. Der Bürohengst des Jugendamts konnte sich der Kraft seiner Argumente kaum mehr entziehen.

„Aber Sie wohnen doch in Bamberg."

„Ich versichere Ihnen, wenn dem Kind je irgendwas fehlt, bin ich schneller aus Bamberg da als Ihr Paragraphenreiter aus Ingolstadt."

„Uns fehlt allerdings noch ein aktuelles Gesundheitszeugnis", murmelte der Beamte, während er in der Akte blätterte. Er gab tatsächlich nach!

„Ja, daran soll's nicht scheitern. Da gehen wir gleich im Anschluss hin."

„Ja, das müssten sie schnellstmöglich nachreichen." Der Beamte hatte den Satz kaum fertig gesprochen, da stand Hannes schon und schüttelte ihm bestimmt und verbindlich die Hand. Theresa rappelte sich auch auf.

„Herzlichen Dank. Wann bekommen wir schriftlich Bescheid?"

„Ja, wenn... sobald... ich meine, wenn die Unterlagen vollständig...."

„Wunderbar. Vielen Dank für ihre Hilfe."

◆

„Meinst, des hat highaut?", fragte Theresa, als sie wieder drunten auf dem Kopfsteinpflaster standen.

„Des haut hin", versicherte Hannes. „Wo is jetzt der Kinderarzt?"

„Glei die nächste Straß, aber unser Termin ist erst um zwoa."

„Na, dann haben wir ja gut Zeit", sagte Mathilde.

Die Krögers führten Theresa und die Kinder zum Mittagessen aus. Brigitte aß wie ein Wolf, der Klara mussten mit großem unterhalterischem Aufwand winzige Kloßstückchen gefüttert werden. Bald entkam sie Theresas Griff, schlüpfte unter den Tisch und versuchte, die zur Stabilisierung der wackelnden Tischbeine untergeschobenen Bierdeckel zu entfernen. Die Großen gaben ihre Fütterungsversuche auf, damit sie selbst in Ruhe ein paar Bissen genießen konnten. Theresa und Brigitte hatten nicht auswärts gegessen, seit Sam weg war. Brigitte schwelgte in Schnitzel und Bratkartoffeln.

„Hoppsala, wem gehördn des Negerla?", ertönte die Stimme einer Bedienung, die gerade beinahe mit einem vollen Getränketablett über Klara gestolpert wäre.

„Die ghörd uns!" Brigitte schlüpfte wie geölt von der Sitzbank unter dem Tisch hindurch, um ihr entwischtes Schwesterchen einzufangen.

Um zehn vor zwei saßen sie im Wartezimmer des Kinderarztes.

Der Arzt wehte mit flatterndem weißem Kittel hinein, grüßte freundlich, neugierig, erfreut, mal einen ‚interessanten' Fall in seiner Praxis zu haben. Brigitte wurde auch gleich mituntersucht, sie war ja kaum jemals bei einem Arzt gewesen. Binnen fünf Minuten war sie fertig.

„Wunderbar, alles gesund, widerstandsfähig. Bisschen dünn für ihr Alter."

„Sie isst aber wie ein Scheunendrescher."

„Na, solange sie gut isst, ist das dann nicht weiter schlimm. So, jetzt aber zu unserer Toxi."

„Sie heißt Klara", berichtigte Theresa trocken.

„Klara. Gut. Den Film haben Sie aber bestimmt gesehen, oder?"

„Ghört hab i davon", machte Theresa in einem Ton, der um ein Ende des leidigen Vergleichs bettelte. Jeder benannte ihr Kind ungefragt nach der Hauptfigur des schmalzigen Spielfilms, der dem deutschen Kinopublikum gelehrt hatte, was von diesen schokoladenbraunen Kindern zu halten sei: Im Grunde ja furchtbar süß, arm dran, von Geburt an zu einem schwierigen Leben verdammt, unschuldig an der spektakulären Verantwortungslosigkeit ihrer Eltern.

Der Arzt gab sich unheimlich Mühe mit Klara, der das gar nicht behagte. Sie rutschte und wand sich auf dem Behandlungstisch, ergriff jede Gelegenheit zur Flucht, wollte ihre Zunge nicht rausstrecken und sich vor allem nicht in die Ohren schauen lassen.

„Lebhaft, ja?", interpretierte der Arzt, während er versuchte, Klaras Beinchen lange genug still zu halten, um mit seinem kleinen Hammer ihre Reflexe zu testen.

„Musikalisch wird sie bestimmt auch sein, und sozial sehr umgänglich", prophezeihte der Doktor nun. „Das ist das schwarze Blut in ihr."

„Ja", sagte er am Ende der Untersuchung und klatschte sich dabei zufrieden auf den schmerbäuchig gewölbten Arztkittel. „Alles im normalen Bereich. Keine Mängel, keine anormalen Entwicklungen."

„Erstaunt Sie des wohl", schnappte Theresa, nur mit Mühe ihre Verärgerung unterdrückend, während sie Klaras Strumpfhöschen mit solchem Schwung wieder hochzog, dass die Kleine kurz vom Boden abhob.

„Nicht unbedingt", erwiderte der Arzt gelassen, Theresas Unmut ignorierend. Er suchte etwas in einer chaotischen Schublade, fand es schließlich, und reichte Theresa ein vergilbtes Heftchen.

„Diese Handreichung finden Sie vielleicht hilfreich. Sie ist schon älter. Wurde damals gedruckt, als nach dem großen Krieg im Zuge der Rheinlandbesatzung viele Mischlingskinder geboren wurden, Sie wissen schon, von afrikanischen Soldaten aus den französichen Kolonien gezeugt. Beachten Sie bei der Lektüre allerdings, dass die Situation damals ein wenig anders war. Die sogenannten Rheinlandbastarde waren ja damals vorwiegend die Kinder vom Vergewaltigungsopfern oder Prostitutierten. Die Väter waren wilde, unterernährte Legionäre aus dem afrikanischen Busch. Die Mischlingskinder heutzutage stammen ja eher von gesunden Vätern aus einem wohlhabenden Land, und sie haben teils liebende Mütter. Aber lesen Sie die Broschüre trotzdem, das eine oder andere trifft sicherlich auch heute zu."

Theresa standen heiße Tränen der Empörung in den Augen. Sie wusste gar nicht, worüber sie sich mehr ärgern sollte, wie verächtlich dieser Mensch die Fremdenlegionäre beschrieb, oder dass er Sams und ihre Situation mit ihrer verglich.

„Nein, danke", lehnte sie ab und ließ sie die Broschüre zurück auf den Schreibtisch des Arztes fallen.

♦

„So, hier is des blöde Gsundheitszeugnis", sagte sie schroff, nachdem sie aus dem Ärztehaus kamen und Hannes und Mathilde wieder in einem Cafe trafen.

„Das geben wir gleich beim Jugendamt ab", sagte Hannes zufrieden. Mathilde sah die Erregung in Theresas Gesicht.

„Und dann bringen wir euch nach Hause. War ein langer Tag."

Visitor

Jason showed. After more than two years.

Sam pretended that they were having a normal relationship. He maintained a conversation.

"Stupid thing to go to jail fo'," Jason said.

"Remember what happened to *you* when ya walked down the street with ya medals in forty-five, Jason?"

"I remember."

"I'm learnin, ya know. It's so weird, I was never a physical man. But somehow I responded physically couple of times in a row. That's gotta stop. I gotta control that. That lady in Montgomery a couple of weeks ago, she did it right. She went on that bus, sat down on purpose, calmly, and let them arrest her without any fuss. That's the way to do it."

"How d'ya even know what's happenin in Alabama."

"News travels. But that's the way to do it. Same way Gandhi did it."

"Who?"

"Shit, Jason, you gotta get into these things more. He was this scrawny little leader in India, wouldn hurt a fly, and in the end that man freed this entire huge country with no other weapons but persistence and justice."

"Oh. Yeah, I know who ya talking 'bout."

"That's the way to do it, that's how people in Montgomery are doin it, and that's how I'm gonna do it as soon as I'm outta here."

Jason was not comfortable with the conversation. He was kneading his visitor's pass. With those maimed fingers of his. Sam had almost forgotten about that.

"And how are *you* doin?" Sam decided to inquire.

"All righ, I guess."

"Still workin at the plant?"

"Hmhm."

"Well, what's new, tell me."

"Well," Jason shrugged. "Gettin married in the fall."

"Ya kiddin me," Sam said, rising from his chair in genuine joy. The guard flicked a hand at him, he sat back down. "Congratulations, man!" Since the guard would not let him get up and hug his brother, he took Jason's mangled hands in his and squeezed them hard.

"Who is she? Do I know her?"

"No, ya doan know her. Jus a girl from the plant."

Sam was taken aback at Jason's lack of enthusiasm.

"Well, that's... that's great."

Jason shrugged. "Was 'bout time I settle down."

"Well, I ... I wish ya both all the happiness in the world, man."

"All the happiness one can get in this world, huh."

A girl at the plant. No one was opposing *their* union. Smooth sailing. Yet Jason did not seem to experience even a fraction of Sam's fierce passion. *Was 'bout time* to tie the knot.

Nonetheless, Sam felt encouraged to share his situation with his brother now.

"Jason," he said in a solemn tone, to make sure this part of the conversation would not just drown in triviality. "There's sumthin ya doan even know. Mother doesn know, either. I got a woman, too. I got a whole family over there. And I need to get them over here as soon as I get out."

Jason did not seem very surprised. Sam leaned forward:

"Jason, I'm gonna need money when I get out. I need a plane ticket, or I'll take a ship, I doan care, and then I'll need four more tickets to get us all back over here."

"Four?"

"For maself, ma woman, ma daughter, and ma step-daughter."

"They white!?"

"They're German, fcourse they're white! Cept ma

baby daughter, fcourse. I ain even seen her yet."

"Oh, ma word," Jason now animated himself. "Ya can't bring'em over here."

"I wouldn stay down here. We gotta go up North, anyways, where the climate's more like Germany. Cuz the plan is to grow Bavarian hops for a livin."

Jason came to the conclusion that his brother had lost his mind. He made a move to get up.

"Ya gonna help me?"

"With munny, ya mean?"

"Yes. I saved up what I could at the mill, but since…."

"Ya mean, am I gonna give ya ma hard-earn munny so ya can go back over there and drag a couple more people into your misery?"

"Jason…."

Jason left the visitor's room.

Rückkehr

Brigitte sah ihn anfangs gar nicht kommen. Was sie zuerst bemerkte, waren die Bäuerinnen an den Fenstern und in den Türrahmen, die an so einem Samstagnachmittag, nachdem der Gehweg gekehrt und das Mittagessen abgeräumt war, so rein gar nichts Sinnvolles zu tun hatten. Brigitte sah, wie sich das gelangweilte Aus-dem-Fenster-Starren plötzlich mit Interesse füllte, die molligen Arme mit den schuppigen Ellbogen sich ein bisschen besser abstützten, Hälse sich reckten. Sie alle blickten in dieselbe Richtung, weder finster noch freundlich, aber *erkennend*. Denn auf der Hauptstraße lief, in einem guten Anzug, ein Mann, der zu einem der Dorfkinder passte wie die Faust aufs Auge. Wer gerade bei einander stand, flüsterte und deutete.

Ein heftiger Instinkt packte Brigitte, sie wollte zu ihm rennen, direkt in seine Arme. So oft hatte sie ihn in Gedanken schon diese Straße herunterkommen sehen, hatte fest daran geglaubt. Hatte versucht, diesen Glauben auch in ihrer Mama wach zu halten. Und jetzt lief er da wirklich. Doch etwas hielt sie zurück. Sie tat ein paar Schritte von der Straße weg, hinter einen Busch der Langeneders, von wo aus sie sehen konnte, ohne gesehen zu werden.

Mitten auf der Straße spielten noch die Kleinen, zu deren Beaufsichtigung Brigitte eigentlich abkommandiert war. Unter ihnen war auch Klara. Gleich würde

Sam in Sichtweite kommen, und er würde Klara sehen, zum ersten Mal. Brigitte sah ihre Schwester mit ganz neuen Augen an – so wie er sie sehen würde:

Aus Klaras streng geflochtenen braunen Zöpfen lösten sich vorwitzige Löckchen. Ihre weißen Kniestrümpfe waren schmutzig, denn sie spielte selbstverloren in den Pfützen der Dorfstraße. Rotes Röckchen, karierte Schürze, weißes Blüschen — im Gegensatz zu Brigitte, die ihre Kindertage in speckigen Lederhosen verbracht hatte, zog Theresa Klara immer herzig und gewissenhaft an, selbst wenn das Kind dann den Tag im Matsch verbrachte. Klaras emsige, bronzefarbene Ärmchen waren dünn, ihr Lächeln aber pausbäckig und ihr Augenaufschlag sanft und neugierig. Im Arm hielt sie die Paulina, mit dem grob zupackenden Beschützerinstinkt einer Puppenmama. Erst dieses Jahr hatte Brigitte ihre heißgeliebte unverwüstliche Hohlplastikpuppe, die sie von Sam zur Kommunion bekommen hatte, feierlich der Klara vermacht.

Sam erkannte die Puppe als Brigittes und die braunen Rehaugen der Puppenmutter als seine eigenen. Sein Schritt verlangsamte sich. Brigitte beobachtete gebannt den Augenblick, in dem Sam klar wurde: Da spielte *sein* Kind.

Er schritt auf sie zu. Die älteren unter den Kindern begriffen, dass hier etwas Bedeutendes vor sich ging. Sams Schritte teilten die Kinderschar wie ein Pflug, nur die Allerkleinsten spielten ungestört weiter.

„Wie heißt du, Maus?"

„I bin die Klara."

Ihr Stimmchen war aus Zucker.

„Klara", ließ es sich Sam langsam auf der Zunge zergehen. Er versuchte, den Namen genau so zu sagen wie das Kind, mit diesem knackenden K, fast lautlosem L, den glasklaren As und dem rollenden R dazwischen.

Sam ließ sich nun auch auf den Boden hinab, steckte ein Knie in den Matsch, das andere Bein stellte er im rechten Winkel auf, und darauf setzte er das Kind, das kaum Gewicht hatte in seinen Männerhänden. Sie ließ es geschehen. Ihr ruhiger Blick ruhte in stiller Neugier auf seinem Gesicht.

„Ick kenn deine Puppe", sagte er.

Sie sah ihn erwartungsvoll an. Er fuhr fort:

„Des is die Paulina."

Jetzt lächelte Klara ein bisschen.

„Woher woaßt denn du des?"

„Weil die Paulina hat ghört der Brigitte mal. Stimmt's?"

„Ja", freute sich Klara vorsichtig.

„Aber jeds die Brigitte is zu groß für eine Puppe und jeds sie ghört dir."

Während ihr kleines Gesicht sich nickend hob und

senkte, blieben ihre klugen Augen fest auf Sam fixiert.

„I will eds zu meiner Mama", beschied sie, als der eindringliche Blick des Fremden ihr zu viel wurde, und sie wand ihr kleines Sitzfleisch von seinem Knie.

„Ich auch. Ich will auch zu deine Mama", stimmte Sam zu und hob das gerade von seinem Knie entwischte Kind auf seinen Arm, in dessen Beuge sie passte wie angegossen. Klara ließ sich in Richtung Winklerhof tragen und legte dabei ihr Köpfchen schief auf seine Schulter, so dass sie sein Gesicht beobachten konnte. Brigitte löste sich aus dem Gebüsch und folgte den beiden. Andächtig betrachtete sie den Griff, mit dem Sam das Mädchen hielt, so besitzergreifend, mit solcher Selbstverständlichkeit.

„Du. Bist du wohl mei Papa?"

Sam hielt inne, sichtlich erschrocken über so viel Scharfsinn, der so glöckchenhell aus so einem winzigen Kirschmund kam. Brigitte wunderte es nicht. Sie kannte ihre Schwester und deren messerscharfen Kinderverstand.

„Die Brigitte sagt immer, irgendwann kimmt mei Papa."

„Ja", antwortete er ihr schlicht. Sie gingen ein paar Schritte. Klaras Blick ruhte weiter auf ihm, sie verarbeitete still und aufmerksam. Sam packte sie noch fester, sie passte so wunderbar in seinen Arm. Klara ließ Paulina fallen. Als Sam sich nach der Puppe umdrehte, hatte

Brigitte sie bereits aufgehoben.

"Sweetheart." Sams Blick füllte sich augenblicklich mit Tränen.

„Du bist lustig", sagte Brigitte, während sie sich in seiner Umarmung vergrub, so dass sie zu dritt in einem engen Knäuel standen. „Über die Klara weinst ned, aber wennsd mich siehst, heulst los."

„Weil jeds, wo ich dich seh, ich weiß, es is kein Traum."

Als Sam seine lange Gestalt unter den niedrigen Türrahmen duckte, ließ die alte Frau Winkler in augenblicklichem Erkennen ihr Geschirrtuch auf die Arbeitsfläche gleiten. Sie murmelte einen fast lautlosen Gruß und verließ die Küche, machte Raum für den ungestörten Moment, den ihre Schwiegertochter und der unerwartete Gast nun brauchten. Im Gehen bedeutete sie Brigitte mit einem Kinnschlenker, ihr nach oben zu folgen, doch Brigitte rührte sich nicht von Sams Seite. Sie war Teil dieser Begegnung, Teilhaberin dieses Schicksals, das gerade so eine steile Kurve nahm.

Theresa stand noch an der Spüle, in einer roten Schürze mit winzigen Karos, einem blauen Kopftuch und abgelatschten braunen Pantoffeln. Sie schrubbte energisch an hartnäckigen Krusten in der Auflaufform, spürte gar nicht, dass soeben die Welt in der alten Essküche stehen geblieben war. Erst als sie den sauberen Bräter ihrer Schwiegermutter zum Trocknen reichen wollte, merkte sie, dass die gar nicht mehr neben ihr stand. Sie drehte sich um.

Da war Sam, auf seinem Arm Klara, die sich an ihn schmiegte wie ein Kätzchen. Brigitte stand dicht daneben, tastete mit einer Hand nach Sams Hosenbein, als könne er plötzlich verschwinden, wenn sie ihn nicht festhielt.

Die Auflaufform zerschellte auf den kalten Fliesen.

Theresa stand da, die Finger kraftlos, ihre Lippen zugepresst.

"I'm takin y'all with me", grüßte er sie.

„Wo warst du die ganze Zeit", fragte sie tonlos. Sie wischte sich die seifignassen Hände an der Schürze.

"I was in jail."

"Jail? Du meinst… *Gfängnis?*"

"Can we sit?"

Brigitte packte zwei Esstischstühle an den herzförmigen Löchern in der Lehne und zog sie vom Tisch weg. Sie selbst hüpfte auf die Eckbank auf der anderen Seite. Sam ließ sich nieder, Theresa blieb mitten in der Küche stehen.

"Ya know how it is. I tole ya how it is over there. I got attacked, I fought back, I got arrested, I got sentenced."

Theresas Erwiderung war so bitter trocken, dass ihre ersten paar Worte krächzten: „Ma lässt sich doch ned verhaften, wenn ma Frau und Kinder hat, die oan brauchn. Da bringt ma si doch überhaupt ned erst in so a Situation."

"Ya had to be there to understand how it happened."

„Und trotzdem kommst hier reinspaziert und sagt, du willst uns *dahin* mitnehma."

Er sah auf den Boden, der noch nicht gewischt war. Seine Tochter hielt er immer noch fest im Arm, die ließ es sich weiterhin gefallen.

"Not to *that* place."

„Da, wo du herkommst, könntn ja die Klara und ich no ned amol aufd selbe Schul gehn," warf Brigitte ein, Sam und Theresa gedanklich einige Schritte zu weit voraus.

„Woher willstn überhaupt wissn, dass ich ned längst irgendoan Vertriebenen gheirat hab? Wennsd mir koan einzign Brief gschriebn hast?"

"I's gone 162 weeks, and I wrote twice as many letters. I can't say the same of you."

„I hab dir jede Woche gschriebn, Sam. Da drüben liegt der Umschlag, den i heit zur Post bringa wollt." Sie deutete auf einen kleinen uralten Sekretär beim Fenster. Sam stand auf, setzte Klara vorsichtig auf den Boden, ging hinüber und las die Adresse in Theresas zierlicher, angestrengter Bauernhandschrift.

Zum ersten Mal, seit Theresa die Auflaufschüssel zerdeppert hatte, sahen die beiden sich richtig in die

Augen. Es waren nicht *sie* gewesen, die den Kontakt miteinander gebrochen hatten.

"Ma mother", verstand Sam mit kummerschwerer Stimme. "She kept ya letters from me. And where ya reckon *my* letters ended up?"

„Wohin hastn gschriebn?"

"Waltraud, of course."

„Der Metzger Ahrendt hat's rausgschmissn. Aber die Post hätt er eigentli weiterleitn solln."

„Der Ahrendt", sagte Sam vielsagend. Sie nickten beide. Freilich hatte Ahrendt die *unzüchtigen* Briefe nirgendwohin weitergeleitet.

Theresa streckte linkisch eine Hand aus, ins Leere. Mit einem Satz war Sam bei ihr, ergriff die kraftlose, vom Abwasch rotgescheuerte Hand, und mit ihr das Angebot, das in dieser unbeholfenen, schwermütigen Geste steckte.

„Komm, gehmer was spieln", flüsterte Brigitte und schleppte Karla hinaus in den Hof.

*****

Other books by the same author:

HELLO ABLE FIVE – THE JOURNEY OF ALBERT TORREELE

THE TRUE STORY OF A BELGIAN OFFICER IN WARTIME BRITAIN

During his birth on Christmas Day 1916 under a circling, grenade-dropping German warplane, Albert Torreele was blinded in one eye by a panicked midwife. That did not stop him on his tenacious path towards officerhood. He graduated from the Royal Military Academy in Brussels just in time to lead an ill-fated platoon straight into the German onslaught of May 10, 1940. A single shot that should have left him crippled sent him on a grueling odyssey, through his tumbling country to the edge of the hell of Dunkirk, and across the English Channel to the charming seaside town of Tenby where the Belgian forces regrouped and prepared for another chance to fight. Finding old friends and true love in Wales, Albert and his comrades of the Free Belgian Forces set their minds on a single goal - cross the English Channel, take back their home and free their families.

POPPY DAYS - MOHNBLUMENZEIT

A NOVEL IN GERMAN AND ENGLISH

Als Panzerketten kreischend neben ihm zum Stehen kommen, weiß der versprengte Soldat Hannes: für ihn und seinen Freund Ludwig ist der Krieg vorüber. Der Krieg schon - nicht aber der ganz normale Wehrmachtswahnsinn, den die deutschen Offiziere im englischen POW-Lager Salisham auf absurde Weise aufrechterhalten. Ein paar unvaterländische

Briefe geraten in die Hände der Briten und das Leben zwischen den Fronten wird richtig gefährlich.

Physically and emotionally maimed, Baron Sandwell returns home from Italy to find his wife Ernestine completely altered by her service on the Home Front. To make matters worse, a new appointment by the War Office makes him the reluctant commandant of a POW camp. When a lynched body dangles in front of his office window, Sandwell realises that he must be more than a prison keeper. He and his wife set out on a mission to wrench the hearts and minds oft he infantrymen from the grip of their Nazi officers. As the prisoners' eyes slowly open, the Sandwells begin to believe that they and the prisoners can win the peace. And yet disaster strikes again. Who is behind the mysterious attacks in Salisham Camp?

TALE OF A TURNCOAT– DER ABTRÜNNIGE

A THRILLER IN GERMAN AND ENGLISH

Als Halbfranzose Valentin zum ersten Mal Maries Gesicht im grellen Licht der Verhörzimmerlampe sieht, ist ihm klar: sein langweiliges Dasein in der Schreibstube eines kleinstädtischen deutschen Gestapo-Stützpunkts in der Normandie ist vorüber. Mit der Identität eines amerikanischen Piloten will er sich in Maries geheimes Netzwerk einschleusen. Nachdem er kläglich auffliegt, ist er zu einem gefährlichen Doppelleben verdammt.

A dutiful, straight-headed American pilot is downed over occupied France and captured by a capricious, vain young German spy. Their ruin is the steely-cold enchantment of a French underground warrior and her impossible quest.

Find more transatlantic books at

www.transatalantic-passages.com